Some Like It Hot-Buttered

Jeffrey Cohen

BERKLEY PRIME CRIME, NEW YORK

THE BERKLEY PUBLISHING GROUP
Published by the Penguin Group
Penguin Group (USA) Inc.
375 Hudson Street, New York, New York 10014, USA

Penguin Group (Canada), 90 Eglinton Avenue East, Suite 700, Toronto, Ontario M4P 2Y3, Canada
(a division of Pearson Penguin Canada Inc.)
Penguin Books Ltd., 80 Strand, London WC2R 0RL, England
Penguin Group Ireland, 25 St. Stephen's Green, Dublin 2, Ireland (a division of Penguin Books Ltd.)
Penguin Group (Australia), 250 Camberwell Road, Camberwell, Victoria 3124, Australia
(a division of Pearson Australia Group Pty. Ltd.)
Penguin Books India Pvt. Ltd., 11 Community Centre, Panchsheel Park, New Delhi—110 017, India
Penguin Group (NZ), 67 Apollo Drive, Rosedale, North Shore 0632, New Zealand
(a division of Pearson New Zealand Ltd.)
Penguin Books (South Africa) (Pty.) Ltd., 24 Sturdee Avenue, Rosebank, Johannesburg 2196,
South Africa

Penguin Books Ltd., Registered Offices: 80 Strand, London WC2R 0RL, England

This is a work of fiction. Names, characters, places, and incidents either are the product of the author's imagination or are used fictitiously, and any resemblance to actual persons, living or dead, business establishments, events, or locales is entirely coincidental. The publisher does not have any control over and does not assume any responsibility for author or third-party websites or their content.

SOME LIKE IT HOT-BUTTERED

A Berkley Prime Crime Book / published by arrangement with the author

PRINTING HISTORY
Berkley Prime Crime mass-market edition / October 2007

Copyright © 2007 by Jeffrey Cohen.
Cover art by Stacia Krause Stojanoff.
Cover design by Annette Fiore.
Cover logo by Stacia Krause Stojanoff.
Interior text design by Laura K. Corless.

ISBN: 978-0-425-21799-3

BERKLEY® PRIME CRIME
Berkley Prime Crime Books are published by The Berkley Publishing Group,
a division of Penguin Group (USA) Inc.,
375 Hudson Street, New York, New York 10014.
The name BERKLEY PRIME CRIME and the BERKLEY PRIME CRIME design
are trademarks belonging to Penguin Group (USA) Inc.

PRINTED IN THE UNITED STATES OF AMERICA

10 9 8 7 6 5 4 3 2 1

To my two greatest influences:
my father and Harpo Marx.
Alas, neither got the chance to read it.

ACKNOWLEDGMENTS

I am a very lucky man. I get to do what I love to do for a living, and I have a great support system, which as always is headed up by my unparalleled wife and constantly amazing children. There are no better.

This time out, however, I had help from many different people, and they each deserve much more than thanks (but that's all I can afford). For help getting Elliot's story seen, thanks to Julia Spencer-Fleming, Ross Hugo-Vidal, PJ Nunn, and Bruce Bortz.

Extremely special thanks are due to a very special person: Linda Ellerbee, whom I had never met nor spoken to before *As Dog Is My Witness*. She has become, I think, a friend. Anyone who recommends your book to the *Today* show is a friend, but Linda is also as gracious and open as they come.

For help in finding the right poison for poor Vincent Ansella, my thanks to Kay Lancaster, P.J. Coldren, and especially Luci Hansson Zahray (otherwise known as "the Poison Lady"), who gave me the information I ended up using, which I've probably messed up herein. *She* knows what she's talking about, even if I don't.

And for enormous amounts of information on how a projection booth works, what it costs, and all that sort of thing, I am indebted to Denise Brouillette of the Paramount Theatre in Austin, Texas; Robert Bruce Thompson, Bert Sandifer, Carl Brookins, and John Stewart (not of *The Daily Show*), also of the Paramount in Austin. I wasn't even in the A/V club in high school, so they have literally taught me everything I know, as selflessly as is humanly possible.

I'd be a total swine (an awful thing for a Jewish boy) if I didn't acknowledge my incredible agent, Christina

Hogrebe of the Jane Rotrosen Agency (and all I met there), without whom this book wouldn't exist, and the terrific editor of the Double Feature Mysteries, Shannon Jamieson Vazquez, without whom this book wouldn't have been nearly as good.

❁ ❁

*Something peculiar,
something for everyone: a comedy tonight!*

—Stephen Sondheim,
A Funny Thing Happened on the Way to the Forum

❁ ❁

1

❀❀❀❀❀❀❀

Dying is easy. Comedy is hard.
—attributed to every dying English actor
since Richard Burbage (1567–1619)

TUESDAY
Young Frankenstein (1974)
and *Count Bubba, Down-Home Vampire* (last Friday)

The guy in row S, seat 18, was dead, all right. There was no mistaking it. For one thing, he hadn't laughed once during the Blind Man scene in *Young Frankenstein*, which was indication enough that all brain function had ceased. For another, there was the whole staring-straight-ahead-and-not-breathing scenario, and the lack of a pulse, which was good enough to convince me.

"Were you the one who found him?" I asked Anthony (not Tony, mind you), the ticket taker/usher/projectionist. Anthony, a Cinema Studies major at Rutgers University, was nineteen years old, and a film geek from head to toe (sorry, Anthony, but it's true). He was wearing black jeans, a T-shirt with a picture of Martin Scorsese on it, and a puzzled expression that meant he was wondering how to work this event into his next screenplay. Anthony shook his head.

"Sophie found him," he said, indicating our snack stand attendant/ticket seller/clean-up girl, who was standing to one side, biting both her lips and ignoring her cell phone, which was playing a Killers song by way of ringing. Sophie was, in her own high school junior way, freaked out. I considered gesturing her over, then realized she wanted to stay as far away from our non-respiring patron as possible, so I walked to her side instead.

"It's okay, Sophie," I told her. "Just tell me what happened."

She avoided looking toward the man, who appeared to be in his early forties, maybe five years older than me, and was dressed for a late April evening out in Midland Heights, New Jersey: pink polo shirt, with the proper reptile depicted on the left breast, tan khakis, no socks, and penny loafers that looked to have last been shined during the Clinton Administration. His box of popcorn was still on his lap, although there was very little left in it. The popcorn had spilled onto the floor at some point, but the carton remained in his hands.

"I was picking up the wrappers and whatever," she said, her usual teenage indifference betrayed by her wavering voice. "I saw him sitting there as the people filed out, and I didn't think anything about it. You know, some people just sit there and wait for everybody else to leave. But then they all, like, left, and he didn't move. And when I went over to see . . ." Sophie fluttered her left hand in a gesture of futility, and then it went to her mouth. She didn't want us to see her cry; it would ruin her image. Sophie was the Midland Heights version of Goth, which is to say, she wore all black and straightened her hair. But her clothes were clean and pressed, her makeup leaned toward pinks (which didn't have much effect on her pale complexion), and her shoes were open-toe sandals. She was about as Goth as Kelly Clarkson, but she was in there swinging.

"Okay," I said. "Did you call 911 like I asked you to?" It had been the first sentence out of my mouth when Anthony had informed me someone had died laughing—or in this case, *not* laughing—in our theatre. Sophie nodded earnestly, just as her cell phone stopped playing music. "Good. I think everyone had better stay put until the cops get here. They'll want to talk to us."

"Mr. Freed?" Anthony refuses to call me "Elliot," even

though Sophie, three years his junior, does. He thinks that just because I once sold a novel to a film company, and the movie was actually made, that I now have a direct line to Quentin Tarantino and must be treated with every respect. He's wrong. I looked at him. "Should we close his eyes or something?"

I think Sophie's hands went to her belly at that point. Not that she actually *has* a belly, but if there were one, that's where it would be. Sophie actually looked a little like a girl scarecrow dressed for an evening out at Dracula's place.

I shook my head. "No. Don't touch anything. Once the police get here . . ."

"When are they *getting* here, already?" Sophie asked. Her voice made her sound like she was about eight years old. "It's been *hours*."

I smiled with one side of my mouth. "It's been nine minutes, honey. Take it easy. Do you want to go and wait in the lobby?" She nodded, and was out the door in roughly the same amount of time it takes a Pauly Shore movie to go to DVD.

Anthony and I spent a few uncomfortable moments staring at each other, then he broke the tension by staring at the ceiling, while I completed a close study of the exit sign to the left of the screen rather than look at him or our less animated guest. Normally, Anthony would be asking me about some obscure movie he'd seen in class that week, and I'd be telling him I didn't know much about it, but let's say we were a touch preoccupied at the moment. A dead guy staring at a blank movie screen will do that to you.

Luckily, we heard the sirens just seconds later, which gave us a clear agenda, even if we didn't know what it would be yet. The people who handled these situations had arrived.

The EMTs got inside first, rolling a gurney and acting like it was an episode of *ER*. Clearly, we idiot civilians couldn't be trusted to tell when someone was dead, and it would be in their purview to resurrect my guest and show us all how ignorant we had been. Even medical people spend too much time watching television, and sincerely believe they, too, can be heroes in every possible situation. I had given up that attitude two years earlier, when my wife the doctor had decided she'd prefer to be married to another doctor. And then six months later, married him.

"Stand aside," the taller one said, despite the fact that neither Anthony nor I was standing anywhere near the stiff in row S, seat 18. The EMT and his partner rushed to the seat and blocked my view as their arms flailed and they barked orders at each other. After a few moments, the second EMT, eager for his role in the drama, looked dolefully at me.

"This man's dead," he said solemnly. If he'd said, "He's dead, *Jim*," he could have been DeForest Kelley on *Star Trek*; that's how perfectly final his words were.

"No kidding," I told him. "I thought he just wanted to get into tomorrow night's show without paying a second time."

He stared at me a moment, but was unable to react to my insubordinate behavior with anything except surprise. It was lucky for him that the police arrived at that moment. It was probably lucky for me, too, as I was feeling sorry about being so snotty, and was about to apologize.

Two uniformed Midland Heights police officers walked through the open door to the auditorium, a blond woman in her mid-thirties and a youngish man who looked to be of Indian or Pakistani descent. They nodded to the EMT, who had just pronounced the dead man dead, and the blond officer took a look at the guest of honor, who was now considerably more disheveled than he had been, but no more animated.

"What do you think?" she asked the taller EMT, who was probably the senior technician. He was about forty, and the flecks of gray at his temples gave him that look of authority that works so well in commercials for Lipitor and other cholesterol-lowering drugs.

He puffed himself up at the sight of the attractive cop. "Heart attack," he said. "It's just a guess, but it looks like it hit him so fast he didn't even blink before he was dead."

The blond officer turned to me. "Did you notice him during the film?" she asked.

"Nice to meet you, too," I told her. "I'm Elliot Freed. I own the theatre."

Her eyes widened a bit, and she almost smiled. "I'm sorry. It's my first dead movie patron."

"Mine, too."

She nodded. "That's Officer Patel," she said, indicating her partner, "and I'm Officer Levant."

Officer Patel was questioning Anthony over to one side. "I've never met anyone named Levant before." I'd seen Oscar Levant in some old movies, and was wondering if she were some descendant.

"It used to be Levine, they tell me."

My eyebrows probably rose. "You don't look it," I told her. I can say that because I *do* look it.

She pursed her lips, but not in a nice way. "My ex-husband," she said. "Given name is Baldwin."

"I didn't mean to react that way," I apologized. "I'm a little shaken up."

"Don't worry about it," she responded. "It's understandable. Now . . ."

"I noticed he wasn't laughing, during *Young Frankenstein*," I told her.

"What scene wasn't he laughing at?" She seemed to mean it.

"The Blind Man scene," I answered.

Levant looked surprised. "You should have called us sooner," she said.

Really? Could I have saved his life if I'd taken the talents of Mel Brooks more seriously? Levant smiled at my worried expression. "Calm down," she said. "I'm kidding. You'd think the owner of a theatre that only shows comedies would have a better sense of humor."

"I usually do, when everyone who walks in walks out after the movie is over. I'm not used to the police knowing the Mel Brooks oeuvre so well. Officer, I really didn't notice anything unusual about . . ."

Patel, who had put on latex gloves and approached the

body, was reading the driver's license from the wallet he'd extracted from my deceased guest's side pocket. "Mr. Vincent Ansella," he said.

". . . about Mr. Ansella at all, until Anthony told me something was wrong." I gestured toward Anthony, who was seated in row R, seat 2. He looked like, well, like he'd been in the same room with a dead body too long, and he was staring at Officer Levant in a way that made me notice how well she filled out her uniform. I'd never seen Anthony look like that at anyone before. I turned toward Levant again. "Any way we can get Mr. Ansella out of here now? I think my staff is getting a little spooked."

Levant shook her head. "I'm sorry, Mr. Freed," she said. "We'll have to wait until the detectives have been through."

I sat down. Row U, seat 1. "There have to be detectives, even when it's, um, natural causes?"

Levant nodded. "Procedure. We're never sure about anything until the autopsy, so then if anything looks suspicious, the detectives have seen the scene."

"They've seen the scene?" I smiled at Levant with the left side of my mouth. I'm told that's my rakish grin. Okay, so I'm not really told that, but nobody's ever specifically told me it *isn't* rakish.

"You'd prefer if I said they've surveyed the area of the myocardial infarction?" Levant responded.

I didn't have the time (or the wit, to be honest) to retort in an amusing manner, because the rear door opened wide, and a very large African-American man who looked like Colin Powell's stunt double walked in, dressed in jeans and a denim shirt. Behind him, Sophie slipped through the half-opened door with another uniformed cop behind her. She looked even paler than usual, which, for Sophie, is saying a lot. There are polar bears with more pigment in their faces than Sophie.

Levant noticed the plainclothes guy immediately, and her face lost its playful expression. "Chief," she said.

Okay, so he was the head of the Midland Heights Police Department. He walked up to me and put out his hand. "Barry Dutton," he said.

"No," I told him. "Elliot Freed. But I get that a lot."

The chief smiled. He reminded me of someone, I thought someone from television, but I couldn't remember who. "I'm Barry Dutton," he said. "I'm the chief of police. Sorry for your trouble tonight."

"More his trouble than mine," I said, indicating the guest of honor.

Chief Dutton surveyed the scene: the man's body was now slumped to one side in his seat, the popcorn box at a forty-five-degree angle in a hand that was only going to clamp more severely around it, his mouth wide open, his eyes the same, staring at a gigantic Teri Garr who wasn't there. "Heart attack?" he asked Officer Levant.

"EMT says it looks like," she answered. "Mr. Freed here says nobody noticed anything unusual during the movie, except that the man wasn't laughing."

"The first movie or the second?" Dutton asked.

"We're showing *Count Bubba, Down-Home Vampire*, so I try not to be in the auditorium during the second movie," I said. "I noticed he wasn't laughing at the first."

Dutton suddenly looked interested. "What movie?" he asked.

"*Young Frankenstein*," Levant told him.

The younger EMT's eyes narrowed, as if someone had told him something mentally taxing. "Isn't that *old*?" he asked.

"It was followed by the new Rob Schneider," I explained. "If you come for the classic, you can stay for the new comedy for free." The truth is, one ticket buys you admission to both films, since we show the classic first, but it sounds better if you say something's free. People like that. In theory.

"Now, Rob Schneider is funny," the EMT said. "But why go to a theatre to see some old movie you can get on DVD?"

Since there was a dead man in the room, I decided against explaining the communal experience of watching a comedy among others who might laugh. Levant stifled a grin.

Dutton gave the EMT a look that said "Less Roger Ebert,

more Dr. House," then turned to me. "You noticed him not laughing during the first movie and you didn't do anything?"

I blinked. "He's allowed to have bad taste."

"What about between movies? Anybody notice if he got up, talked to other people, *moved*?"

"We run a series of trailers and reminders to go out to the snack bar during the break," I told him. "We barely raise the lights between movies, so it's possible nobody would have noticed."

"Why don't you shut down in between shows?" Dutton didn't seem suspicious so much as curious.

"Frankly, we're not always sure we'll be able to get the projector started again after we turn it off," I told him honestly. "We like to keep it going."

"Do you recognize him?"

"No, but I didn't even sell him the ticket."

"Who did?"

I gestured toward Sophie, who looked like a Goth deer caught in Goth headlights. Her eyes were wider than I'd ever seen them, at least in the three months I'd known her, and she seemed awfully scared. I walked to her side. "Sophie sells the tickets," I told Dutton, and then turned to her. "You didn't know the man, did you, Sophie?"

She shook her head a little and looked like she might cry. I had a sudden urge to adopt her, which might or might not have been met with her parents' approval.

"Don't worry," Dutton told her. "Nothing bad is going to happen."

"Can we move away from . . . him?" Sophie asked in a tiny voice, pointing at the audience member least likely to return for another visit.

"Of course," Dutton said. We shuffled up the aisle toward the auditorium doors, and stopped about thirty feet from the EMTs and their patient. On the way, I saw Dutton take Officer Levant aside and say something to her quietly. Maybe he thought Sophie might be more comfortable talking to a woman, because Levant stepped between us and smiled gently at Sophie. "Did you notice if the man was alone or with somebody when he bought his ticket, Sophie?" she asked.

Sophie shook her head a little. "I don't really remember, but I think he was alone," she said.

I gestured to Anthony, who had been avidly watching the EMTs put Mr. Ansella in a body bag, no doubt filing it away for use in a movie one day. Anthony's a nice kid, but nothing has ever happened to him that he wouldn't someday write into a script. He walked over to us with his hands in his pockets, staring at Officer Levant with an odd expression I took to be lust. She looked discouragingly at him, and I felt for the kid. Looking at the officer under different circumstances, I might have had the same expression. On Anthony, it was strangely touching in its hopelessness.

"Anthony is the usher, and he keeps an eye on the house during the show," I told Levant and Chief Dutton. "Was Mr. Ansella sitting with anyone, Anthony?"

Anthony seemed to be considering the question, or maybe he was thinking about the incredible leap forward in special effects technology that *The Lord of the Rings* trilogy represented. All I know for sure is that he furrowed his brow. "I don't think so," he said. "I mean, I wasn't paying special attention to the guy, but I think I remember a woman sitting next to him during the first movie, but not the second one. Blond, I think."

"Just sitting next to him, or with him?" Dutton asked.

"I don't know. I wasn't really paying attention to them, and it's really dark in here during the movie. I see most of it from the projection booth," Anthony told her.

The taller EMT walked over to Dutton. "I think we've about done it, Chief. Can we take him out of here?"

"How long's he been dead?" Dutton asked.

"I'm not the ME, but I'd say two or three hours."

Dutton nodded, and said, "Take him. But tell the ME to take a look right away. I want to be able to tell Mr. Ansella's next of kin what happened to him for sure."

The EMT popped a stick of gum into his mouth and

walked away, giving Dutton a mock salute. I hoped it was sugary gum. Anyone who thinks Rob Schneider is funnier than Gene Wilder deserves tooth decay.

Officer Patel walked over carrying a sealed plastic bag. "I've got his personal effects, Chief," he said. "Wallet, cell phone, keys, a couple of ATM receipts. No prescriptions that would indicate a medical condition; nothing special."

Dutton nodded. "Bag some of the popcorn," he told Patel. "It was the last thing he ate. Maybe got some stuck in his throat or something; the ME might want to see if it matches what he finds." Patel took another plastic bag from his pocket and walked back to row S.

Dutton looked at me, then at the area where Mr. Ansella had been seated. He turned to me and asked, "Do you sell cheddar popcorn?"

It took me a moment to realize he was serious. "No," I told him. "We pop our own. It's butter or nothing."

Dutton took another look at the scene as the ambulance personnel prepared to roll Ansella's body up the aisle. Sophie looked absolutely horrified, and Anthony, fascinated. With Dutton's approval, I told them they could go home, that I'd close up. I don't think it took an entire second before Sophie was out the door. She was only a few moments behind Mr. Ansella's body.

Patel gave row S one last examination, taking the rest of the popcorn box with him in another plastic bag as an afterthought.

Dutton looked up at the balcony. "Was there anybody up there?" he asked.

"No. The balcony is a little shaky, and I don't keep it open. Besides, we didn't have what you'd call an overflow crowd tonight," I told him. Dutton took that in, and then stuck out his hand and smiled.

"Sorry again for the trouble," he said. "Good night, Mr. Freed." He turned toward Levant. "Officer." Patel walked up the aisle behind Dutton, checking at the door to make sure they hadn't overlooked a Junior Mints box that might be evidence in Ansella's heart attack. They hadn't, so he exited, too.

Levant watched as I got the broom from the lobby and swept up what was left of the popcorn.

"This bothers you," she said. "You put on a good show, but it bothers you."

"Of course it bothers me. I bought the theatre because I wanted people to have a good time. I wasn't prepared for one of them to have his *last* time here. How many people have a heart attack while watching Cloris Leachman?"

Levant raised her left eyebrow. "It's not your fault the man died."

"I know, Officer Levant—"

"It's Leslie."

"I know it's not my fault, Leslie. I'd just prefer the guy died of natural causes somewhere else."

She nodded, and turned to walk up the aisle. "I have to go file my report, Mr. Freed."

"Elliot. And thanks. Sorry we didn't get to meet under less morbid circumstances."

"I'm sure we'll meet again, Elliot," she said.

"What do you mean?"

"I was watching Chief Dutton," she said, as if that explained things.

I nodded, but I'm sure I looked puzzled.

"He saw something," Levant said. "I'm willing to bet you that was no heart attack tonight."

2

○◌◌◌◌◌○

I went up to the projection booth, rewound the films, and then finished cleaning up the theatre quickly; I admit, it was a little spooky being there by myself. I turned out the light on the marquee, which I should have done an hour before, and locked the front door when I left. I'd come in early tomorrow to clean up behind the snack bar.

My bike was chained up to a strong water pipe in the alley next to the theatre. I carried the front wheel, which I keep in the office of the theatre, and attached it once I unlocked the bicycle. I checked my watch before I got on; it was twelve fifteen in the morning.

I'm probably the only New Jerseyan left who doesn't drive a car. It's not that I don't see the utility of it—I have a driver's license, and make sure I keep it current—but I don't own a car, and I don't want one. They cost a lot of money, they break down often, they have to be parked on a regular basis, and they pollute what's left of our air. Everybody talks about doing something to help the environment; I'm doing what I can. Mostly.

There were few cars on Route 27 going south this time

of night, but I stuck to the sidewalk on the Albany Street Bridge into New Brunswick. I guess a bike lane is too much to ask for in a state where people hop into their cars to go from one room to another. Besides, the bridge is too narrow as it is, so adding a space for bikes would make it impossible for people to drive the Hummers they so desperately need in case New Jersey is attacked by the Visigoths.

It was cool but not cold out, and I was glad I had my *Split Personality* crew jacket on, although I don't like to be reminded of the experience that went into making that movie. Not that I was actually involved. I sold the book to the producers, the producers hired the writers, the writers changed the characters, the plot, and the title, and then the producers put in a credit that the resulting abomination was "based on the novel *Woman at Risk* by Elliot Freed." Which I suppose it was. It says so on IMDb. It also said so on the check, and I cashed it.

I'd spent two years of my life writing that book, and before that, another two years researching it: talks with private investigators, police detectives, victim rights advocates, psychologists, and prosecutors. Hollywood turned it into what they like to call an "erotic thriller," which meant that the main character was naked a good deal of the time for very little reason. I have nothing against naked women (damn it!), and as I said, I had—as my grandfather used to say—"no kicks coming." I had indeed cashed the check.

Once I had gone through the novel-to-film process one time, I was not anxious to do so again, and didn't feel like I had another book in me, anyway. Despite the movie, sales of the first book hadn't exactly set Oprah's heart aflame, and publishers were resisting the temptation to break down my door with offers of a fat advance on the next one. Which was just as well, since I didn't have a burning desire to sit myself down and start typing ten hours a day again.

Also, the movie deal had provided me with something I'd never had before: money. Enough of it that I didn't have to work very hard for quite some time. Enough that I could evaluate exactly what it was I wanted to do with the time I have remaining on this planet. And writing more novels that people didn't want to read wasn't it. Unfortunately, it was a lot easier to determine what I *didn't* want than what I did.

I've always loved the movies. Well, not including the *Split Personality* experience, but I was trying hard to block that out.

Specifically, I'd always loved comedies. The Marx Brothers. Mel Brooks. Billy Wilder. *Gene* Wilder. Laurel and Hardy. Buster Keaton. Woody Allen, before he decided he was Ingmar Bergman. Did I happen to mention the Marx Brothers?

But I couldn't *do* anything for the movies. Not after seeing how the writers on *Split Personality* were treated. (I'd say they were treated like shit, but in Los Angeles, with all the colonics they're into out there, they treat shit a lot better than screenwriters.) So that was out.

Since I'd never had the dream of being a director or an actor, and I was as adept at technical skills as I was at seducing women, working in the film business from the creative side was beyond my reach. And the business side of virtually anything had never interested me. Add to this the fact that almost *any* job in the movie business would have required a move three thousand miles west, and it seemed smarter to take my Hollywood-based windfall, invest wisely (as soon as I hired someone to invest it for me), and live a life of modest means off those investments and whatever commercial writing work I could get. After all, my ex-wife was actually paying *me* alimony (that would teach her to go to medical school!), and I had inherited my parents' house in Midland Heights, mortgage free, when they moved to an "active adult community" in Manalapan. They'd saved enough to give me the house and still put a down payment on the condo they bought. You'd think this would teach me something about the value of savings. At least, you'd think that if you didn't know me very well.

But I had gotten restless in the four-bedroom, two-bath Victorian with the wraparound porch. If Sharon and I had stayed married and had children, it would have been a perfect place to live. But we hadn't, and I didn't even have a dog to use the fenced-in backyard. It seemed greedy to deprive some lovely family of their dream house, so I put the place on the market, insisted the broker sell it to people who had at least two children, and rented myself a town house on the Raritan River in New Brunswick.

It seems that some ambitious real estate developers had noticed that New Brunswick, a city in decline in the 1970s and '80s, was turning into a hub for theatre, restaurants, and health care. Figuring people would now want to live here, they built a good number of luxury condominiums right on the river to cater to the postgraduate crowd from Rutgers University, as well as the professors and support staff who work there. Unfortunately, the people who bought the condos, like the person from whom I was renting, soon discovered that New Brunswick school funding hadn't improved much since the 1970s and '80s, the city still had the same crime as any urban center, and whaddaya know, even with theatres, it wasn't Broadway. So they moved out and rented to people like me, who didn't care and liked the city just the way it was. Living in New Brunswick, an unattached single person like myself can walk to the train that goes into Manhattan, eat well without cooking, and admire a view of an extremely muddy and smelly river outside his window whenever the mood strikes.

The money from the sale of the house and the book left me with quite a bank account (since my parents refused to take the half of the proceeds I offered), and renting meant the lack of a large mortgage payment every month. So I suppose it was only a matter of time before I inquired about the availability of the Rialto, the lone, long-abandoned movie theatre in Midland Heights.

In typical cagey fashion, I invited the real estate agent, Virginia Squeo, out to lunch, letting her believe I might be interested in looking for a new home in town (nobody in New Jersey, especially real estate dealers, believes that you *want* to rent). I figured I could casually ask about the Rialto, just as a passing whim of a guy at loose ends. Ginny surveyed her salad and my steak sandwich, decided I was getting the better of the deal, and gave me a list of houses in the area that might interest me. But she'd known me a few years, and she saw the cursory glances I gave the photos she was showing me.

"You don't want a house," she said, eyeing me. "Why did you call me?"

"I'm interested in you as a person," I said.

"No, really."

There was no point in trying a deception; I'm just no good at it, or I'm out of practice. "What's the deal on the Rialto?" I asked. "I saw your name on the sign out front."

Ginny's eyes lit up like a pinball machine when you've knocked the ball all the way around the glass and into the "triple bonus" hole. *"The Rialto?"* she asked. "You're interested in the *Rialto*?" Heads turned three tables away. Ginny was already counting the bonus money she'd probably win in the office pool for lining up a sucker on the least-sellable property on the board.

I maintained my level of cool, which was equivalent to that of the average jalapeño pepper. "Just in passing," I tried to croon, but sounding much more earnest than I should have. "I just thought about owning a movie house, and it seemed like fun."

"Fun?" She snorted. "You think owning a single-screen movie theatre in this era of multiplexes would be fun? Elliot! You'd lose your shirt in six months."

"Maybe." I nodded. "But right now, I have some money, and if the place is in some kind of working order, maybe I could make something out of it. It's something I've always wanted to do, and if I don't take the chance while I have this windfall, I'll never really know, will I?"

I spent the next two hours talking the Realtor into selling me a property she was desperate to get off her hands. We negotiated on price, and I did better than you'd expect, since the owners of the building had been listing it for years, and I was the first person to express an interest in buying it outright. I held out for some reductions and some renovations, and got them. And a few months later at the closing, I paid cash. I owned the Rialto, from its leaky roof to its mouse-infested basement.

Once over the Albany Street Bridge tonight, it was mostly downhill toward my condo. The streets in this section of town, with few businesses open at this time on a weeknight, were relatively empty, and it didn't take me long to get where I was going. Entering the development, you'd have thought you were in a tiny suburban town, the Epcot Center of New Jersey. Each townhouse sported its own young tree in front, brick facing, and brightly painted door. The idea that only a block to the east there was a bustling city of forty-nine thousand people was downright surreal.

I carried the bike up the front steps, all six of them, and unlocked my very green front door. Inside, there was no sound, which is what I'm used to, and I locked up again behind me, because this is New Jersey, and that's what you do.

I left the bike in the foyer and walked into the kitchen for a quick snack before going to bed. Strangely, Mr. Ansella's premature departure from this earth had not blunted my appetite. Luckily, I bike a lot, or I'd have trouble getting through that eye-catching door.

The message light on the kitchen-wall phone was blinking, which is unusual. Most people know they can find me at the theatre during the day, and anyone who doesn't know me is usually put off by my voice-mail message, which says, "I'm not in. If I don't know you, don't leave a message, because I won't call you back. It's nothing personal." So, after a night in which I had to deal with a corpse in row S, I was more than a little shaky as I reached for the playback button.

"Mr. Freed, we just met, but I think I know you well enough to leave a message," the deep voice said. "This is Chief Dutton of the Midland Heights Police Department, and I'd appreciate it if you would call me back as soon as possible. I'll be waiting at the following number." And the rumbling voice gave a local phone number, which I assumed was his home or cell, given that it did not end in a "00," and was probably not the department's headquarters.

This was not good news. I dialed the number immediately, and the phone was answered on the first ring. That didn't bode well, either.

"Barry Dutton."

"Chief, this is Elliot Freed. I just got your message. I assume this is about Mr. Ansella?"

"Yes it is, Mr. Freed. Thanks for calling back. I'm afraid there's been a wrinkle in the case since we left the theatre tonight."

A wrinkle? What kind of cop uses the word "wrinkle" about a heart attack? "Is there a problem, Chief?" I asked.

"I'm afraid so. I got a call a few minutes ago from the medical examiner's office in New Brunswick. They're not issuing a report for quite some time, but something leapt out at them immediately on the arrival of the body."

Images from *Alien* were hard to repress. Something *leapt out at them* from the body?

"It was just a heart attack, wasn't it?"

"No, it wasn't," Dutton said. "Mr. Ansella was murdered. There appears to have been some kind of poison used on his . ... um . . ."

"His what?"

"His popcorn."

3

Chief Barry Dutton seemed even larger in daylight. The next morning, when we had agreed I could come in without an attorney (luckily, Dutton didn't see any reason why I would poison a customer—yet), I sat in his extremely utilitarian office, between a file cabinet and a vinyl sofa that must have been left there by the set decorator on *The Nutty Professor* (the original Jerry Lewis version).

"I know you, don't I?" he asked. Not a reassuring way for a cop to open a conversation. "I thought so when I met you last night." He made a show of snapping his fingers. "You wrote that book that they made into that movie."

I suppressed the impulse to tell him how eloquent he was, and said, "Yeah."

"Meet a lot of police officers, doing the research for the sex picture?" I couldn't decide if he was James Earl Jones or Yaphet Kotto. Right now, he was leaning toward Mr. Jones, in his Darth Vader mode.

"It wasn't a sex picture when I sold them the book," I said. "I tried to accurately portray the police I met."

But his face was already wearing a mischievous grin

that said he'd been kidding. "I read the book, and thought it was very good," Dutton said. "Never saw the movie." Maybe I was being too hard on him. He had a Yaphet Kotto quality, especially in his jollier *Homicide: Life on the Street* episodes. Yes. Kotto, for sure.

"Kind of you, Chief," I said. "Thank you."

"So. Why are you poisoning your customers' popcorn?" Wow, he could really segue.

I said something like, "Ahhhh . . ." Don't feel bad. Not everyone can match my quick wit.

Dutton smiled. "Take it easy, Mr. Freed," he said. "Since you've done your homework, you understand that I have to look into every possibility. If there was something in all the popcorn at your theatre . . ."

"Then I would have had a lot more people staying through the end credits, Chief. If the county coroner . . ."

Dutton stopped me. "We're required to say 'medical examiner,' " he said. "I think it started around the time of *Quincy*."

So, our chief of police had a sense of humor. That was going to make this easier. "Okay, so if the *medical examiner* found something that caused Mr. Ansella to keel over halfway through the first movie, anyone with a decent popcorn habit would now be residing in the next drawer over from him, wouldn't they?"

Dutton nodded. "Yes, I'm assuming this was done to Ansella and Ansella alone. That's what leads me to believe it was done deliberately, and that's what makes it a homicide and not a very, very odd accident."

"So why am I here?"

"I've already called the Middlesex County prosecutor, and they'll be sending investigators over. I need you to understand why we're going to have to close your theatre for a day or two."

Close the theatre? Just when, after six months in business, we were starting to establish . . . Okay, so we hadn't actually been starting to establish anything in terms of attendance, but having the place closed for two nights certainly wasn't going to help. There had to be a way I could avoid that.

"Why do they need so much time when you and your officers were in and out of the theatre in less than an hour?" I asked.

"I thought we were investigating a heart attack," Dutton said. "Now it's a murder. I've had officers watching the building since last night to make sure the scene isn't contaminated. I'm taking the municipal responsibility for this case myself. For the duration, I'll be the primary for Midland Heights, and the county prosecutor will be sending someone to handle it from their end. We do that with any major crime. We're a small force."

"Chief, I understand the problem, but can't the investigators get through with any physical investigations they need to do before we open at eight o'clock tonight? Comedy Tonight is still a new business in town, and we're going to have a hard time building a following if we have to shut down with no advance notice. I'm already advertised in this morning's *Press-Tribune*."

Dutton picked up a sheet of paper from his desk, and actually put on a pair of half-glasses to read it more clearly. It was charming.

"In the past week, you've had a grand total of two hundred and fifty-two ticket-buying customers in your theatre," he said. "That's over a seven-day period, and on Friday and Saturday nights, you averaged a total of fifty-seven and a half people per evening." He put the paper down and looked over the half-glasses at me. That was not so charming.

"Yeah, but we made the half-person pay full price," I answered. Okay, I was embarrassed to hear those figures, and not on top of my game. So write your own joke and insert it there.

"I promise you, I'll see to it that your business is closed for the shortest length of time possible," Dutton said, ignoring my attempt at hilarity. "And we'll reimburse you for your advertising costs on anything you can't cancel. But we'll also need the full cooperation of your staff and, of course, you."

"My *staff* consists of a Rutgers kid who's still trying to understand *The Cabinet of Dr. Caligari* and a high school girl who can't scratch Goth together on her best night," I told him. "A half hour with each of them will be enough to wipe their minds clean."

"And you?" Dutton asked.

"I was stupid enough to buy the Rialto and rename it Comedy Tonight," I told him. "I am the innovator who brought old movies back to a market flooded with DVDs. I am the genius who refuses to screen Academy Award contenders because the Academy is resolute in its failure to recognize comedy. I'm the marketing master whose theatre brought in two hundred and fifty-two patrons in a seven-day week. I have exactly one regular customer, a man with a life so full he shows up to watch old comedies *seven nights a week*. Exactly how much useful information do you think you'll be able to get from me?"

"It's a decent point," the chief nodded. "Maybe we'll be done faster than we anticipate."

I remember thinking on my way out of the office that the interview could have gone better. Maybe I should have brought donuts. I'm told cops like donuts.

4

◦◖◖◖◖◖◦◦◖

"**Why** is this bothering you?" My wife—sorry, *ex*-wife—Sharon sat across from me at the outdoor portion of C'est Moi!, a cafe whose name is fifty-six times more pretentious than its food. I was having a caesar chicken wrap and Sharon was wolfing down huge bites of a reuben sandwich and maintaining her figure, which bugged me. "It's just a couple of days out of your life. Your business won't be hurt that badly."

"It's the principle," I told her, not looking up from my food so I could avoid seeing her roll her eyes. "The cops think they can simply shut me down just because a guy chose to have a heart attack in the middle of a Mel Brooks movie."

"It wasn't a heart attack, and you know it." Sharon brought her eyebrows down in a V that should have made her look like a Klingon, but didn't. "They have to investigate. Your problem, Elliot, is that you want this to be a freedom-of-speech issue, and it's not."

"You've always been good at pointing out what my problems are."

Sharon and I have lunch once a week, usually at C'est Moi!, but sometimes elsewhere. We frequented a diner in Highland Park called Penny's until it changed hands, and now we stay in Midland Heights, where my business and her practice exist within a couple of blocks of each other.

It started as a way to keep our divorce from being a typical, no-holds-barred, knockdown event in which the two people forget what it was they liked about each other to begin with and merely try to inflict as much damage as possible. But I still find talking to Sharon a way to define my strengths and weaknesses. I specialize in the "strengths" department, and she handles the rest.

I didn't say it was a perfect arrangement.

"Don't be snippy, Elliot," she said. "I know you're frustrated. But I can't believe it's the police closing your theatre for a couple of days that's getting you so angry."

"Stop saying, 'your theatre' like that. It makes my business seem like a cute little toy I've decided to play with that you think is just adorable, but that I'll outgrow."

"What should I say?"

"You should say '*the* theatre,' or 'Comedy Tonight.' I realize you don't appreciate the name I've chosen, but it illustrates what the place is about."

"Okay, fine. So, what's *really* bothering you, if it's not the police closing Comedy Tonight?"

Ah, who was I to argue? She was right (as was irritatingly often the case)—I *was* more worked up about losing two nights' worth of negligible business than I should have been. I just hadn't had the time, nor the inclination, to think about it long enough to understand why.

"I guess I'm insulted," I said finally. "Some person decides to off poor Mr. Ansella, whoever he was, and they go out of their way to do it in my theatre. I mean, poisoned popcorn? That's not a crime of passion; that's not an impulse buy of a murder. It's not a question of someone seeing an opportunity to get rid of a guy they really don't like and then possibly regretting a rash action later. This person had to plan it. Go over Ansella's schedule. Determine he was coming to my theatre last night, maybe lure him there."

"You just said, 'my theatre.' How come it's okay when you do it?"

I ignored her, which was another one of the issues in our marriage. "They had to decide how to kill him—poisoned popcorn. That was a decision *based on* his coming to Comedy Tonight—see, I said it correctly—and they used *my business* as the place to do it. They had to find a poison that wouldn't be detectable in popcorn, or one that would work so quickly that the bad taste wouldn't matter. And they had to get it onto his popcorn somehow, *knowing* that he'd order popcorn at the movies, and get him to eat it, then scurry away before they could be discovered. They did it on my watch, and they counted on my not stopping it."

There was a long pause. *"Scurry?"*

"Would you prefer 'slink'?"

She frowned. "So you're choosing to take it personally that whoever killed Mr. Ansella didn't just pour the poison into his coffee or do him in at the Laundromat? You think that the fact they killed him at . . . *Comedy Tonight* . . . was a personal affront to you? Geez, it's all about you, isn't it, Elliot?"

"Well. Not *all*." I felt sheepish, except for the woolly part.

"Maybe you need a life outside your theatre. Maybe you should start dating again. You said there was a blond cop? Was she cute?"

"You just want me to remarry so you can stop paying alimony."

She made a face like Donald Duck does right before he says something unintelligible. "Yes, Elliot. That's why I ask. Because between Gregory and myself, two practicing physicians, we really can't afford your alimony." Sharon could have left it there, but she was unable to resist. She mumbled, "Not that you actually *need* it . . ."

"Ha!" I am a man of few syllables.

My ex is not someone who is easily dissuaded. After all, it took six years of marriage before she divorced me—she probably kept thinking the following year would be better. She regrouped and dove back in. "I sincerely believe that you would be a happier man if you were seeing someone good for you," she said, putting a hand over mine. This was awkward, as I was actually reaching for one of her french fries.

"You want to assuage your guilt over leaving me for an anesthesiologist," I said. "A man who is paid large sums of money to put people to sleep."

She took her hand away, and I got the fry. "You're impossible," she said.

"On the contrary, the fact that you see me makes me possible. Highly improbable, perhaps."

"Lunch," said my ex-wife, "is on you."

"It's your money." I smiled.

5

❁❁❁❁❁❁❁

The Middlesex County Prosecutor's Office wasted no time
in sending someone to Comedy Tonight a mere six hours
later. I had already been waiting in the theatre—looking
for odds and ends I could repair quickly—for four hours
when the investigator, Detective Sergeant Brendan O'Donnell, announced himself ready to begin his work. There
were Midland Heights officers scouring the place—a couple of them had let me in when I proved I was the theatre
owner. They told me to stay away from "the crime scene,"
so I was sticking to the front of the auditorium, repairing
some broken seats in row C. I had briefly seen Officer
Leslie Levant, but she was in the lobby, and I was in the auditorium. It was going to be one of those days.

When not taking orders, the Midland Heights cops had
little to do with O'Donnell. They were the local cops, and
he was the investigator from the prosecutor's office. For a
force as small as Midland Heights', it was necessary to
bring in the County Major Crimes Unit on a murder, but
that didn't mean they were happy about it. They answered
his questions when he asked—which was a rarity—and

otherwise did little in the way of investigating besides searching under seats (although it was unclear what was being sought) as O'Donnell had directed them to do.

Sophie, who had come directly to the theatre from school, had gotten over her obvious horror of the night before, and was back to displaying the kind of overpowering level of blasé that only a teenage girl can muster. To look at her, you'd think Sophie wouldn't be especially concerned if Godzilla had entered the auditorium and demanded a really, *really* large soda.

Part of her demeanor could be attributed to the presence of her parents. Ron and Ilsa Beringer were trying hard to support their daughter, and by doing so, were in the process of embarrassing her to the point of physical violence. On Sophie's part. They stood with O'Donnell and me in the auditorium, while their daughter cringed at virtually every word they spoke, moaned frequently, and generally gave off the vibe that the ground should swallow them up.

Sophie wandered over toward Anthony, who was sitting and reading a copy of *On Location*, a publication for directors and crew. Anthony is nothing if not an optimist. Sophie started talking quietly to him, in an apparent attempt to forget her parents were in the room.

"She couldn't sleep a wink last night," Ilsa told Sergeant O'Donnell. "She cried for hours. The poor girl." Ilsa cast a glance in my direction that was not entirely friendly, while I wondered exactly how this had become my fault. "I held her in my arms for half the night." Sophie was trying as hard as she could to sink into the floor, and I think she had made it up to her knees at that point. "I can't understand why she'd ever set foot in this *place* again." Apparently, my providing her daughter with (semi) gainful employment was merely a ruse to traumatize her. I must have known someone was going to check out in my theatre the night before. After all, I was the *owner*, wasn't I?

I moved closer to where Sophie and Anthony were talking, noticing that Sophie's pseudo-Goth face appeared a little agitated. *"Just don't tell them anything, okay?"* I heard her hiss.

"They're your parents," Anthony said. "They'll understand."

"Have you ever *had* parents?" Sophie saw me walking over and straightened up, made her face impassive. I ushered Sophie back toward O'Donnell, who had more questions for her. She stared at her shoes.

Meanwhile, Ron patted his wife on the shoulder. "Come on now, Ilsa," he said, somehow speaking without actually moving his lips. "You know she's got to get right back on the horse." Really, the man had a future in ventriloquism if he wanted one.

"I don't know anything about a *horse*."

Anthony, sitting with his feet up on a seat in row G (which I'd asked him not to do, since it leaves marks, and our seats aren't in such great shape to begin with), put his head back and closed his eyes. He didn't want to embarrass Sophie, so he'd pretend he was asleep. He's a nice kid.

O'Donnell, however, wasn't interested in anybody's feelings. He stared past Sophie's parents and spoke to her directly. "Are you *sure* he came in alone?" he asked.

"I'm not *sure* of anything," Sophie said, her tone Gothful and disinterested. "How can we be certain of our own existence?"

"Don't be rude, Sophie," her mother admonished. "Mr. O'Donnell's simply trying to do his job."

O'Donnell ignored her, which was a talent I was hoping to develop. "We need to establish whether or not the man was here alone or with someone else who might have poisoned him. So I'll ask you again, Sophie. Do you remember whether he came in with another person, or by himself?"

"I don't look at every face," she said, staring into his. "But I *think* he was alone. I *think* he bought one ticket. And I *think* Fargo is the capital of North Dakota. I can't be sure." (She was wrong: the capital of North Dakota is actually Bismarck.)

"And I *think* that you'll have to do better than that if you want to get home at a decent hour today," O'Donnell said, seeing her Goth and raising her a Bad Cop. "Think hard, and I'll come back to you." He waved his hand, and Sophie and her parents walked to a corner near the exit. Sophie looked like she wanted to keep going, but her mother stood between her and the open door.

Through the auditorium door, I saw Officer Levant call over Officer Patel and ask him something, pointing to the basement door. Patel shrugged, then nodded his agreement. Reluctantly, I diverted my attention from Levant, who demanded attention even in a cop's uniform, and toward the guy running the investigation, although he wasn't as much fun to watch.

Sergeant O'Donnell glanced at Anthony, who by now really was asleep in perhaps the only two adjacent unbroken seats in row H. O'Donnell shook his head slightly, as if convincing himself not to do something he really wanted to do, and beckoned to me. I decided not to hide my resentment at the way he had talked to Sophie.

"You swept up after the cops left last night?" he asked.

"Yeah," I nodded. "Glad to see that you reserve the threats for the sixteen-year-old. She's just putting on a brave face, O'Donnell."

"*Sergeant* O'Donnell."

"You're not going to earn respect with me by browbeating that slip of a girl," I told him.

He curled his lip. No, really. "How am I going to get anywhere if your staff won't cooperate with me?" O'Donnell asked.

"Cooperate? Nobody's done anything *but* cooperate. Do you seriously believe that a high school junior poisoned Mr. Ansella at the movies because she had nothing better to do that night?"

"Of course not."

"Then why are you treating her like a suspect?"

"Because I don't know who the suspects are yet." Damn it, he had a point. O'Donnell sighed dramatically, which didn't fit his manner. "I don't think *anyone* on your staff is a criminal, Freed," he began.

He was interrupted by Officer Patel, who walked into the auditorium with an air of urgency I had not seen the previous night. Sophie and her parents, in the corner, were arguing, probably about her attitude (I distinctly heard the word "*Moth*-errrr"). The two cops took notice of Patel, but kept flashing their lights under the seats in row B. O'Donnell and I were the only other people in the room, unless you counted Anthony, who was snoring ever-so-slightly by now.

"You'd better take a look downstairs," he told O'Donnell. "There's something you're going to want to see."

Downstairs? I hadn't been in the basement in days, maybe weeks, now that I thought about it. The door was always locked when we were open for business. How could Mr. Ansella's murder have anything to do with my theatre's musty old basement?

"I'm coming with you," I told O'Donnell. He didn't object, but then again, he didn't say anything at all. He gestured to the two cops with the flashlights, and they followed him.

Patel seemed anxious to get O'Donnell downstairs quickly, so we didn't waste any more time. I noticed Sophie and her parents follow us out of the auditorium. Anthony was perfectly happy, his legs up on row G, seat 12. It would have been cruel to disturb him.

At the door to the basement was the open padlock, whose key I had given the officers when I arrived. The light was on in the stairwell, and Patel led the way. At the top of the stairs, O'Donnell pointed to Sophie and her parents. "Stay up here," he said. There was no protest. Even Sophie looked like she'd prefer it that way; the look from last night was back in her eyes.

O'Donnell followed Patel and I followed O'Donnell. The stairs were narrow, and frankly, I was curious, but in no hurry to confront whatever had gotten Patel so excited. He hadn't blinked once the whole time he was in the auditorium.

Officer Leslie Levant was at the bottom of the stairs, looking considerably more serious than she had the previous night. This was alarming, as the previous night there had been a dead body in the room. I tried to catch her eye, but she was looking straight ahead, following Patel with her eyes.

The basement was, well, a basement. I didn't keep anything perishable or edible down there, as I couldn't completely vouch for the absence of nonhuman forms of life.
There were some tools; some broken seats; access to the
electrical, heating, air-conditioning, and water systems;
cleaning supplies; and a good deal of dust and grime.
Cleaning the basement of Comedy Tonight had always
seemed somehow superfluous, like polishing the decks of
the *Titanic*.

Had I known we'd be entertaining down here, I might
have reconsidered that position.

I might also have noticed the rows of large cardboard
cartons to which Patel was now leading O'Donnell and, by
extension, me. I definitely hadn't put them there, and to the
best of my memory, had never even seen them before. But
Patel was just about panting in anticipation.

"You see?" he said to Sergeant O'Donnell. "There are
close to two hundred boxes. Almost ten thousand in all."

"Ten thousand *what*?" O'Donnell and I said, almost in
unison.

Patel opened the flap on one of the cartons and pulled
out a small jewel case. Levant came up behind me and
stood a little to my left. I didn't see her, but I could tell she
was there.

"These," Patel said. "Almost ten thousand of *these*."

O'Donnell held up the jewel case, the size of a CD or
computer disc, and I caught a look at the artwork on the
front cover, which made my stomach fall to an area somewhere around my left knee.

"Okay, I give up," O'Donnell said. "What do some CDs
have to do with . . ."

"They're not CDs," I broke in. "They're DVDs. And
they have the artwork from the poster I have hanging outside my theatre right now."

O'Donnell's face was impassive as he thought that over,
and then his eyes widened and his head tilted back just a
bit. "So that means . . ."

"Exactly," I said, although it sounded like my voice was
coming from another part of the room. "Officer Patel has

found close to ten thousand pirated copies of *Count Bubba, Down-Home Vampire.*"

"You know, Freed, pirating copyrighted material is a federal offense. If we discover that these were being offered for sale outside the state of New Jersey, I'd have to bring in the FBI." O'Donnell was looking at me, but he was really watching his career advance by about seven steps in an afternoon.

"Is there a reason you're telling me that, O'Donnell?" I asked defiantly, while feeling about as defiant as the average ladybug.

"*Sergeant* O'Donnell." He left out "of the Middlesex County Prosecutor's Office," which I considered a friendly gesture.

"Why did you point that comment at me, *Sergeant*?" I asked.

"Well, as you keep pointing out, it's your theatre," he said.

"Honestly, with a murder investigation going on, if I was keeping pirated movies in my basement, do you think I'd be stupid enough to leave them here waiting for you? I had lots of time to get them out of here, if I'd known they existed to begin with."

"There have been cops watching the theatre since last night. And to tell you the truth, I just met you a half an hour ago," O'Donnell answered. "I have no idea how stupid you are."

"I'm . . ."

"He's not stupid, sir," Officer Levant stepped forward and volunteered. "It's not that I know he wouldn't pirate movies, but given the choice, he'd certainly have pirated *Young Frankenstein* instead."

We'd barely spoken the night before, but she'd definitely gotten a strong sense of my character. Because that's exactly what I would have done. I began to see Leslie Levant in a nonofficial light.

"Not as profitable," O'Donnell countered.

"I own a movie theatre that only shows comedies, and half of them are classics made before you were born," I told him. "Do I sound like the kind of a guy who worries about what's *profitable*?"

"You sound like the kind of a guy who could use some extra income," O'Donnell said. Somehow, alimony from my ex-wife didn't seem the type of thing I wanted to mention in front of Levant, so I said nothing.

It was Officer Patel who broke both the silence and the glares being traded between O'Donnell and me. "Well, if it wasn't you, Mr. Freed, could it have been one of the people on your staff? Do they have the key to this area?"

"No, but they know where I keep it, and they could get at it if they wanted to." I took a breath. "Hey, wait a minute, neither of my staff did this."

O'Donnell cocked an eyebrow. "Oh, really?" he asked. "And how do you know that? You told me you've known them for maybe four months. You can vouch for their integrity?"

"I've known Anthony for five months, and Sophie for three," I said. I pushed air through my lips in a scoff. "Sophie's sixteen years old. She's more concerned with finding black clothes to wear than selling pirated DVDs."

"She has to pay for those clothes with something," O'Donnell said.

"Please. She has the pittance I pay her, and, oh yeah, the money she gets from her parents, who own three different hybrid vehicles for the two and a half drivers in the family. I don't think Sophie has tastes *that* expensive."

"How about the other kid?" he asked.

I hadn't wanted to think about that one. Anthony, budding young filmmaker that he was, always needed money for his latest project. He would have had access to the equipment to dub the film, not to mention to the projector and the film itself, and he knew every piece of technology ever invented by its first name. It could have been him.

"It couldn't have been him," I said.

O'Donnell nodded with great sarcasm, the unofficial State Language of New Jersey. "Let's go ask him," he said.

After directing Patel to stay with the cartons, O'Donnell led Levant and me upstairs. Sophie and her parents were still in the lobby, where Sophie was busying herself with washing down the frames for the Coming Soon posters, and her parents were finding the tiny spots she missed before she had a chance to check for herself.

We walked directly into the auditorium as I tried to think of ways to a) accuse Anthony of video piracy and send him to a federal penitentiary, and b) wake him. As it turned out, neither of those tactics would be necessary.

Row H was empty. So were all the other rows and seats. Anthony was gone.

6

❀❀❀❀❀❀

It had been useless to search for Anthony, I realized the next morning as I was biking back into Midland Heights from New Brunswick. He had turned off his cell phone, never gone back to the off-campus apartment he rented with three other Cinema Studies majors, hadn't called his parents (and the police calling them had made for a truly memorable experience, I'm sure), and had no girlfriend, which wasn't a tremendous surprise. Most women wouldn't flock to Anthony until he had won his first Golden Globe Award.

If he were behind the pirated videos, did they have anything to do with Vincent Ansella's murder? How did the two fit together, if at all? And how much longer did this mean Comedy Tonight would have to remain closed? (Not all my impulses are altruistic.)

Sergeant O'Donnell had again questioned Sophie and her parents, but they insisted they hadn't seen Anthony leave the auditorium, and I believed them. The officers had followed us out of the auditorium when we left, assuming Anthony was asleep, and he'd probably gone out one of the side exits, which the cops had been using all day. Normally, those doors set off an alarm, but I'd turned off the bell at the request of the police.

See? It pays to show that fire exit announcement before every movie.

I had no idea where to start looking for Anthony, although O'Donnell had been skeptical about that the night before. I'd shown him my records, which listed Anthony's parents as the "in case of emergency" contacts, and his address on Guilden Street in New Brunswick as his local address, but the investigator had insisted I must know of some other contact in case Anthony didn't show up for work one night.

"Anthony hasn't missed a day of work since I hired him," I'd told O'Donnell. He wasn't happy about that, either.

I rode up Edison Avenue past the Dunkin' Donuts to Comedy Tonight. My father, Arthur Freed, stood in front of the theatre, ahead of me as always, dressed in polyester slacks, a belt, and a double-knit shirt that was less wrinkled than the tuxedo I'd worn at my wedding. I stopped the bike just at the door.

"I thought we were painting today," I told my father. We get together once or twice a week to do repairs and continue the restoration of Comedy Tonight.

He looked puzzled. "We are."

"You dress better for painting than I would to apply for a bank loan."

Dad chuckled. One of his many virtues is that he thinks I'm funny, even when I'm being perfectly serious. The man hasn't raised his voice to me once since I was fourteen, and that's mostly attributable to the fact that even when I was doing my adolescent best to infuriate him, Arthur Freed thought I was a riot.

I unlocked the front door and let him inside. Today we were working in the auditorium, not the lobby, since I didn't have to worry about patrons smelling paint fumes or getting ladders out of the way in time for the show. Not today. Maybe not tomorrow. *(But soon, and for the rest of my life?)* In fact, who knew when? Now that evidence of a second

crime had been found on the premises, it was anybody's
guess when Comedy Tonight could reopen.

When my father retired from the retail paint and wall-
paper business, he probably didn't expect to spend this
much time immersed in the decoration of a rapidly deteri-
orating movie palace. Okay, movie house. Movie fixer-
upper. But he had offered to help, in his typically genial
way, and I had accepted as much to hang out with Dad as to
get his expertise, which was considerably more expert than
my own. I had pretty much given up painting in kinder-
garten when they switched us from fingers to a brush.

I'd bought the Rialto slightly less than a year ago, and
for six months after the transaction closed, I had prevailed
upon friends, called in every marker I'd ever issued, downright blackmailed a few people, and when absolutely necessary, paid others to help renovate the place. I'd been
intelligent enough to have a structural engineer come through
before the closing, and while there were a few questions here
or there (chiefly in the balcony), I was assured in writing that
the place wasn't likely to slide off its foundation anytime
soon, and probably wouldn't need much beyond the kind of
cosmetic work you might expect in a seventy-year-old structure that hadn't undergone much maintenance in the past
decade.

There had been beams in the ceiling that needed replacing; cracked (and, in some cases, missing) plaster facades;
floors that needed to be sanded, filled, and refinished; seats
that flat-out needed to be replaced; and the entire lobby
(except the snack bar), from carpet to art deco ceiling, had
needed to be completely redone, thanks to Hurricane Floyd's
trip through the area in 1999.

My father, freshly retired practically at the moment I
bought the theatre, was always there supervising, since the
union workmen wouldn't let him up on the scaffolds to do
the work himself. He had spent forty years with painters,
wallpapers, carpenters, and contractors, and he had spent
the same forty years owning a home that practically had to
be rebuilt on the day he purchased it. My mother had complained about his constant work on the house when I was a

boy, but never missed an opportunity to point out his hand-
iwork to visitors. It was never fancy, but it showed crafts-
manship and imagination. I was sure the family living
there now appreciated his efforts.

Maybe that was part of what had attracted me to the
Rialto. Today's theatres look like large college dormitory
rooms: they're square, functional, and impersonal. It's a
good thing they have a screen and seats, or you'd think you'd
entered the largest police interrogation room in the world.

The Rialto was built during a more creative age. Movies
were being made by people who wanted to make movies,
and were happy with the money that came in. Today,
movies are made by people who want to make money, and
are happy with the movies they make to achieve that end.
There's a difference, and it shows in the theatres as well.

The over-the-top architecture evident in the Rialto
wasn't terribly unique in its day, but in today's world, it is
nothing short of astonishing. Plaster moldings and appoint-
ments around the auditorium (a uniplex) were only part of
the deal. Lighting was discreet but impeccably placed to
highlight the impressive features of the room, and there was
a real, huge chandelier (which I'd had to have reinforced, as
we were not planning on a nightly showing of *The Phantom
of the Opera*), and a cupola that held it, as well as paintings
on the ceiling reminiscent of the frescoes of Rome, only
less religious. Cleaning the paintings themselves had taken
two whole weeks. You can't just go up there with a huge
bottle of Windex and expect that kind of thing to survive in-
tact. I know that now.

I unlocked the utility closet and started removing the
painting supplies: ladders, drop cloths, brushes, rollers,
buckets, and so on. My father pitched in with the smaller
items, since I gave him a stern look that said "Remember
your heart" whenever he reached for a ladder or a five-
gallon bucket of paint. I'd have stopped him from reaching
for anything at all, but whenever I did, he gave *me* a look
that said "Remember your head, because I'll hit it with a
hammer if you treat me like an old man." Every relationship has its give-and-take.

Setting up the ten-foot ladder under a green exit sign over a side door, I assessed the room. Besides the painting, which would take weeks, if not months, to complete, there was still the matter of a new sound system (what was state-of-the-art in 1954 sounded very much like two tin cans and a string today); various patches in various walls; many, *many* new seats; and about six miles of new carpeting, of which we currently had none.

My father studied my face closely. "Stop looking at the negative," he said. "Think about how much you've already done. Think about what it looked like when you bought the place."

"How can you tell what I'm thinking?"

"What are we, strangers? I lived with you for more than twenty years; you pick stuff up." He kneeled to stir a large bucket of paint. "But something else is bothering you. You want to tell me about it?"

"Not really."

He gave me another look, and I told him the whole story. He knew about Vincent Ansella's unfortunate (and apparently premeditated) demise from yesterday's newspaper, and was upset I hadn't told him myself. Now I explained about the discovery of myriad copies of a Rob Schneider movie, months before they would become $9.99 specials in the cutout rack. My father listened with careful attention, but still managed to get the paint ready, as well as a three-inch brush for my use at the top of the ladder.

I climbed up, a roller tray full of paint balanced in my left hand, my right tightly gripping the ladder. I'm not crazy about heights, even low ones, and since this ladder was not new, it wasn't at the top of my confidence chart.

"So, what do you think I should do?" I asked Dad as I reached the top of the ladder and the end of the story simultaneously.

"Do? Why do you have to do anything? Aren't the cops working on this?"

I nodded, not looking at him, but at the small gargoyle over the exit door, which was the target of my paintbrush today. "Sure, but once Anthony went MIA, they probably decided that he's guilty, so even if he shows up today, they're not going to look at anybody else. And with the discovery of the pirated copies coming so close to a murder in the theatre, they're going to look for a connection as hard as they can, and find one whether it's there or not."

My father got to work on some baseboards. Dad is a meticulous man, and he spread newspaper on the floor where he'd be working, despite the fact that he has never spilled a drop in my presence for as long as I can remember. "So you believe this boy isn't involved, is that it?"

"It's not in his character. He doesn't care enough about money, and if he did, he'd find another way to make it. Anthony isn't the type."

"So why do you think the cops won't figure that out?"

"Because they're cops, and they're going to look for the simplest answer. I don't blame them; they don't know Anthony, and all the circumstantial evidence seems to point to him. What throws me is his running away; it's not what I would have expected." I had to reach over a bit to get the gargoyle's nose, and I stopped talking. I have to concentrate when I'm leaning off a ladder.

My father took this as an indication that he should talk. He doesn't know me *that* well. "You've known this kid what, five months? And already you think you can guess what he'll do in any situation? Talk to his parents; I'll bet they have something to say about it that you won't see coming."

I leaned back and caught my breath, the gargoyle's nose now a lovely clean shade of white. "So you think I should ask questions? Get involved?"

"I didn't say that. But knowing you, and knowing the way you feel about this poor man dying in your theatre, you're *going* to get involved, so you might as well do it right." Dad wields a paintbrush like Carlos Santana plays a guitar: there is no wasted movement, and a finger is never put in the wrong place.

"The cops will be pissed," I said.

"Don't underestimate the cops," he admonished. "And don't let your mother hear you talk like that."

"Oh, for pete's sake, Dad."

"The cops will figure it out, Elliot," he said slowly, concentrating on the impeccably straight line he was painting. "Anything you do will be strictly to make yourself feel better. Hey." Dad stood up, holding something between two fingers. "What's this?"

"What's what?" I started down the ladder, happy for the excuse.

"It's evidence," said a voice behind us. Sergeant O'Donnell was standing halfway up the aisle. "That looks very much like a drug vial, Mr. Freed." Swell. Maybe the next time O'Donnell showed up, I could arrange to be holding a bloodstained carving knife.

My father stared at the small glass tube in his hand. "Really!" he said. "How did you know my name?"

O'Donnell walked toward Dad. "I didn't," O'Donnell said. "I was talking to him." He pointed at me.

"My son," said Dad. He finds the oddest times to exhibit fatherly pride.

"Please hand me the vial without touching it any more than you already have," said O'Donnell, holding out his hand, which was now gloved. "I don't want to lose any prints it might have on it."

I walked to Dad's side. "What do you think this has to do with anything, O'Donnell?" I asked.

"*Sergeant . . .*" O'Donnell began, and then gave it up. "I don't know anything yet," he answered after a moment, taking the vial and putting it in a plastic bag. "It depends on what that white powder inside might be. If it's your average recreational drug, I'd just assume someone in your audience felt the movie needed a little help."

"Come on. Rob Schneider needing help from drugs? That's crazy talk."

He didn't even smile. "But if it's whatever was found on Vincent Ansella's popcorn, that would be another story," O'Donnell continued. "I'm hoping that your father's prints aren't the only ones on the vial."

"I didn't do it," Dad said.

"Nobody thinks you did, Mr. Freed." O'Donnell looked at me as a couple of uniformed cops entered through the auditorium doors. "You'll stay closed until we know more," he said. "This place continues to be a crime scene."

"Swell," I answered. "We'll put that in the ads."

7

✿✿✿✿✿✿✿

The cops threw Dad and me out on the street with a comment about "contaminating the crime scene," so we had a quick lunch then parted ways. I was covered with speckles of paint, and Dad looked like he could be teeing off at Augusta. Some guys have it, and then there's the rest of us.

I rode home and took a shower. Small white dots fell off me, giving the strange impression that I had a weird skin rash I could wash off, but I felt better when I was done.

O'Donnell had actually ordered me not to return to my own place of business without asking his permission first, which was both insulting and understandable. But what he expected to find there was a mystery. Another one I could add to my list.

This left me with remarkably little to do. I had eaten already. Most people I knew were at work. The two young people I worked with on a daily basis were either at school or missing and presumed guilty. My wife was married to someone else. Daytime television can be hazardous to your mental health and, worse, didn't include baseball this afternoon.

I considered calling the Midland Heights Police Department, but I couldn't think of a plausible reason to ask if Officer Levant was on shift right now. She wasn't listed in the New Brunswick area phone book, which meant nothing. But calling the cops as a dating technique was a little too blatant a tactic for a guy just sticking a toe back in the pool after a divorce.

So I turned on the computer, scoured through my address book, and came up with the number for Margaret Vidal, which I dialed carefully, on the assumption that she would know if I misdialed her number the first time. She's a stickler for accuracy.

"Homicide. Sergeant Vidal."

"Ah, Meg, you charmer," I said. "The very sound of your voice is enough to thrill me down to my socks."

That voice added a growl now. "Is this my ex-husband?"

"Not yet. Meg, it's Elliot Freed."

I could hear the relief spread through the phone. "Jesus, Elliot! Stop sounding like my ex-husband. You practically gave me an embolism. What's up? Working on a new book?"

Meg had been my most reliable source of cop info when I was writing *Woman at Risk*. The first female detective on the Camden, New Jersey, police force, she let me follow her through a homicide investigation that I'd rather not describe, as it interferes with my digestion when I think about it. She'd answered every question, and had only gotten testy when I did something unbearably stupid—which was about once an hour—and we eventually achieved the kind of closeness that two people who know they're going to drift apart in a very short time can have. We held nothing back.

I'd seen her divorce coming, and if she'd seen mine, Meg had been kind enough not to point it out. If she hadn't been six years older than me and endowed with good taste (and if we hadn't both been married to other people), we might have been an item, but we weren't, and never considered it. That gives a man and a woman a real freedom to be themselves.

"If I ever tell you I'm writing another novel, Meg, you have my permission—no, my sincere request—to come and blow my brains out with your service revolver."

"I'd never do that, Elliot," she said warmly. "They'd catch me."

"You could plant another gun in my hand, make it self-defense," I suggested.

"It's sweet how you're always looking out for me," Meg answered. "So, you've called me for the first time in two years, and we've bantered. What do you want?"

I gave her a very quick rundown on my activities, my ownership of Comedy Tonight, and Vincent Ansella's untimely departure from this earth. "So here's what I want to know, Meg: how do you investigate a homicide?"

I could hear her brow furrow. "Okay. Get a pencil and paper, and write this down, because it's complicated."

What could I do but comply? "Okay. I'm all set, Meg. What do I do?"

"Let. The. Cops. Handle. It."

I'd actually written down *Let the* before I stopped. "That doesn't help me."

"Yes, it does. Professionals will find the answers. You won't. Don't get in their way. Do you trust the detective on the case?"

I thought about Dutton, then O'Donnell. "One seems good, but he's an administrator, the local police chief. The county guy might know what he's doing, but I can't tell. He irritates me."

"He irritates *you*?" Meg is a riot when she wants to be.

"Imagine such a thing," I said.

"Elliot, I'm not kidding. You're not the guy for this. You're intuitive, and you have a good eye for what's wrong at a crime scene; I know that. But you're not as smart as you think you are, and you have no practice. You can get yourself in trouble."

"They've already closed my business. How much bigger can the trouble get?" I asked.

"Suppose you find something out—by accident," she said. "You could piss off somebody who knows where you work and has access to poison. Is that worse than your movie theatre getting closed for a couple of days?"

"I dunno. We were showing *Young Frankenstein*. It's practically a crime against humanity to shut that down."

Meg sighed, which is not an uncommon sound when I'm talking to women. I consider it a plus, so long as the sigh doesn't become a groan. "What does Sharon say?" she asked.

"We, um . . . that is, Sharon and I . . ."

Her voice got very quiet and low. "I'm so sorry, Elliot," Meg said.

We caught up for a while longer, she admonished me a time or two more, and I hung up, promising to call sometime when I didn't have police questions. We both knew I was lying, but it was a sincere lie, if such a thing were possible.

I knew Meg was right: I shouldn't investigate Ansella's murder. But maybe investigating film piracy was exactly the job for a theatre owner. Sure: I had a background in movies. I'd have knowledge and abilities that those trained in crime detection wouldn't have. I'd be invaluable to . . .

Nah. That argument didn't even sound convincing to *me*.

This left me with few options for the rest of my day, so I read the newspaper.

I won't comment on the national headlines, as some people think that I'm a . . . what's the term? Oh yes, a throwback/liberal/bleeding-heart/tax-and-spend/pansy/unpatriotic/left-wing fanatic. Which is ridiculous. I've never taxed anyone in my life, unless you count my ex-wife's patience.

Locally, Midland Heights mayor Sam Olszowy was resigning his office to "spend more time with his family," which meant that the Middlesex County prosecutor was about to indict him for tax fraud. A special election was being quickly organized, but candidates hadn't been selected yet. In Midland Heights, whoever wins the Democratic primary will win the election, but in this case, there wasn't going to be a primary. Therefore, whichever candidate the Democratic Party decided to nominate would take the prize—which was by my count a part-time job whose only benefit was a parking space with your name on it in the municipal parking lot, where no one ever parks unless they're interested in being mayor. It's cyclical.

The entertainment section boasted a number of ads for new movies, and my tiny one for "Comedy Tonight: The Only All-Comedy Movie Theatre in New Jersey!" (I could have also listed it as the only all-comedy movie theatre in the Western Hemisphere, or on Earth. I'm only limiting myself because I have no idea if there are any all-comedy movie theatres on Jupiter.) Of course, I couldn't pull the ads in time to make a difference, and the two dozen people who were planning on attending tonight would become disappointed ex-almost-customers. Even my only "regular," a guy named Leo who showed up every night no matter what was playing, would probably desert me out of a sense of abandonment. My business plan was not exactly being executed with colossal skill. As if I *had* a business plan.

In the sports section, a good number of teams had beaten other teams in games. I didn't especially care which, but it's always fun to watch some baseball when you can. It's the only sport that can't exist without elegance.

That left the obituary page, and I found myself reading it, something I very rarely do. I told myself it was out of boredom, but the item at the bottom left-hand side of the page was the real reason I was scanning the newspaper at all.

Vincent Ansella, forty-three, insurance executive, had left a wife, Amy of Piscataway; a mother, Mrs. Olivia Ansella of Little Ferry; and a sister, Lisa Ansella Rabinowitz of Red Bank. No children, which I confess made me feel a little better. Apparently, his whole life had been about insurance, since the four-paragraph obit mentioned little else. Once captain of his high school track team, he had still run six miles a day. Until recently. Very recently. Two nights ago.

Because the medical examiner's report wasn't complete, the body hadn't been released to Ansella's family yet (the obit didn't mention this, only saying he had "died very suddenly"). But there was a memorial service planned for the next day at Carmeliso's Funeral Home in Edison.

Suddenly, Ansella wasn't just a dead guy to me anymore. I hadn't actually considered his life before, well, his death, until now, and it was gnawing at me. The guy had died under my roof, if you wanted to see it that way. I owed it to him to find out a little bit more about who he was.

I didn't want to bother his wife. I decided to call the office where he had worked, Mutual Life, Home, and Auto, in Bridgewater. I didn't know who his supervisor was, so I asked for the actuarial department, where the obit mentioned (at great length) Ansella had been a vice president.

It would have been, let's say, awkward to explain to the receptionist that I was the guy in whose theatre Vincent had been murdered, so I decided on a slightly less scrupulous approach. Okay, I lied outright.

"Hi, this is Elliot Freed of the *Press Digest*," I said, making up the name of a newspaper on the spot, and mumbling just a bit. "I'm following up on the death of Vincent Ansella, and I'm wondering who I should be talking to there." Let them decide.

"Hold on," the receptionist said, no doubt looking for someone to take this problem off her hands. I waited through two recorded explanations of an exciting new term life product while she no doubt ran around the office trying to foist me off on the least suspecting actuary.

Just when I was considering getting the insurance, but unsure who my beneficiary would be, the phone clicked back to life. "This is Marcy Resnick," a rather tentative voice said. "Is there some way I can help you?"

I reiterated the bogus story about being with a newspaper, although I think this time I was working for the *News Digest*. I'd have to work at my phony profession a little more diligently next time. "I'm just trying to get some background on Mr. Ansella," I added. "We're considering running a follow-up piece." I felt the "considering" would ease the blow when Ms. Resnick went to pick up her fictional newspaper the next morning and found no fictional article there. No doubt she would assume that not only was the story unworthy of print, but the company had decided to fold the whole publication, having decided that the public no longer had a right to know anything. It's a philosophy that has worked wonders at Fox News.

"Well, I don't know what I could tell you," she said. "We weren't exactly close friends."

"Did he have any close friends at the office?"

"Not really," Resnick said. "I don't like to say it, with him being gone, and all . . ."

Oh, go ahead and say it, I thought.

". . . Vincent wasn't really the kind of guy who told you much about himself," she continued. "He was very friendly, but he kept it casual. Everybody liked him."

"So you don't know much about him, I guess," I said. I wasn't really sure what I was looking for, anyway, and might as well terminate this conversation.

"No, not much he ever told me," she answered. "Listen, I don't like talking this way on company time. Do you want to meet for lunch or something?"

That was just what I needed, an hour's worth of conversation with a woman who didn't know anything about the subject I wasn't sure what to ask about. Not to mention, I'd already eaten lunch. There had to be some way to get out of this gracefully.

"Well, I don't want to take up your time," I said.

"Oh, it's no bother. I was going to go for lunch in a half hour, anyway."

I sighed, but inwardly. "Why don't you give me the directions?" I asked.

�❁�❁

Moe Baxter wasn't pleased to see me hanging around his auto repair shop on Edison Avenue. "You leeching off me again, Freed?" He moaned, his voice a rusty hinge. "Why don't you just buy a car?"

"Don't you see how this is a better deal for both of us,

Moe?" I grinned. He was going to give in, like he always did, but we had a ritual to perform, and Moe was giving it his all. "I get the ride I need for the afternoon, and you get someone reliable to test out the cars you repair. It's a mutual benefit. This way, you don't lose valuable time from one of your mechanics, and I don't charge you a dime."

"*You* don't charge *me*? I like that! I should charge you a rental fee. What happens if you smash up the car, Mr. Mutual Benefit? Which, by the way, is the name of the insurance company that's going to sue my ass."

"I'm the best driver you ever had, Moe, and you know it. Besides, if the car undergoes any damage at all, I'll pay to have it repaired. You get paid to fix the same car twice. How's that?" We had been through this at least once a month for the past six years, and had honed the routine down from twenty minutes to two.

He threw me a set of keys from a pegboard he had on the wall. "The red Mazda," he said, pointing. "Watch for a shimmy in the front wheels."

"I'll report back in excruciating detail, Moe," I told him.

He closed his eyes and sighed. "I know, I know."

I had plenty of time to evaluate the ride on the way to Bridgewater. Moe's employees had done their usual impeccable job, and there was no sensation of shaking in the steering wheel or the front end at all. Once satisfied on that score, I decided to evaluate the stereo system, although Moe hadn't asked me to do so. I considered it a value-added service for Moe. What are friends for, anyway?

The CDs in the console leaned heavily toward Willie Nelson and Johnny Cash, which would have been fine if I was trying desperately to become depressed. Luckily, the owner of this fine Japanese vehicle was also an aficionado of movie soundtracks, and had an Elmer Bernstein collection I found impressive, especially for carrying around in a car.

If you're driving with a purpose at all, you can't beat

the music from *The Magnificent Seven*, even if it does remind a person of Marlboro ads, back when there were Marlboro ads.

I met Marcy Resnick at an Applebee's on Route 22 West, just beyond the Bridgewater Commons, a fancy name for a fancy mall in a relatively fancy town. And yet, still room for an Applebee's (and for that matter, room for Route 22, the least fancy road in the state). You have to love Somerset County.

Marcy waved to me from a corner table, and we shook hands. I had brought a small cassette recorder to embellish the fiction of being a newspaper reporter. We had given each other rudimentary physical descriptions to recognize each other by (she had shoulder-length brown hair and was wearing a gray suit, and I looked exactly like me), and I had gone so far as to wear the *Split Personality* jacket, assuming (correctly) that no one else in the area would have one, or would at least have the good taste not to wear it in public.

I had resigned myself to not finding out anything useful (especially since I had no idea what constituted "useful"), so I settled down to order a beer—which was what I figured a reporter would drink—and to watch Marcy, an attractive woman in her early thirties, eat a shrimp salad.

It came as something of a surprise when she opened the conversation with, "I didn't want to say this over the phone, but Vincent was definitely not acting like himself lately."

Instinct immediately led me to push the record button on the cassette unit. "What do you mean, not acting like himself? Was he depressed?"

"No." She shook her head. "Although Vincent was usually a happy sort of a guy; not in an annoying way, like one of those chipper little secretaries who is always wearing a pin to commemorate some holiday or another, but just . . . happy. He was glad to be alive. Things were always good for him. He never told jokes—he hated jokes—but he liked banter. He was always using lines from Tracy and Hepburn movies, or the Marx Brothers." Damn. Now I liked the guy.

"So, what happened?" I asked her.

Again, Marcy shook her head. "I don't know. He stopped being happy. He wasn't *sad*, you know. He didn't mope around. But if you asked him how he was, he'd say, 'Fine.' Before, he'd say something cute, like 'That's kind of a personal question, isn't it?' He'd just lost his spark."

"But he wasn't depressed."

"No. He seemed more . . . *mad*, I guess. Angry. He started sniping at the other actuaries. Not a lot, but he'd kind of jump down your throat if you made a simple mistake. It was the kind of thing he'd have laughed off a few months before; but now, he'd just lose it."

"Any idea what changed?" I had taken three sips of my Anchor Steam, before remembering that I was driving Moe's client's car. Hell, I weigh 185 pounds; I should be able to handle one beer.

"I don't like to gossip . . ." Marcy said. But the look in my eye encouraged her. "There was talk around the office that he had, you know, trouble in his marriage."

"His wife was cheating on him?"

"No. I heard the other way around, but I don't know if it's true." She backed off. "You know what they say about speaking ill of the . . . you know."

"I'm sorry," I said. We sat for a few moments in silence, and I finally got up the courage to say, "Were there rumors about whom he was cheating with?"

"Of course. But no consistent ones. Everyone from his secretary to Julia Roberts, to . . ."

"You?"

"I've heard that was going around, but nobody said anything to my face." Her face was, at the moment, pinched and angry. "In any event, it wasn't true." That led to an even more awkward silence. And Marcy looked down at the table.

"You've already eaten, haven't you?" she asked me.

"I'm afraid so."

She smiled a sad smile. It was actually a very nice smile. "And you're not really a reporter, are you?"

My eyebrows might have raised a bit. "How could you tell?"

Marcy smiled another half-smile. "Most reporters probably would have put a tape in the cassette deck," she said.

8

We sat and talked for quite some time after that, as I had to explain myself to Marcy, which is something I'm not terribly skilled at doing. She didn't really understand why I was pursuing information about Ansella, but then neither did I, which made explaining it that much harder.

Finally, she realized she was overdue back at her office, and I needed to bring the car back to Moe, so we parted ways in the Applebee's parking lot, doing that awkward-handshake-when-you're-not-sure-if-you-should-hug thing that adults do if they have social skills deficiencies, like I do. Ask my ex-wife.

On the drive back to Midland Heights, I ditched *The Magnificent Seven* for a Susan Werner CD I found in the console. I couldn't sing along with a voice that feminine, but I could appreciate it, and it fit my mood, which was somewhat wistful but also a little bit amused.

What I had discovered about Vincent Ansella had been less a relief and more a cattle prod: he was another rabid comedy fan, and someone had offed him when he should have been in his element. Something had been bothering him lately, possibly involving his marriage. I can't say that kind of issue is completely alien to me, either. He didn't like jokes. I don't like jokes. Friends send me e-mails containing what they think are hilarious jokes all the time, because they figure the "comedy guy" must love these things. I hate jokes. I like wit, not contrived stories that end with someone making an obscene pun or confusing his wife with a horse or something.

Let's face it: if I had been Italian, drawn to actuarial tables, and dead, I could be Vincent Ansella.

Meanwhile, I was, in fact, the owner of a theatre that couldn't open, with a projectionist who had vanished into thin air upon being suspected of video piracy. And I was tooling around Central New Jersey in a borrowed car, looking into the life of a man I had never actually met while he was, you know, breathing. I'm sure Sharon would have been able to define exactly how this scenario showcased six or seven character flaws, but I was at a loss as to how to do so myself at the moment.

I dropped the car off with Moe, reported on its complete lack of a shimmy and the quality of the sound system, which could have used a subwoofer, and was given an extensive lecture on leaving the car the way the customer had brought it in. I thought that was silly, since the customer had taken the car in to have something done to it that would make it *different* from the way it was brought in, but my point of view was, as usual, discounted. I thanked Moe and left.

I rode my bike from Moe's shop to the Midland Heights police station, a short, squat building that could just as easily house the tax assessor's office, the public works department, and the water department. All of which it did.

I told myself the trip was based on the strong desire to help Anthony, to punch holes in the awful accusations being made of him, and to see that truth and justice would, indeed, prevail. And I *did* want to help the kid, but who was I kidding? I was riding over there as an excuse to "run into" Leslie Levant. Sly dog that I am.

I chained the bike to a rack in front of the building, but

left the front wheel on. Somehow, walking around with a bicycle wheel at the age of thirty-seven doesn't really impress the ladies the way it did at, say, fourteen. Funny how life moves on, isn't it?

There was a small waiting area right through the front door of the police headquarters, where a dispatcher sat behind bulletproof glass, apparently dispatching things. It's not a huge confidence-builder that the police department feels the need to reinforce its own reception area with bulletproof glass, but I guess if someone's going to fire at people, this would be the area for it. I'm told that a gun was once shot within town limits, but that was to start a 10K race, and doesn't really count.

The dispatcher, a painfully thin African-American woman in uniform, was talking into her microphone as I entered, so I waited until the orders to de-tree someone's cat or investigate a mysterious lack of froth on the cappuccino at the local coffee bar was given, then walked up to the small area of the glass where holes large enough to carry sound (and air) were drilled through. Just then, I noticed Chief Dutton through the window of the locked metal door to my right. The dispatcher looked at me.

"Can I help you?"

I thought of saying "That's a good question," but the gun on the woman's hip had a tranquilizing effect on my sense of humor, and instead, I answered, "Yes, please. Is Officer . . ."

Before I had the chance to make myself sound like a sophomore with a nasty crush, Dutton opened the door and called to me.

"Mr. Freed! I was just about to call you."

He was? "Can't be parking tickets, Chief," I said. "I don't have a car." I don't know why, but Dutton's shoulder holster didn't intimidate me nearly as much as the dispatcher's hip model, even if she was behind glass that could stop a bullet. I mean, I don't *think* anyone has invented one-way bulletproof glass, have they?

Dutton chuckled, sort of, a rumble that made me think of the late Peter Boyle in, well, *Young Frankenstein.* I can't imagine what had brought that film to my mind this week. "No, I just have a question or two for you. Would you come through, please?" He gestured inside. I looked at the dispatcher, as if to verify with her that it was okay for me to obey her boss, and she, inexplicably, nodded. I walked into the station, and followed Dutton down the hall.

We entered Dutton's office and both sat, after he indicated that I should. "Was there something we missed earlier, Chief?" I asked.

"No, it's just that things have developed a little bit, and I'm trying to make certain of a few things. Are you absolutely sure you don't know Anthony Pagliarulo's whereabouts right now?"

"No. I've tried everywhere I could think to look. He's nowhere to be found, so far as I can tell. Why, is he in more trouble?"

Dutton ignored the question, and pressed on. "No girlfriend?"

"Me, or Anthony?"

He smiled impatiently. "For now, Anthony," Dutton said.

"Have you *seen* Anthony?"

"I'll take that as a no. Any siblings in the area?" He caught himself in time. "Anthony, not you."

"Neither of us, as far as I know."

"Has he been having money troubles? Asked you for a raise recently?" Dutton's eyes narrowed a bit.

"You've seen my box office receipts. I'm barely making the payments on the Milk Duds. No, Anthony hasn't mentioned any financial problems. I don't think he even notices I pay him every two weeks." Okay, so Anthony had always wanted to make his own movies, but that would take millions; even if he were in on the piracy scheme, he wouldn't have made anything close to that. I figured the police must have had something more that pointed to Anthony in connection with the pirated videos, but I couldn't imagine what.

"So it's not sex, and it's not money," Dutton said. "What's left?"

"I can't answer that, because I don't know what we're talking about. Anthony's not the type to pirate DVDs of a bad movie, Chief. He'd sooner digitize a copy of *The Grand Illusion* and distribute it for free on the Internet."

Dutton leaned forward just a bit. "Has he done that?" he asked.

"No! Chief, it doesn't make sense. A man is poisoned in my theatre, and you seem more concerned about a few copies of a comedy written by six chimpanzees and an escaped mental patient. If you really want to witness a crime, you should watch that movie. You should arrest the people who want to buy it, and get them help."

Dutton leaned back in his chair and closed his eyes for a moment, measuring how much he should tell me. "You don't think it's a little more than unlikely that a man was killed in your auditorium at the same time a piracy operation was going on in the basement? This goes beyond a few pirated DVDs, Mr. Freed," he said.

"I suppose this is a bad time to ask you to call me Elliot."

He smiled, sincerely. "Elliot, believe me. We're doing everything we can about Mr. Ansella, but it's mostly out of my jurisdiction. Detective Sergeant O'Donnell is investigating for the prosecutor, and we're assisting. In the meantime, if there's anything more you know about the packages we found in the theatre basement, I'd really appreciate the help."

I searched my mind, but ended up shaking my head. "I haven't a clue, Chief," I said. "When Officer Patel led us down into the basement, it was the first time I'd been there in I can't tell you how long. And it was the first time I'd ever seen those boxes."

He stood up. "Well, then, I'm sorry to have wasted your time." Dutton leaned over and extended his hand.

There was something about his dismissing me that was just not right. He called me into his office just to ask if there was anything else I hadn't told him? There had to be another motive behind Dutton's sudden interest—and his Dr. Hibbard jovial attitude.

"What are you not telling me?" I asked. "What did they find in that vial in my auditorium?"

He had the nerve to look insulted. "Honestly, Elliot, you can't imagine that the chief of police would share details of a case with a civilian."

"Sorry." I shook his hand. "I wasn't aware there were national security issues at stake."

"You'd be amazed what a chief can't share," he said. "In some ways, even the uniformed officers have more freedom to talk than I do. Now, if you don't mind, I have to meet with the mayor about keeping my job when he is replaced by someone hopefully a little less obvious in his corruption."

We nodded at each other, and I walked out, more confused than I was when I walked in. The very definition of municipal government.

Luckily, when I closed Dutton's office door, I walked almost directly into Officer Leslie Levant, who was making her way toward me, having spotted me first.

"Elliot," she said, "did the chief call you about Anthony already?"

"Actually, I was here to see . . ." I almost said, "I was here to see *you*," but instead I finished the sentence with, "if there was any way for me to help Anthony out." Okay, I'm a coward. Now you know.

"It doesn't look good right now," she answered. "When they find him, I bet he'll be charged, and piracy can be a federal rap if they prove he sold any outside the state."

Well, if officers could be more open than the chief . . . "What changed between this morning and now?" I asked. "All they have are some boxes of DVDs in the basement."

Leslie looked confused. "Didn't the chief tell you?"

"Tell me *what*?"

She pulled me to one side of the corridor to stand closer, a move to which I did not object strenuously. There are some forms of police brutality that are not entirely offensive.

Leslie spoke very quietly, but with urgency, especially since Dutton chose that moment to walk out of his office.

Luckily, he didn't look in our direction as he walked down the corridor away from us. "What's changed is that the search warrant for Anthony's apartment came through this afternoon."

"And?"

"And when they searched the place, they found duplication equipment and empty jewel cases. Not to mention DVDs of four more titles: all the new movies that you've shown in your theatre for the past month."

9

○♡○♡○♡○

Leslie walked me outside, clearly concerned that the top of my head might blow off or that I might actually give myself a stroke through sheer will.

"It doesn't make sense! I don't believe that kid would do all this. He never talked about money; he wasn't the type to rail against the system. He wanted to make his own movies, not copy someone else's illegally."

"You can't argue with the evidence," Leslie said in her best police officer voice. "What doesn't make sense is that he'd have all that stuff in his apartment and all those copies in the theatre and *not* be pirating copies. You can't explain it any other way."

"Not yet, I can't. But give me a little more time—"

We both stood and stared for a long moment. Chained to a rack outside the local police station, a few yards from uniformed and gun-toting people sworn to uphold the laws of the state of New Jersey, was my sole mode of transportation. My bicycle.

Missing its front wheel.

"That's . . . that's . . ." I said. Sure, *now* I'd be able to think of something witty to say, but at the time, that was the best I could do.

"Is that yours?" Leslie asked. "Where's the front wheel?"

"That's . . . that's . . ."

"Did you leave it out here so you wouldn't look like a dork carrying it around in a police station? That's so cute."

Not as cute as it might have been.

Although I wanted to file an incident report, Leslie convinced me that finding one bicycle wheel might be a little unlikely, even for as crack an outfit as the Midland Heights Police Department, and besides, I had no way to identify the wheel. She offered, since it was the end of her shift, to drive me home in her personal car, a brand-new Toyota that she kept impeccably clean, which I considered evidence of an unbalanced mind. Without its front wheel, the remaining part of my bike just fit in the trunk, which was lucky, as Leslie informed me in no uncertain terms that she wasn't "about to put that greasy thing on my brand-new seats."

We didn't talk much during the ride. I was overwhelmed, I'll admit, by the whole day—I'd started out with a vague feeling that the Ansella thing would get worse (although not for Mr. Ansella, who had it about as bad as it gets), and it had. I'd gotten myself into a funk by comparing my life to that of a man so well loved someone had poisoned his popcorn, and then my most trusted employee (which, admittedly, wasn't a hard-won title) seemed to be getting deeper and deeper into trouble over a crime that, on top of all the other implications, could ruin my relationship with film distributors and put my fledgling business into more jeopardy.

And now I had a unicycle where this morning I had a fully functioning mode of transportation. I do not ride unicycles. Clearly, things were on a downward spiral.

Leslie parked the car in front of my (very, very green) front door, and got out of the car as I removed the carcass of my bicycle from her trunk.

"I really don't need help, you know," I said.

For a split second she looked like I'd punched her, but

that expression was immediately replaced with a smile. "Of course not," she answered. "I didn't think so."

She followed me as I carried the bike up and we stood on the stoop, looking at each other like two junior high kids doing their best to maintain eye contact when there were so many more interesting places to look. I heard myself exhale.

"You don't have to see me inside the town house," I continued. "I realize you're a police officer and everything, but I've been making it into my house unchaperoned for some time now."

"You sure? You don't need me to look in the bedroom closet for monsters?" There was a shy smile attempting to make itself known on her lips.

"Are you flirting with me?" I decided I'd ask. Best to get these things out in the open.

"No," Leslie replied immediately. Oops. I'd overstepped. "Oh. Um, sorry . . ."

"I'm not flirting with you. *You're* flirting with *me*." And she grinned. "I don't mind."

More awkward silence. I should point out that this is my normal approach to romance, which makes it all the more remarkable that I've ever been on a date, let alone been married for six years. Until eighteen months ago. But I'm not bitter.

"Well." Smooth, huh? "Then you won't mind if I keep flirting." I had no idea what I was talking about.

"I might even flirt back," Leslie said. I began to wonder how I'd know when she did, but that was something to think about another time.

Believe me, Leslie Levant was an attractive woman. Hell, I was willing to bet that without the baton, the walkie-talkie, and, let's face it, the gun, she was a beautiful woman. But I was so far out of practice it was hard to remember what I was supposed to do. Marriage does many things to a man, one of which is to screw up his dating techniques. Mine had never been in the top 70 percent to begin with.

Before my brain started to ponder whether she just

liked me, or *liked* me liked me, I plunged in. "Would you like to have dinner?" I said. I would have asked her to a movie, but my theatre was closed.

Her face lit up, which was what I had hoped for, but really hadn't expected. "I'm really not dressed for it, but I'd love to," Leslie said.

I hadn't actually meant *now*, but what the hell.

As it turned out, my refrigerator held exactly one onion, a pint of half-and-half of dubious freshness, two packages of AA batteries, and a six-pack of Rolling Rock (the freezer had two empty ice cube trays and a quart of Edy's ice cream). So we decided to go to the Harvest Moon Brewery, a microbrewery and restaurant on George Street, which was within walking distance of my town house.

Leslie cut quite the figure in her Midland Heights cop outfit, but I don't think that's why so many of the men in the room were watching her so closely. I started to realize exactly how unlikely it was for me to be sitting with this woman in this place on this night.

My dating history would indicate that this would be where I'd find a way to screw up the situation, so I forged ahead.

"So. Who are you, anyway?" I asked. You have to learn to ease into a sensitive topic if you want to get anywhere with women. Naturally, I had no expectation of getting anywhere with Leslie, and wasn't sure whether I was ready for her anyway. I figured my first date after the divorce should be with someone I found only mildly attractive, so when it didn't work out, I wouldn't be devastated. I was operating here without a safety net.

"Why, aren't I who I think I am?"

Clearly, I was doing well. "I really don't know anything about you. That's what I meant."

Leslie looked blank. "Do you ask out every woman you don't know anything about? That must be very time-consuming."

"I mean, I know your name, and that you're divorced, and that you're a police officer."

"Well, that's not nothing, is it? All I know about you is

that you own a movie theatre, half a bicycle, and a smooth line with the ladies."

I ignored that last part, since I felt that emphasizing my shortcomings would not create a strategic advantage. "So what happened to your marriage?" I asked.

"He was transferred to Salt Lake City and I didn't want to go. We were already drifting apart. I was a cop, and he wasn't crazy about that. I wanted to take some night courses at Rutgers, and he was pissed that I'd be spending even more time away from him. Not to mention, I can't cook."

"Neither can I."

"Well, you choose a fine microbrewery," she said. "So what about you? You were married. What happened to that?"

"How did you know that?"

"We ran a check on you. Your records indicated a divorce."

I scowled. "What, Big Brother doesn't know why my wife left me?"

"Don't get mad. You weren't a suspect. You didn't hand Ansella the popcorn, and as far as anyone knows, you never even met him, so you had no motive. The DVDs are a problem, but you're not the one who disappeared as soon as they were discovered. There's no indication you were making a dime from that operation. You don't own duplicating equipment."

"It's nice to know I wasn't a suspect," I said.

"We have to check on everybody."

I had downed two beers (and one earlier today), which is two more than I typically drink, and it was having the usual effect on me: I stifled a burp. "Since you asked," I said, "my wife is a doctor, and I wasn't. She decided she wanted to be married to someone who could share her whole life, and not just the personal part."

"Divorce sucks, doesn't it?"

I thought about that. "It has its upside. If I were still married, you wouldn't be here with me."

"Maybe I would," she said.

I shook my head. "No, you wouldn't. I didn't cheat on her."

"Another difference between you and my ex," she said.

"Is there any chance Anthony isn't involved in this piracy thing?" I asked.

She shot her eyes around the room, as if looking for the direction in which the conversation had gone. A lot of blondes are in the blue-eyed family, but Leslie's were closer to green. "Nice segue, there, Elliot." She thought for a moment. "I don't know. We're not supposed to say that someone's guilty until they're convicted, but . . ."

"It's all circumstantial."

"Sometimes circumstances lead you to the truth," she said.

I didn't like the way the conversation was going. I switched gears again. "So, what kind of first date am I?" I asked.

She grinned. "I've had worse."

10

╰╮╭╯╰╮╭╯╰╮╭╯

The memorial service for Vincent Ansella had a few surprises attached to it. First of all, the guest of honor was indeed present, so the medical examiner must have released the body just in time.

Given the circumstances, the mood at the service was not as somber as one might expect: Ansella's mother, eschewing the traditional widow's weeds some Italian-American ladies of a "certain age" might favor at such a hideous occasion, wore a well-tailored black suit and carried a white handkerchief she rarely seemed to need; and Ansella's wife, Amy, didn't weep at all throughout the service, although she didn't look thrilled to be there, either.

It was also a little surprising that Amy had been Vincent Ansella's wife. She was small and slim, and strikingly beautiful, not the kind of woman you'd have expected to be married to a rather ordinary-looking insurance man. Then again, you wouldn't have expected to find me sharing a beer sampler with a Midland Heights cop last night, so what you'd expect isn't always relevant.

In the end, I'd chickened out, and hadn't even kissed

Leslie. She didn't seem offended or disappointed, which was a little worrisome, but we had made vague references to what we would do "next time." I had stuck a toe in the dating pond, and it hadn't been bitten off by a crocodile. That's the Elliot Freed version of "progress."

I wasn't surprised to see Marcy Resnick in attendance at the service, along with a group of people whom I assumed were from Ansella's office. We didn't have time to talk before the service began, as I arrived late, but we smiled and nodded at each other from across the room.

It was also a small surprise that Ansella's service was held in the funeral home, and not a church, but I attribute that to my own preconceived notions. There would be no mass, no priest, no obvious religion of any sort. People who wanted to speak were encouraged to do so, but aside from a brief announcement by the funeral director, there was no one who seemed to be in charge of running the show.

Perhaps the biggest surprise was that I was in attendance at all, seeing as how I'd never met the man. I'd had to stand out on Edison Avenue in a jacket and tie to catch the bus, and had arrived just in time. But there was an eerie connection between Ansella and me, and in some twisted way, I felt that this would be as close to attending my own funeral as I could ever come while really being able to enjoy it. So to speak.

I took a seat in the last row inside the funeral home, which was by my estimate about two-thirds full. When you're in the theatre business, you estimate crowd sizes reflexively. This made me envious, as I'd never actually seen my own movie theatre two-thirds full. But maybe I was being petty. Besides, the funeral home didn't have as many seats as Comedy Tonight.

There were a good few testimonials, and a few not-so-good ones, and I was getting to know quite a bit about actuarial tables, which didn't make me feel better. Yes, I was only thirty-seven years old, but I was male, and my family had a history of heart problems, and . . .

My mental connection to the guy in the polished mahogany casket with brass handles was fading—I loved my

business, but it wasn't all there was in my life. I had . . .
um . . . well, there was my ex-wife, although she was married to someone else now; and my parents; and hey, I'd had
a date last night with a woman I barely knew, and even
though she was wearing a gun, I thought it went well . . .

Okay, so my business *was* pretty much all there was in
my life. My novel, now four years old, and the film that
was made "from" it, rarely entered my thoughts, and paved
no path to any kind of future. At least Comedy Tonight
wasn't all about how long the average person would live
under the proper circumstances.

Anyway, the speeches had a decided bent toward
Ansella's professional life. The quick wit and easy manner
Marcy had described weren't really mentioned. Nobody
who spoke seemed to know Vincent very well. Although
Marcy did not stand to speak, she did dab at her eyes a bit
during the service, which was more than I could say about
Ansella's wife or his mother. Ansella's sister, Lisa Rabinowitz, was dealing with two small children who were
wandering up and down aisles (one of them, an adorable
little girl, seemed especially intent on not paying attention
to her mother), so she didn't seem to have time to be sad.

The current speaker, a woman who had worked with
Ansella at the office, finished her remarks by saying that he
was "accurate in his estimates, until the one that mattered
most," choked, and left the podium. There was the embarrassed silence that ensues at such events, when each person
in the gathered assemblage wonders a) if he or she should
be the next to speak, and b) if no one is going to speak
next, is it time to eat?

After a few seconds, a compact, barrel-chested man
with a head almost completely free of the need for sham-
poo stood from his second-row seat on the aisle and composed himself for a walk to the podium. He stood and
looked at us all when he got there, closed his eyes for a
moment, opened them again, and exhaled.

"I'm Joe Dunbar," he said. "Vince Ansella was my best
friend." That seemed to take a good deal out of him, as if he
were addressing his first meeting of Alcoholics Anonymous

and had made the startling revelation that he belonged in their ranks. "I met Vince in the third grade, when we were eight years old. The first thing he ever said to me made me laugh.

"We were waiting outside the school before the first day of class, and a girl I knew told me that Vince was in our class that year. I walked up to him and asked, 'Are you Vincent Ansella?' and he said, 'Yeah, but it's not my fault.' I don't know why, but I was eight, and that cracked me up, and we ended up sitting next to each other in class.

"I knew Vince for thirty-five years, and he kept making me laugh. He loved comedy, and he made me go with him to every movie that came out that might be funny. He kept me up late nights during high school, not drinking and messing around like other kids, but watching the Marx Brothers on late-night TV, because he had just discovered them. When we went to college, and we were in different states, he used to call me whenever a Peter Sellers movie was going to be on TV, to make sure I was watching.

"He could never get enough of something that made him laugh. As you know, his favorite movie was *Young Frankenstein*, and he spent his last few minutes on earth watching that. I'm sure it made him laugh over and over again. He made me see it about eighteen times . . . no, nineteen, now that I think about it, and I think he liked it more when I laughed, because it meant we shared a sense of humor.

"After we both got married, we only lived ten minutes away from each other, so all four of us used to go out to the movies together. Vince never wanted to see anything serious, and we all went along with him. He kept us all laughing. My heart goes out to his wife, Amy, and to his mom and his sister, Lisa, but I bet they have lots of funny stories about Vince to remember even now.

"Vince spent his time doing his job dealing with insurance and actuarial tables, but in his heart, he was all about comedy. The job took his time, and he did it right, but it wasn't what his life was about. His life was about what makes people laugh, about comedy, and seeing as much of it as he could. So I'm glad he was able to do that, because his life was so short, it makes me feel better to know he spent it well."

Dunbar had held himself together that long, but it was as much as he could stand. He closed his eyes tightly, trying to will the tears back into their ducts, but it was no use. He stumbled back to his seat next to a blond woman who under other circumstances would have been described as "brassy." Since everyone now understood that the *real* eulogy had been delivered, we waited for the pallbearers (who naturally included Dunbar and a man I took to be Lisa Rabinowitz's husband, since he had been trying to corral the children with as limited a success rate as she) to gather.

When Ansella had been taken from the room, and his family had followed him out, the rest of us rose and walked from the building.

It was a lovely day, not a cloud in the sky, and I stood in the sunshine for a long moment, trying to absorb all I'd heard and seen that morning. A voice behind me said, "It really makes you think, doesn't it?"

Marcy Resnick was one step above me, so when I turned, I was looking up at her, and squinting into the sun. "Marcy," I said. "Yeah, it makes you think."

"Here I thought Vincent was all about the job, and it turns out he was into comedy movies more than anything else. You don't know anything about another person." She stepped down so I was able to look at her without craning my neck.

"I'm not sure I know all that much about me," I said. "Another person would be too much to expect."

The coffin was rolled into the back of the hearse by the pallbearers, and the driver closed the door on it and walked back to wait by the driver's side. It was a nice day, and there was no reason for him to sit in a stuffy car with a dead man.

"Are you going to the cemetery?" Marcy asked.

"No. I'm still a little surprised I came here. Besides, I don't have a car, and I have to get back to not run my theatre. How about you?"

She shook her head. "I'm heading back to the office. It's still a working day. But I should say something to his wife." Marcy started down the steps toward Amy, and I followed.

"Well, I'm glad I got to . . ."

A loud scream of "No!" cut me off, and we both looked toward the limo, where Amy Ansella, her face contorted with . . . well, that sure looked like rage, was shoving Joe Dunbar away from her. Dunbar, for his part, looked positively stunned, and hadn't even put up his hands to defend himself. The blond woman standing next to him, presumably his wife, seemed horrified. Dunbar was bent over slightly, had probably been leaning over to embrace his dead friend's wife, but she had pushed him away, and his arms were still spread, either in shock or from the blow she'd dealt him. Amy might be stronger than she looked.

"Get *away*! Get away from me, you bastard!" she screamed, as everyone in the funeral party stood as still as statues. "Don't you *ever* talk to me again!"

I don't know why, but I walked down the steps toward them, even as the rest of those gathered stood still as statues. I haven't a clue what I was trying to accomplish. It was too fast, and too strange. I guess I was thinking that if a fistfight broke out, I could try to break it up.

Dunbar sputtered something I couldn't hear, but Amy was having none of it. "Go away!" she bellowed again, and Dunbar started to back off. The blond woman with him couldn't decide whether to look astonished or angry. "Get away from us, and stay away!" Amy yelled.

I looked toward Marcy, who had stayed where I'd been standing, but she was just as astounded as the rest of us. My glance at her may have been the only movement among the twenty-or-so people outside the funeral home, aside from my continuing to inch my way down toward the pavement. I was still operating on autopilot. But even traffic on the street seemed to have stopped in a surreal tableau that suggested time itself had paused for this moment.

"Maybe I won't go see her just now," Marcy muttered.

The limo driver finally snapped back into real time and realized he had the power to end this astonishing scene. He walked around the car and opened the rear door for Amy, who was still staring at the retreating Dunbar.

I was close enough now to hear the Widow Ansella, in a slightly less hysterical tone, fire a parting salvo in Dunbar's direction:

"Murderer."

11

⚬◌◌◌◌◌⚬

"She said 'murderer'?" Sergeant O'Donnell looked surprised. I'd anticipated this would be old news, as I'd assumed he would've had a man at the funeral, but apparently I'd either overestimated the county investigator or his department's budget.

"Quite clearly," I told O'Donnell. "To be fair, Dunbar looked awfully shocked when she said it."

We were in my office at Comedy Tonight, a former broom closet I had cleaned out, given my belief that brooms can stay in the regular closet with all the other cleaning implements and just get over themselves. There was a small assemble-it-yourself desk (which I had assembled myself, after only three calls to the manufacturer and one to my father), a phone, a watercooler, and a single chair, which O'Donnell was now sitting in, having commandeered the office as his temporary headquarters. Standing next to him, I felt rather like someone had taken over my territory, a feeling I remember having quite often during the divorce proceedings.

"Well, he might have simply been surprised she said it

out loud, or surprised she knew it was him." O'Donnell chewed on a pencil, which I realized with some revulsion was one of mine. Companies send me free pencils and pens all the time with the business name on them, secure in their odd belief that I will give them as gifts to my "clients."

"Yeah, or she might have been putting on a nice public display of accusation to shift the suspicion from herself," I suggested.

"Uh-huh," he said, with great noncommittal flair.

"You did suspect her, didn't you?" I might as well accuse somebody of something; it seemed all the rage around here these days.

"I'm sorry, am I required to keep you up-to-date on our investigation, Freed?" O'Donnell leaned back in my chair and eyed me with something that couldn't be described with any word other than "suspicion."

"I thought I'd come by and share information with you, O'Donnell, but if that's your attitude, I'll keep it to myself next time."

"It's *Sergeant* O'Donnell, and what makes you think there'll be a 'next time' you'll have anything useful to tell me?" he asked. I ignored him, because coming up with a clever retort would have required more effort than I had energy for at the moment.

"Did you get a report back on that vial my father found here, or are you not allowed to tell me whether I'm under suspicion as a major drug dealer?" At least that had a little zing to it.

"Oh, we got the report, okay." O'Donnell smirked. "I'm sorry to say, we don't think you're dealing coke in anything but overpriced cups that are mostly filled with ice."

"I've got to make money *somewhere*," I told him. "The studios take all the receipts on the movie. Anyway, what is it I *am* dealing? I've been out of the business for so long, I can't remember which felony I was committing on a regular basis."

O'Donnell picked up a paper from my desk and held it out far from his face so he could read it. I felt like telling

him that real men like Chief Barry Dutton aren't too inse-
cure to use reading glasses.

"It's a substance called clonidine," he said, reading
from the paper. "It's an alpha 2-adrenergic blocker" (it
took him a couple of tries to say "adrenergic") "used to
treat high blood pressure, and sometimes attention deficit
disorder. Crushed up into a powder and given in a large
enough dose to someone who doesn't need it, clonidine
makes a healthy person's blood pressure drop until his
heart stops."

"So it was this clonidine that killed Vincent Ansella," I
said.

O'Donnell nodded. "Sprinkled on his popcorn. He
probably never even noticed it. And anyone with high
blood pressure might have a prescription for it."

"Do any of the suspects have high blood pressure?" I
asked.

"Strangely, Sherlock, I haven't had time to check on
everyone yet, because I haven't ruled out *anyone* as a suspect except Ansella himself. Besides, anyone who wanted
to kill him could have *known* someone with high blood
pressure, and stolen enough to do the job."

"I don't suppose you've checked whether Ansella himself had a prescription?"

"Well, then you suppose wrong." O'Donnell didn't
have enough room in the small office to pat himself on the
back, but I'm sure he made a mental note to do so once he
got back out into the real world. "Ansella didn't have high
blood pressure. In fact, aside from being dead, he was in
excellent health."

"Not to mention, he probably wouldn't take his prescription medication sprinkled over a large buttered," I
noted, mostly to myself.

"Probably not."

"Any prints on the vial?"

He grinned. "Besides your father's? No. But I'm letting
him go because he's only got one reason to be in the theatre."

"Speaking of which, when can I have my theatre back?"

I asked. "I saw a bunch of your storm troopers retreating from the place. I assume you haven't found anything else on the premises I need to know about."

O'Donnell's eyelids fluttered at the term "storm troopers," but he kept it to himself. "As a matter of fact, we didn't," he said. "We're pulling out of here. You can have your theatre back tonight."

He stood up to leave, and a thought occurred to me. "What about his wife? Did Amy Ansella have a prescription for clonidine?"

Sergeant O'Donnell's face closed, and he said what cops always say when you've hit on something they wanted to take credit for themselves. "This is an ongoing investigation," he said. "No comment."

12

❀❀❀❀❀❀❀

FRIDAY
Horse Feathers (1932)
and *Bootylicious* (today)

"**You** think I just have extra wheels for this thing lying around the store waiting for you?" Bobo Kaminsky, the largest bicycle store owner in Central New Jersey (and no, that doesn't mean he owns the largest bicycle shop), stared down on me with what was supposed to look like disdain but instead resembled bemusement.

"Come on, Bobo, it's a twenty-six-inch wheel and you've got hundreds of them. Who's a better customer for you than I am? I need the wheel by tonight so I can ride home from the theatre after the show."

"You could take a cab." But he was already looking through his stock in the back room where we were arguing, trying to match the right width to the frame I'd dragged in from Sharon's car. Sharon, cursing slightly under her breath, had demurred at the idea of seeing Bobo, and driven away almost before I'd managed to get both feet and one wheel onto the sidewalk.

"A cab. Very nice, the owner of Midland Cyclery telling me to take a cab." I was sure he'd find what I needed. Bobo was annoyed because his solution to every problem I've ever brought into his place is that I should upgrade to a four-thousand-dollar bicycle. Bobo is among those who believe that I made millions off of Hollywood and am being obstinate about spending·my fortune.

He scanned a rack of wheels, then turned and walked to the other side of the room to scan another. "So what's with this guy who croaked at your place?" he asked in his usual delicate tone. "I hear you can't trust the popcorn."

"You can trust the popcorn," I bristled. "Whoever did it brought the poison with them. Come on, Bobo, move it. It's already one o'clock, and I've got to get the place ready to open by seven."

"You come in here asking a favor and now it's 'move it, Bobo'? Why don't you go out to Sports Authority or Sears and ask *them* to move it with the wheel on this twenty-year-old bike?" Bobo's glasses, hung on a chain around his neck, were making a clicking sound as he moved from rack to rack.

"Because they wouldn't have it," I recited.

"You're damn right they wouldn't have it," he agreed, then looked at the rack and checked a stock number. "Ah! Here we go!"

He pulled out a wheel, tire already on, and beckoned to me. "Give me the frame," Bobo said. I handed it over, and he carefully maneuvered the wheel into the fork and locked it in. "Perfect. Am I good or am I good?"

"It's a bicycle wheel, Bobo. You didn't cure erectile dysfunction."

He waved a large hand. "Been done," he said.

Once again mobile, my next stop was 91 Guilden Street, where Anthony shared an apartment with three other Rutgers students. It was about as typical as college apartments get: not much in the way of cleanliness, furnished in early garage sale, and plastered with posters, in this case Hitchcock's *Vertigo* (a highly overrated movie in which Kim Novak is scared to death by a nun), Scorsese's *Raging Bull* (what the heck was he raging about?), and, for a welcome change of pace, Jessica Simpson in a very small bikini. Probably a shot from *The Dukes of Hazzard* (no comment).

The kid who'd answered my knock was about six foot three and weighed almost as much as a box of Cocoa Puffs. He had a mountain of curly brown hair, frizzier than mine, and looked very much like a used Q-tip. He introduced himself as Danton, and I introduced myself as me. I had no idea whether Danton was a first or last name, but figured that was his business.

We sat at the kitchen table, and from where I sat I could see a ceiling fan in the living room. From each blade was what I thought at first might have been mosquito strips or fly paper, but which turned out to be pieces of yellow crime-scene tape. College hasn't changed much.

"Anthony hasn't been here since Wednesday, Mr. Freed," he said. "I told the police. Of course, we're in and out to classes and whatever, but I haven't seen him, and the other guys said they haven't, either."

"There are two other roommates?" I asked.

"Yeah. Me, Anthony, Lyle, and Dolores."

I must have looked surprised. "Dolores?"

Danton grinned. "She's just a friend."

"Any sign that he's been here? Extra laundry piling up, cereal bowls in the sink, that sort of thing?"

He looked around the room at the debris that cluttered every square inch and the dishes piled up on every flat surface. Danton smiled, and looked me square in the eye. "Not that I've noticed," he said.

"How about his classes? Would anybody notice if he didn't show up for class for two days?"

"His profs, maybe. Some of them are big lectures, two, three hundred people, and they wouldn't know if one kid was there or not. But he's got a thesis advisor who also teaches his directing course. If he checked in with anybody, it'd be Dr. Bender."

I made a note of Bender's name, and asked if I could see Anthony's room.

Danton gestured toward a door with paint peeling off. "Be his guest."

Suffice it to say that Anthony's bedroom was everything you'd think it would be if you'd ever held a sixty-second

conversation with Anthony. The bookshelves were lined
with tomes such as *The Films of Quentin Tarantino*, *M.
Night Shyamalan: The Man and the Myth*, *Martin Scorsese's Cinema*, and, unexpectedly, *John Ford's West*. The
walls had more movie posters, including ones for *Taxi Driver* and *Mean Streets*, but the bed, thankfully, was not done
up with a John Woo comforter.

The contents of the drawers and closets had been deposited on the floor, but it was hard to say whether the
work had been done by the police or was simply a product
of the typical college student's high regard for house-
keeping. Clothing, mostly jeans and T-shirts, was available
for the grabbing from pretty much any area of the room. I
chose not to think about Anthony's underwear, which is a
policy of mine.

Alas, there was no clue, no piece of evidence, no neon
sign reading "Break Glass to Exonerate Anthony" in the
room. But it had been worth looking.

Danton gave me directions to Dr. Bender's office. I
thanked him for his help, and within ten minutes was
carrying my bike up the stairs (fool me once, shame on
you . . .) of Murray Hall, a very old brick building on the
Rutgers quad.

The good doctor's office was on the second floor, thank
goodness, and he was in when I knocked. I brought the bike
in with me, which made the room a tight fit, but doable.

Bender was about ten years older than I am, with a gray
ponytail that showed how anti-Establishment he was and a
beard that showed what he had eaten for lunch. Looked for
all the world like a piece of turkey salad.

He shook my hand. "So you're the man trying to keep
comedy alive in Central Jersey," he said in a hearty voice
that had probably seen formal training. The man could have
narrated audiobooks by Faulkner or Hemingway. "Anthony
talks about you incessantly." I love academics.

"He's a nice kid," I told Bender. "That's why I'm so
concerned about him."

He nodded with what Woody Allen once described as

"heaviosity." "Yes," Bender said, "it's very distressing that Anthony is implicated in this piracy business."

"You haven't seen him since Tuesday?" I asked.

"In class Tuesday, yes," Bender replied. "From what I understand, no one has seen him. I'm quite worried. He's been acting strangely lately, secretive. He should have checked in on his thesis yesterday, and it's extremely uncharacteristic of him to miss a meeting. He's completely immersed in his research."

"You haven't heard from him at all?"

He shook his head. "As I told the police, there's been no contact with me since Tuesday morning. He was in class at ten a.m., and I haven't heard from him since."

"Well, if you do, would you be so kind as to let me know?" I handed him a Comedy Tonight business card.

"Certainly," Bender said. "Whatever I can do to help, but I doubt he'll contact me first. Surely he'll call his parents, or his employer." He eyed me carefully.

"I hope so," I said. "But knowing Anthony, he may be more concerned about his thesis than his own safety." I stood to leave. "By the way, what *is* the topic of Anthony's thesis?" I hoisted my transportation over my shoulder, to better facilitate leaving without knocking over piles of papers.

"A classic film by Vittorio De Sica," Bender said.

"Not . . ."

"Yes. *The Bicycle Thief.*"

It figured.

Since I'd have to assume Anthony's duties as well as my own for tonight's—and all foreseeable nights'—show, I got back to the theatre around four. I'd called Sophie's cell phone, and although her parents were divided on whether it was a good idea, she would be back at work tonight, which meant I didn't have to do *everything* for everyone. I got the distinct impression that Sophie had acted aggressively obnoxious enough to ensure that her parents would want her out of the house as much as possible. That's my Sophie.

I unlocked the theatre door and went in without turning

on the marquee lights just yet. There was a good deal of preparation to be done, especially since the theatre hadn't been open in days.

First, I vacuumed the rug in the lobby. I didn't want the carpet to smell musty, so I sprinkled some cleaning powder over it and then sucked it up again. It made me feel like I was running one of those vacuum cleaner demonstrations you see in Red Skelton comedies from the 1950s, where a bag of dirt is thrown on the rug and then nothing works right. Luckily for me, Red was nowhere to be seen, and the vacuum worked just fine.

I stocked the snack bar with candy, but didn't start the popcorn machine yet. It was too early, and you want the smell to be fresh when people arrive. I'm not much for popcorn myself, but I do like the smell. And people buy more when it doesn't smell like foam rubber with butter on it.

We use a real old-fashioned popcorn popper, not content to work with the pre-popped stuff that comes in enormous bags. If you're going to re-create the real theatre experience pre-megaplex, you have to do it right. Within a budget.

It was well after five when it occurred to me that since this was the first night of the show, the film itself would still have to be spliced to the trailers we were showing (complete with vintage drive-in movie plugs for the snack bar and the number of minutes until showtime, but decidedly *without* the annoying TV commercials blown up to full-screen size for projection in a theatre that modern movie houses have adopted). Anthony usually did that, then threaded the first reel up on the projector. I knew how to do it, in theory, but he was a magician. I went up early to the projection booth, assuming it would take me a while to remember the procedure and get everything ready in time.

I unlocked the door to the booth (you can't be too careful; since the movies are only rented, not owned by the theatre, they're our most valuable assets—not that my precautions had apparently deterred the movie pirates) and turned on the lights. I stood there for a long time, staring ahead with what must have been a really puzzled expression on my face.

The projector was threaded with the first reel of the Marx Brothers' 1932 classic *Horse Feathers*, which had been spliced to our pre-show reel of trailers. Everything was perfectly set up for my flick of one switch to set the show in motion. It had been done expertly, and the rest of the reels were threaded in order and ready to roll.

Anthony was in the house.

13

◇◇◇◇◇◇◇

After a thorough search of the premises, beginning with the basement and moving up through the lobby, the office, the auditorium, the closets, and even the balcony, I convinced myself that Anthony was no longer in the theatre, although I had to concede to myself (since I was the only one in the conversation) that there were plenty of places to hide, and a one-man search of the building left open the possibility of his moving from hiding place to hiding place without a huge amount of effort.

Still, the effect of that threaded projector was just a little spooky.

By the time Sophie arrived at six, I had gotten the place into a semblance of order and replaced last week's two-sheets with this week's in the outside displays and the lobby. Sophie began by getting the snack bar together (which meant moving everything I thought I had gotten in order, but hey, she ran it on a daily basis), all the while looking at me from under hooded lids, silently accusing me of messing with her stuff. Some people are so territorial.

Suddenly, it occurred to me to take a shot. "You haven't heard from Anthony, have you?" I asked Sophie.

"Anthony?" Either she was trying to remember who Anthony was, or she thought my question was idiotic. I was betting on the latter, but with the "well, *duh*" inflection Sophie puts on every sentence, sometimes it's hard to know.

"Yeah, Anthony. Tall, thin? Used to run the projector until he vanished?"

"I *know* who Anthony is. I just can't imagine why you'd think I heard from him, Elliot."

That wasn't much of a surprise; the three-year difference in their ages is a wider gap than it would be for someone as ancient as, say, me.

I focused a lot more attention on the carpet sweeper I was using. There was nothing to sweep, as I'd already vacuumed, but it made a good prop. "I don't know; you guys work in the same theatre, I thought maybe you were friends."

"Friends are impediments." She must have learned that at the Goth Girl meetings. I wondered if they had a secret handshake, but maybe hands were impediments, too.

"I heard you two talking the day Anthony . . . left," I told her quietly. "I heard something about not telling your parents."

She stared at me.

"I'm not your father, Sophie, but if you know something about this that you're not telling the police . . ."

Sophie stared at me some more. This time, I believed, with genuine confusion in her eyes.

"So I guess not, then." Clearly, I was such an enormous fool that I was not worthy of a response, but I decided to take one last stab. "Anthony never taught you how to run the projector, did he?"

"The one upstairs?" *No, the projector I carry around in my back pocket.* I nodded. "Why would he do that?"

Sometimes, talking to a person is less informative than not talking to them. It doesn't make sense, but it is true.

We opened the doors at seven, although the show wouldn't start for forty-five minutes. Sophie had the popcorn machine going, so the lobby smelled wonderful, and with all the lights on and the marquee illuminated, it really did present at least a glimpse of the image I was trying to project. With another few years of restoration, and a whole lot of money, maybe I'd be able to complete the vision.

A few people were already starting to wander in before seven fifteen, so I went upstairs to recheck the projector (still not entirely comfortable with its being so well prepared by an unseen hand). Then I put up the velvet ropes at the entrances to the balcony, since Anthony usually watched those stairs before starting the projector, and I couldn't be in more than one place at a time. I'd have to be ripping tickets at the auditorium doors before the show started.

I walked back downstairs and stopped in awe on the third step from the bottom. It was hard to believe my eyes.

The place was packed. The lobby was full of people, and from what I could tell, the auditorium was already at least half full. I'd never seen so many customers in the theatre at the same time. This had to be at least ten times the usual house. The lines at the snack bar, where Sophie was simultaneously selling tickets and overpriced goodies, were backing up.

Immediately, I wondered whether I had ordered enough popcorn to accommodate the box office for tonight. We'd never needed nearly this much before.

I ran to Sophie's side and started selling tickets, announcing to the crowd that the line just for snacks should shift toward Sophie. She began dealing in food exclusively, looking overwhelmed, but Goth.

"Where'd they all come from?" I wondered aloud.

"They're here because the guy died," Sophie said, shaking her head at how stupid I am. Of course.

Things were moving so quickly that I barely looked at the people to whom I was selling tickets. They became hands that handed me money, and to which I handed tickets for the two films being screened tonight, sometimes with change. The hands were young and old, male and female, of various skin tones. The money was all green, except for one wise guy who tried to pay in Susan B. Anthony dollar coins.

One of the larger, darker hands hesitated a moment when I handed him change, then spoke in a deep, resonant voice. Well, the *hand* didn't speak, but you get the idea.

"Looks like you got quite a turnout tonight," said Police Chief Barry Dutton.

"I really wasn't expecting it," I told him. "Thanks for coming."

"Not at all. I figured I helped close the place down, so I should help reopen it. Hope it wasn't too much trouble."

I looked up into Dutton's face, which was smiling. "On the contrary; I guess having a man die in the house is good for business," I told him. "Go figure."

"Hopefully, you won't expect someone to be murdered every night just to keep your business going," Dutton said. I'm pretty sure he was kidding.

"I'd prefer to get by without it," I answered. "It's nice to see you, Chief, but . . ." I gestured toward the long line behind him.

"Of course," Dutton said. He walked toward the auditorium doors, where two tall African-American women, who must have been his wife and daughter, were waiting. With them was a short white man and his very attractive wife and two children, a tallish boy with a slightly gawky look and a girl who was so small she could have been anywhere from five to thirteen. When Dutton joined them, the short man said something that made the chief laugh, and they all went inside.

I continued to sell tickets until I noticed a striking blond woman a few places back in the line. It took me a moment to recognize her out of uniform, or without a microbrewed beer in her hand.

Leslie was wearing a skirt, slit up the side to great effect, and a low-cut blouse that completely negated any thought of the police officer who had questioned me the night Ansella died. I blinked a few times, and tried to remember where I should be looking. Tickets. That was it: I was selling tickets. Yes.

Leslie gave me a quick peck on the cheek when she got to the front of the line. "I was hoping I wouldn't be the only one in the theatre tonight," she said. "Guess I didn't have to worry."

The only thing I could think to say was, "You look amazing."

"Of course. You've never seen me dressed as a girl before, have you?" She stood back and let me take in the view, which was worth taking in.

"If that's a disguise, I never want to see the way you really look," I said.

"That was a compliment, right?" Leslie asked. I nodded. "Good," she continued. "I appreciate the thought . . . I think. See you inside?" She tried to hand me a ten-dollar bill.

"Your ticket is on the house," I told her.

She looked annoyed and walked away. Women make no sense.

When the line began to wind down a little, I gave control of both concessions back to Sophie and walked into the auditorium to assess the crowd.

It was astonishing. Virtually every seat was taken. If I'd had confidence in the balcony, I could have opened it and come close to filling the seats up there, too. I considered it, then thought about the possibility of 250 Midland Heights residents falling twenty feet to the floor on top of 250 *other* Midland Heights residents, and made the more prudent, but perhaps less profitable, decision to turn the overflow crowd away. But I thought about it.

This was what I had envisioned when I opened Comedy Tonight. It was what I had wanted when I first flashed on that For Sale sign in front of the Rialto and called Virginia Squeo on an impulse. It was, perhaps, what I had been hoping to do all my life.

The fact that the success had come about because someone had poisoned Vincent Ansella's popcorn did dampen the feeling a little but, I confess, only a little.

Time to head back up to the projection booth and get started. On my way out of the auditorium, I almost knocked over a large bucket of buttered popcorn. Behind the bucket was my one and only loyal customer, Leo Munson.

Leo, in his early sixties, would have been a great "grizzled old Indian fighter" in a Howard Hawks Western, the kind of part generally played by Walter Brennan or Ward Bond. He always had some white stubble on his face, but never grew a beard, thus creating a look perfected in the 1980s by Don Johnson. You almost expected him to be wearing a captain's hat, but Leo was bald as a cue ball and proud of it. He once told me that "every hair I've lost is an experience I wouldn't give back for anything. They can keep the hair." I didn't know who "they" were, but I appreciated the sentiment.

"I was afraid you might not have a seat for me tonight, Elliot," he said.

"Always a seat for you, Leo, even if you have to sit up in the projection booth with me."

"You know, I came by both nights you were closed. The ad kept running in the paper." Leo had come to Comedy Tonight literally every night since I opened the place, laughed the loudest, and, until Vincent Ansella, left the theatre last, discounting the staff.

"Sorry about that, Leo. I couldn't change the ad in time, and obviously I didn't know what was going to happen Tuesday night."

Leo thought about that, ate a little popcorn, and then rubbed some of the butter inadvertently on his stubble in thought. "Yeah, that poor fella. Didn't really seem to be enjoying himself, even before he died."

"Yeah, I guess not. Well . . ." I was already turning away when I realized what he'd said, and I practically pulled a muscle in my back twisting to face him. "Leo!" I shouted. "You *noticed* him?"

"Sure. You come every night to see the same movie, eventually you get to watching the audience at key moments. That guy was sitting there with his girlfriend, watching every move on the screen. The girlfriend just about bust a gut laughing at the 'walk this way' gag with Marty Feldman. You'd think they'd never seen it before."

I heard myself say, "Actually, it was his favorite movie," before I regained my senses. "His *girlfriend*?"

Leo clearly thought I had lost what precious little there was left of my mind, as the look in his eye indicated a deep desire to dial 911 and ask for a well-padded ambulance. "Yeah. Big blonde. Gave him a peck on the cheek at one point, then left before the first movie was over."

"Was he dead by then?"

"How the hell would I know? I was sitting behind him. I could see her leave, all right, but I couldn't see his face. For all I know, the guy was dead before the picture and somebody just dropped him in his seat in time for the trailers."

"What scene was it when she got up and left?" I knew he'd remember that. Whenever Leo's view is obstructed, he remembers.

"Puttin' on the Ritz," he said with great certainty.

I needed to be sure of something. "You're sure it was a big blonde? Ansella's wife was a petite brunette, and about as beautiful as you've ever seen." I took a good look at Leo. "Probably *more* beautiful than you've ever seen."

"Don't assume, Elliot. I wasn't born this old."

But I wasn't listening. Could Ansella really have been cheating on a wife that gorgeous?

"If she's that good-looking, then it sure as hell wasn't his wife," Leo continued. "I'll tell you, Elliot, I couldn't see the guy's face, but the woman kept turning to look at him, and I got a good look at her in profile. She sure don't match your description."

"Not a slim, beautiful brunette? A blonde, huh? Was she . . . brassy?" Could Ansella have been cheating with his best friend's wife?

Leo shook his head. "Not slim, not brunette, not brassy, and just between you and me, Elliot?" He gestured that I should lean forward, and I did, so he could speak softly.

"That was the ugliest woman I have ever seen, bar none."

I was about to ask another question when the house

lights dimmed, which stunned me. The only place from which that could have been accomplished was the projection booth. I could see Sophie from where I was standing, and she looked at me and shrugged.

I rushed over to her. "Who's up there?"

"I don't know," Sophie said, managing not to call me Captain Obvious. Then she got the most delighted grin I've ever seen on her face. "Maybe it's a ghost."

The trailers began to enthusiastic applause, and my gaze instinctively went up to the ceiling. Someone was running the projector, and I was relatively sure it wasn't me.

"Stay right here, Leo," I hissed at him, and even though he complained about missing the beginning of *Horse Feathers*, he stayed.

I ran up the main stairs to the balcony, and turned right to the projection booth door. It was locked, but I pulled the key out of my pocket and burst through the door.

The lights were out in the room, as they should be, but I could see well enough via the illumination of the screen. And what I saw—or didn't see, to be more accurate—made me gasp and sit down behind the projector. There was absolutely no one in the room.

Maybe it *was* a ghost.

14

✿✿✿✿✿✿✿

I went back down and found Leo inside the auditorium, just at the back of the room, laughing as Groucho Marx sang his way through "Whatever It Is, I'm Against It," a song which pretty much changed the course of my life when I first heard it in 1986. I scolded him for leaving the area I'd left him in, and he shushed me, pointed to the screen and said, "Groucho." Who could argue?

Nonetheless, I found Dutton in the crowd (luckily, he was laughing loudly, and his basso tones made him easy to locate) and asked him to come to the lobby for a moment. I dragged Leo out after the song and, over his protests, got him to reiterate his story to Dutton in the lobby.

"You sure it was a large blond woman?" Dutton asked again.

"Why is everybody so shocked at this?" Leo wanted to know. "There's more than one type of woman in the world. I remember this one time in Kansas City . . ."

"I'm not interested in your romantic history, Mr. Munson. Thank you," Dutton said, which was a relief to me, if not to Leo. "Let me ask you this: did you see anyone do anything to Mr. Ansella's popcorn? Did this woman reach over at any point?"

"I wasn't watching the two of them with a pair of binoculars, Chief," Leo said. "I noticed what I noticed, but it *was* Gene Wilder and Madeline Kahn on the screen, after all."

"After all," I echoed. I don't know why.

"So you didn't see any interaction beyond a kiss on the cheek?" Dutton was pushing Leo, thinking there was something the older man just wasn't remembering.

"Nah. That was it." Or, he had been watching the movie.

"Okay. Thanks, Mr. Munson. We might want to get in touch with you again."

"I'm in the book. Now, can I go back inside? I'll bet I missed the speakeasy scene." Leo was halfway through the door.

I looked at Dutton. "Swordfish," I said.

"Very funny. Do you remember anyone else who might have been here that night? Someone who could have seen something Mr. Munson overlooked?"

I made a "yeah, well" face. "Leo's really our only regular," I told him. "I don't recall anyone else of note being here that night. But Sophie sold all the tickets on her own. We don't usually draw like we did tonight."

Dutton nodded. "I'll have to tell Sergeant O'Donnell about Mr. Munson, you know."

"Yeah, that should really move the case along."

Dutton raised an eyebrow. "Don't underestimate O'Donnell. He's not the most personable guy on the planet, but he knows what he's doing. I've worked with him before. Meanwhile, have you heard from your projectionist?"

I had left Anthony—and the rather eerie indications that he'd been in the theatre tonight—out of my summary to Dutton, since I couldn't *really* report accurately that he'd been here. It might have been elves; you never know. Besides, if Anthony *had* been there, what had he done other than his job?

I shook my head. "No word. I spoke to one of his room-mates and a professor today, and nobody's heard from him since Wednesday." That was accurate and truthful. Not complete, but accurate and truthful.

The auditorium door opened, and Leslie Levant walked out and joined us. Dutton, also used to seeing her in uniform, was having a hard time with the substantial amount of cleavage being displayed, and made very healthy efforts to maintain eye contact. Hoping for a somewhat different relationship with the officer than her chief had, I let my eyes roam where they may.

"I saw you get up and walk out, Chief. Is there anything I can help with? A clue on the poisoning?"

Dutton shook his head. "No, thank you, Officer. Nothing to be done right now. I appreciate the offer, though."

He turned to me. "Don't hesitate to call me if you hear from that young man, Mr. Freed. It's important to me and to the department. Is that clear?" His tone was much sterner than before, and caught me off guard.

"Sure," I finally said. "I get a call, you get a call."

"Be sure I do," said Dutton. He hesitated, as if deciding whether to slap me or not, and then walked into the auditorium, nodding at Leslie and her cleavage.

"He's a real laugh riot," I said when the door had closed.

"He's a good cop." Still with the frozen demeanor.

I knew that tactic from my marriage. "Okay, what'd I do?"

She'd been waiting. "You don't comp me at the door, Elliot. I didn't go to dinner with you to get free movie tickets."

"I never thought you did. But as the owner of the theatre, I'm entitled to let friends in free if I want to. And I'm not going to take your money, Leslie. I don't take my ex-wife's money at the door."

"No, you take it in alimony checks."

"It's the principle. After you and I get divorced, I'll be happy to take your money."

She couldn't help it; she grinned. We might have had our first kiss then, but she spotted Sophie looking at her from the snack bar. Leslie straightened up, cop that she was, and nodded.

"All right, then," she said. She turned and walked back into the auditorium.

"Well," I said to myself, giving Sophie the evil eye, "that was certainly . . . satisfactory."

I went upstairs to check on the change of reels, but it had already been accomplished, and the next one was set up. That could have happened within seconds, or within twelve minutes of my previous checking, so it was a decent bet that if it was Anthony, he wasn't commuting in from Pennsylvania to keep the place running.

The light in the projection booth was adequate to make out what was going on, but not to see under the table or in corners, and I couldn't turn on the lights without people in the audience noticing. I had time to kill, since Harpo was playing "Everyone Says I Love You" on his harp, and although the man was possibly the most brilliant mime of his or any age, he was never able to turn me into an aficionado of the harp. Four minutes to search.

"Anthony," I hissed, ducking under the table. *"Anthony! It's Elliot."* I caught myself. *"Mr. Freed. If you're in here, come on out. I promise, I won't turn you in!"*

"That's great," came Dutton's voice from the doorway. "If your promise to him is as sincere as your promise to me, I've got nothing to worry about."

15

✿✿✿✿✿✿✿

A good deal of time was spent with me explaining exactly why I suspected Anthony was around; Dutton threatening to shut down the theatre to search again; me protesting that my business, suddenly booming, would be ruined (and besides, to deprive an audience of Harpo's ride in a garbage cart pulled by horses—the silent Mr. Marx in only his underwear and a scarf that made him look like Julius Caesar—would be beyond cruel); Dutton countering that a suspected criminal was secreted in the building; me countering his counter by saying that all the searching so far hadn't turned up much of anything; and Leslie bringing us to reason by saying that if we'd simply leave the booth and wait for the next reel change, we'd have a chance of spotting the criminal in the act. (When did Leslie come in? I just don't know anymore.)

Dutton took up the position with the best view of the projection booth door, just outside the women's restroom, which could certainly cause an amusing stir in town. Once she covered her cleavage with Dutton's jacket (which fit her like a small tent), Leslie was stationed at the top of the stairs, where she could see not only the door to the booth but also whether anyone was coming up the stairs.

Since I was the owner of the place, and in Dutton's mind the least trustworthy, I was relegated to the first row of the somewhat shaky balcony, in the corner farthest from the staircase, to better ensure my demise should the structure decide to collapse. I could see the door of the booth, but barely, and got caught up in the movie just as Harpo and Chico were busy putting the "tie-onna-the-bed, throw-the-rope-outta-the-window."

Wait a minute! That meant that the next reel change—which would come just when Harpo would be "getting tough" with two nasty football players—was only seconds away. I stood up and headed for Dutton's position.

Dutton wasn't there. Neither was Leslie. I couldn't imagine what had taken them away other than . . . Anthony!

But when I rushed to the booth door and flung it open, I found Police Chief Barry Dutton trying desperately to figure out how to switch from one reel to the next, and Officer Leslie Levant next to him, standing over his shoulder and pointing toward the take-up reel on the first projector.

"I think it's that one," she said.

"You don't mind if I do it, do you?" I asked. "I paid close to a hundred grand for this projection booth, and I'd prefer not to get anything broken."

They looked up, a little embarrassed, and stepped aside. I hit the pedal on the floor when I saw the small white circle appear in the right-hand corner of the screen, and the reels changed smoothly, as they should.

Leslie's arm brushed a pile of papers on one side of the table, and she bent to pick them up. I turned to Dutton.

"Do I tell you how to stop a car for speeding?" I asked.

"I was on the A/V crew in high school," he muttered.

"I was on the baseball team," I said. "Doesn't make me Derek Jeter."

"This is not the major leagues," Dutton said, but without much swagger in it.

"If you two are done comparing the size of your bats,"

Leslie said, "I think I've got something here you should see, Chief."

Dutton ignored the less-than-totally-respectful remark that had been made, and took a step toward Leslie, which was all he needed in the cramped projection booth.

She was holding a small plastic pill bottle, which I couldn't see well from the screen's illumination, but which appeared to immediately intrigue Dutton. He pulled down the sleeve on his shirt and grasped the bottle with his fingers inside the sleeve to avoid leaving fingerprints on it. I walked to his side.

It was a prescription vial, and I could see it had some pills in it.

"What is it?" I asked, but Dutton didn't answer.

"Who has access to this room?" he asked me over his shoulder.

"On normal nights, just me and Anthony," I said. "Tonight we have enough people to start a basketball game. Why?"

"It's a prescription," Dutton answered, still not looking at me. "Thirty pills. Clonidine."

It took me a moment. "The medication that killed Vincent Ansella," I said, and Dutton nodded. "Who is it made out to?"

"Michael Pagliarulo," Leslie said, her voice hushed, and not because she was afraid she'd spoil the football scene for the audience.

I took a deep breath. I remembered the name from an employment application. "Anthony's father," I said.

16

○♧○♧♧○♧

"It doesn't mean anything," I told Leslie in my kitchen that night. She'd given me a ride home on the pretense that I'd "had a rough night," but really she wanted to talk about the new evidence without Dutton around. "All it means is that Anthony's dad has high blood pressure, and the medication he's been prescribed is the same as the stuff that was used to poison Vincent Ansella."

"Sounds like something to me," she said, still in the jaw-dropping outfit she'd worn to the movie but minus Dutton's jacket. "I'll grant you the evidence is all circumstantial, but . . ."

"I've got to look at the circumstances," I said.

"Exactly." She noted my glance. "Not *those* circumstances." Leslie blushed, quite fetchingly.

I got the container of Edy's ice cream out of the freezer and took two spoons from a drawer, then sat next to Leslie. "I'll bet you there were fifty people there tonight with high blood pressure," I told her. "I don't know what percentage of those were prescribed clonidine." I handed her a spoon and opened the container. I'd offered a coffee mug to hold the ice cream, but Leslie said this was a more "communal" experience. I think she was just impatient; she plunged in with the spoon and got the bevy of chocolate chips lurking near the top.

"Maybe," Leslie said, her tongue doing all sorts of interesting things to the ice cream. "But it all looks bad for Anthony, and you need to maintain a distance."

I almost stopped spooning ice cream for a moment. Almost. "A distance? Why do I need to maintain a distance from Anthony? For one thing, how can I know if I'm maintaining a distance when I don't know where he is?"

"I'm talking like a cop now," she said.

"You're not dressed like one," I marveled.

"Nonetheless. The water's getting deep for your projectionist, and you can't tell me you weren't aware he was in the building tonight."

All the clichés are true. I looked away, thus confirming my guilt. "Sure I can," I said.

"Well, not convincingly."

We seemed to have stopped eating the ice cream, so I stood to give myself something to do, and took it back to the freezer. "Okay, so I had an idea he was there. But I never saw him tonight."

Leslie stood, too, carrying the spoons. She opened the dishwasher to put them in, saw it was empty, and washed the two spoons by hand. "You need to stay away from this, Elliot. It's going to get bad."

"It's a couple of pirated DVDs of a bad movie. I don't understand why everybody's so bent out of shape about it."

She dried her hands on a towel. "Because now there seems to be a dead man connected to it, and *that* is a very good reason for everyone to be bent out of shape."

"Anthony has no motive to kill Ansella. He didn't even know the guy."

Leslie raised an eyebrow. "As far as you know."

"You don't know the kid." I waved a dismissive hand. "It just doesn't fit his character. Anthony's the type who would spend six months figuring out exactly how to shoot a murder scene for a movie, but it would never occur to him to do it for real."

"Maybe he's into snuff films," she suggested.

"Anthony? Snuff films would be too real for him. I don't think he's ever seen a documentary he liked. He thought *Fahrenheit 9/11* was a lousy movie because it was too realistic, and he wanted to know who that guy was who kept talking so funny."

"Michael Moore?"

"No."

Leslie sat down on the living room futon. "You have no furniture."

"What's that you're sitting on?"

"My butt."

"And a lovely one it is. Besides that."

"A piece of foam rubber," she said, rubbing her lush behind. "And not a very thick one."

"Well, based on the box office figures from tonight, if we can pull in half that for the weekend, you can come with me and help pick out some furniture on Monday."

"Well, let's see how the theatre does this weekend, then. And think about what I said, all right? About maintaining a distance?"

I walked over but didn't sit down next to her, for fear I'd never be able to get up. She was right about the foam rubber. "Maintaining a distance," I echoed. "From Anthony, or from you?"

She stood in a fluid motion, which I considered an impressive athletic feat on its own merits. "From Anthony," Leslie said.

And then she kissed me.

17

✿✿✿✿✿✿✿

Sharon hadn't even sat all the way down in her seat at C'est Moi! when she gave me a strange look, paused, and said, "You're seeing somebody."

"It's nice to see you, too, honey," I countered. "My lord, but you have a talent for small talk."

Sharon ordered and turned back to me. "So, are you going to tell me about her?" she asked.

"What makes you think . . ."

"Before I was your ex-wife, I was your wife," she said. "Before that, I was your girlfriend. And in order to become your girlfriend, I started out as the girl you wanted to ask on a date. I know what you look like when you're infatuated. My god, it practically radiates from you."

"It's a wonder they let me walk the streets, isn't it?" I asked.

"Are you going to tell me, or not?"

"It's true; I've met someone," I said. "I don't know how serious it is yet." I went on to tell her that it was someone I'd met at the theatre recently (which was technically true), but gave her few details, which irked her. Good. But I'm not bitter.

Not that there were a ton of details to convey, anyway. Leslie and I had kissed a little, then she'd said it was late, and I interpreted that to mean she wanted to go home. I couldn't tell by the look on her face whether I was correct, but Leslie did, in fact, leave. And I was up half the night, kicking myself.

Sharon decided to switch tactics by changing the subject upon the arrival of her club sandwich and my turkey on rye, hold the cholesterol. "So what's going on with your projectionist?"

"Anthony," I reminded her.

Sharon nodded. "Yes. Anthony. Has he shown up yet?"

I recounted for her the seemingly unending string of circumstantial evidence that was building up around my missing projectionist, and my eerie feeling that he had been nearby the night before. Sharon listened intently, as she always does, really paying attention to every word, chewing thoughtfully, but without showing you anything she was chewing. It's an art I intend to emulate as I go through life. I should start any day now.

There was a long moment when I was finished with my tale, and I studied her face, which is something I like to do when I'm in the mood to torture myself. It's the same open, friendly, in some ways beautiful face I remember pursuing and, to my amazement, winning years ago. But now it was one that chose to look into another man's eyes with romantic thoughts, and into mine with the same characteristics as a winter fleece: soft, comfortable, but a reminder that it's cold outside.

"So?" I asked finally.

"So, what?"

"So, what do you think about Anthony?"

She frowned. "What I think is irrelevant. What are you going to do about it?"

I probably looked as confused as Stan Laurel being asked to do logarithms. "What do you mean, what am I going to do about it? What *should* I do about it?"

It was her turn to look surprised. "Seems to me the man I was married to would have been actively looking into this. A guy who works for you is in serious trouble, he hasn't been seen since Wednesday, and he's implicated in a crime that took place in your building. Aren't you the same man who was offended that someone chose his theatre to kill a total stranger in?"

"That's 'in which to kill a total stranger,' and he was a stranger to me, not to the killer, I'm guessing."

"Thank you, Professor Grammar."

"And you may recall that the man to whom you were married is the very same man you chose to divorce, probably for the same exact reasons." Divorce is nothing if not an endless quest for the upper hand.

"Let's keep our divorce out of this conversation. What are you going to do about Anthony?" Sharon's eyes weren't widened any more than usual, but they seemed to be looking directly into my soul, assuming I had one.

"The police have specifically advised against my doing any investigating," I pointed out. Well, one member of the police department had said it was a bad idea, right before she kissed me. That had to stand for something.

Sharon's face got an "aha!" expression and she pointed a finger at me. "Oh, my god, you're dating the cop, aren't you? The one you told me about, from the theatre?"

"Yeah," I said, "and you're sleeping with a bald anesthesiologist. What's that got to do with anything?"

"Gregory isn't bald. His hair is thinning."

"Vertical stripes are thinning. Gregory's bald."

"Let's try to stay on topic, shall we? So your girlfriend is telling you not to help your employee, and you've decided to listen." Sharon took on an expression that made it seem less painful not to be married to her anymore.

"She's not my *girlfriend*; I'm not in the seventh grade. And I'm not investigating because I'm not an investigator. Who died and made me Sam Spade?"

"They're after your projectionist for more than pirating movies now, Elliot; they think he's involved in the murder.

And what about the murdered man? Did that stop bothering you when the cop got into your bed?"

I felt no need to correct her. "We're getting into weird territory here, Sharon. You almost sound jealous."

She went and did the one thing that I'd never be able to forgive—she looked at me affectionately. "Elliot," Sharon said, "you have the strongest moral sense of any man I know. You don't drive a car because you believe in conservation. You run a comedy theatre because you believe in laughter. You didn't contest our divorce because you believe that I have the right to be happy, even if it's with another man."

"I'm still undecided about that one," I said.

She ignored me, which was wise. "I can't believe that a man as decent as you, and with as strong a sense of right and wrong, could just stand by and let this go on. I really can't believe it."

Now, that was hitting below the belt.

18

○○○○○○○

It was surprisingly easy to arrange an interview with Amy Ansella; I didn't expect she'd be alone the Saturday after her husband died, but apparently friends and family had left her to her own devices. Sharon dropped me off at Amy's Piscataway home, and noted the easy walk to the bus stop before driving away, a smug expression on her face. I cursed her quietly as I walked to the door.

The house was nice but unassuming, a Colonial on a street of Colonials, and well kept, much like the woman who answered the door.

Amy Ansella, close up, was not quite as stunning as she had been from a slight distance, but she was still enough to temporarily cloud my brain. Luckily, this time I'd told the truth, so I didn't have to remember the name of a fictional newspaper for which I'd come to interview her. She'd agreed to talk with me anyway.

She ushered me into a very nice living room, with well-polished hardwood floors and a wide-screen TV hung on the wall.

"I'm not sure I understand why you're here, Mr. Freed,"

she admitted as she gestured toward the sofa, but I stood, uneasy and more interested in surveying the room.

"I'm not sure I understand it either, Mrs. Ansella, and please call me Elliot."

Everyone has a yardstick by which they, well, measure other people. For some people it's the religion to which they belong, the political party they support, or the sports teams they root for. With me, it's taste in movies, and judging by the DVD collection that dominated one half of the room, taking up shelf after shelf, Vincent Ansella and I could have been brothers. Or two sides of the same multiple personality disorder.

It took a lot to distract me from a woman like Amy Ansella, but this was a treasure trove: Buster Keaton, Laurel and Hardy, Lillis and Townes, *Fatty Arbuckle*, for god's sake! Of course the Marx Brothers, but even episodes of *You Bet Your Life*, not to mention Woody Allen on *What's My Line* and Peter Sellers in *The Goon Show*. There was a wonderful British comedy miniseries called *Flickers*, with Bob Hoskins and Frances de la Tour, that I would have bet my last quarter wasn't available on DVD, but Vincent Ansella had it. Truly, a man after my own heart.

"Are you here about Vincent's collection, Elliot?"

That snapped me back to attention. "No, I'm not, Mrs. Ansella, but if I were, I'd be awfully impressed. He has titles here that make my mouth water."

"Vincent was a . . . what did he say . . . a *completist*," she said, visibly proud of herself for remembering the word. "When he set his mind on something, he didn't rest until it was done. And his mind was *always* set on classic comedies. But if it's not his movie collection, Elliot, please help me understand why you're here."

She gestured again to the sofa, and, reluctantly, I pulled myself away from the Comedy Museum and sat facing her. Not knowing the nature of the planned visit, Amy had put a pot of coffee and some Oreos on the coffee table.

"I don't want to seem presumptuous, Mrs. Ansella . . ."

"Amy."

I nodded. "But the fact is, it bothers me that your husband . . . died . . . in my theatre. I want Comedy Tonight to be a happy place, and somehow, it seems to be, well . . ."

"Insulting?" Wow. Beautiful *and* able to decipher my babble. Where was she when I was looking for a wife?

"For lack of a better word, yes. I don't want to overstate it, and I'm not interested in adding to your pain, but . . ."

Amy Ansella stood up. She was wearing black, but it was a scoop-neck T-shirt and black jeans that were fitted for maximum effect. In all that black, she could have been Sophie's Goth mother. "Don't worry about my pain, Elliot," she said, although her mouth was tightened, and she walked toward the fireplacc, which had no wood in it. "My marriage wasn't exactly the best there ever was."

"I've heard rumors," I said.

She turned a little too quickly. "From his office? Did Marcy Resnick have the nerve to say something about it?"

How did she know I'd seen Marcy? "Well, she just said there had been rumors," I said, "but she said they were lies."

"She would," Amy spat. "The lying bitch."

"Are you saying that your husband and Marcy Resnick . . ."

"Maybe you don't understand, Elliot. Are you married?"

"I'm divorced."

"Did your wife cheat on you?" Her eyes were not wavering, looking straight into mine.

"Let's just say she married someone else very soon after we divorced," I sidestepped.

"So you do understand."

"When you say your marriage wasn't the best . . ." I wanted to get off my miserable love life, and back to Amy's.

"I meant exactly what you think," she said. "My husband was having an affair with Marcy Resnick."

"What makes you think that, Amy?" I don't know why, but Marcy's denial had struck me as genuine, and frankly, I thought she could have done better than Vincent Ansella if she'd wanted to, at least in the looks department (then again, so could Amy). But maybe I was projecting. Being back on the dating scene had me thinking about a lot of women differently than I had, say, a month before.

"My husband confessed it to me the night he died."

That took a moment to sink in. "He told you he was having an affair with a coworker, then went out to the movies?"

Amy looked down, and I don't think she was considering eating an Oreo. "We fought," she said. "I knew something was wrong, but I didn't suspect . . . or maybe I did. But when he said it out loud, that he was in love with Marcy Resnick, and wanted to get a divorce, well, I didn't handle it well. We had a very loud argument; I'm sure the neighbors heard some of it. And he stormed out. It occurred to me he'd go to the movies; that's what he did to calm down. If a movie made him laugh, he could lose himself in it."

"And while he was there, someone poisoned him." Wait. Did I say that out loud?

Amy Ansella, who had been staring at the floor, looked up suddenly with fury in her eyes. "I know what you're thinking, but it wasn't me," she said.

"You don't know what I'm thinking," I said, "and I have no reason to think it was you. I'm only the theatre owner."

The fury faded, replaced by weariness. "You don't talk like a theatre owner. You talk like a detective."

"Watch enough Bogart and everybody talks like a detective. But I do have one question. At the memorial service, you called Joe Dunbar a murderer. Do you think that Joe killed your husband?"

"I think you need to go now, Mr. Freed," she said. Amy stood up, clearly a signal that I should do the same, and I did.

"But . . ."

"I don't need to explain myself to you," she said, with the loveliest smile I'd seen in some time. "You're only the theatre owner."

19

✿✿✿✿✿✿✿

It was getting late after Amy politely kicked me out of her house, so I caught the bus back to Midland Heights to have some dinner before opening the theatre for the night. My head was starting to hurt from all the things I didn't know, and that was troublesome. Besides, I'd tried calling Joe Dunbar from a pay phone near the bus stop, and he wasn't answering. I left a message.

A sign over one of the front seats asked me if I was "Depressed? Lonely?" I hadn't really thought so, but if they were putting ads up on buses just to ask me that, I figured it was worth more than a knee-jerk reaction. I should consider.

Before this week, I hadn't been even a little involved with a woman since Sharon, and she'd been married to the somnambulist for almost a year and a half now. So my batting average hadn't been great, and I really didn't know what my current status with Leslie was, aside from the fact that she looked terrific and we bantered nicely. We needed to find the time to actually get to know each other.

Yet, as soon as she'd suggested that I shouldn't look into the situation with Anthony and Ansella's murder, I'd begged off, and as soon as Sharon had noted the wussiness of that move, I'd called Amy Ansella to ask for an interview.

Man, I was easily manipulated.

It wasn't a long ride back, and the bus stopped within a block of Comedy Tonight, so I was in my office eating a Quiznos chicken sub an hour before I'd need to start getting the place presentable. I'd done most of the cleaning up the night before, after convincing Dutton I wasn't withholding any *more* information, so the theatre was in pretty good shape. It would be just as difficult tonight without Anthony, but there was nothing to be done about it. Maybe I should teach Sophie how to use the projector. On the other hand, maybe the elves who had threaded it up the previous night would take up permanent residence, and I wouldn't have to worry about it. Maybe . . .

"Mr. Freed?" I wasn't expecting to hear a voice, so it startled me. I didn't exactly do a spit-take, but the ratio of chicken inside my mouth to outside definitely saw a shift in that second.

A rather large man in his late fifties, with a head full of curly dark hair, was standing in the doorway of my converted closet office, and he was enough to fill it up. Carrying an actual hat, he stood nervously spinning it in his hands and barely making eye contact. But his eyes, when I could see them, looked haunted.

"We're not open yet," I told him when my mouth was relatively chicken-free again.

The man nodded. "I know. I came to talk to you. My name is Michael Pagliarulo."

Inside my head, there was a sigh. I hoped there was no outside sign of it. "You're Anthony's father."

Mr. Pagliarulo nodded again. "That's right. May I come in?"

"There's not so much 'in.' Maybe I should come out." I stood, wiping savory sauce off my lower lip, and walked into the lobby to talk to the man, who on closer examination did bear some resemblance to his son around the eyes and mouth. I wondered if Anthony was destined to avoid hair loss as well as his father, and hoped for his sake he was.

"Is there something I can do to help you, Mr. Pagliarulo?"

He shrugged, possibly because he didn't trust his own voice not to waver, then he said, "I don't know what to think. Ant'ny doesn't disappear like this. I've been called twice during the week by the *police*, Mr. Freed. Do you have children?"

"No, sir." But I'd be glad to go out and have some right now if it would make him feel better.

"Calls from the police are the last thing you want when you have children," Pagliarulo said.

"They're not exactly a high point of the day even if you don't," I volunteered, then wished I hadn't.

He prudently chose not to respond. "His mother is beside herself, on tranquilizers the past two days. I don't know what to tell her. Ant'ny would call us if he were . . ."

"There's no point in thinking that, Mr. Pagliarulo. There are plenty of reasons that Anthony might feel the need to stay away right now." For example, he's either involved in a serious crime, or the victim of one (a possibility I hadn't considered until this very moment). There are reasons I never considered a career in diplomacy.

"They called me about my medication last night," he went on. "To find out if Anthony had taken any pills from me. Why would a nineteen-year-old kid need blood pressure pills, Mr. Freed?"

"The police don't think he has high blood pressure," I told Mr. Pagliarulo. "There was a . . . situation here with someone who took the wrong pills, and they're trying to find out where the pills came from."

"The man who died here the other night?" Pagliarulo's eyes were wide with fear for his son, but now outrage was starting to creep in, too. "They think Ant'ny poisoned a man he never met before with my blood pressure pills? That's crazy!"

"I don't believe it either, Mr. Pagliarulo," I said, and I meant it. "But the man died from an overdose of the same medication you take, and they found a prescription bottle of clonidine where Anthony had hidden it."

He waved a hand, dismissing the idea. "Hidden," Mr. Pagliarulo said. "I asked him to fill a prescription for me. He passes by the CVS on his way sometimes, and I was going to see him the next day. He said he'd do it. He used to do that for me all the time . . ." I think that was the moment Mr. Pagliarulo realized what he was saying. "You think the police are going to say he stole pills from me and used them on that man?"

"Let's not get ahead of ourselves, sir," I said. "I don't see any reason they'd think Anthony would do something like that. They just don't have any other suspects right now."

"I wish they did," he said.

"Maybe I can do something about that," I told him. I wasn't going to be intimidated by a cop, no matter how good a kisser she was. And she was good.

"Would you?" asked Michael Pagliarulo, and I was lost.

20

○◌○◌ ○○◌

Joe Dunbar finally called back, but he didn't want to talk to me at his home, so we met at a Dunkin' Donuts in Midland Heights over coffee and reduced-fat muffins late Sunday morning.

I actually had an iced coffee, as it was a warm day, and they put coconut flavoring in it, which always makes me feel like I'm on a tropical island. Unfortunately, the view of Edison Avenue, with its used-car lots and antique stores side by side, doused that feeling just a little.

"I don't know why she'd say 'murderer,'" Dunbar said. "Amy just seemed to turn on me suddenly, but I got the feeling it was planned."

"Planned?" Reduced-fat muffins are really bad, no matter who makes them. The whole *point* of muffins is the fat.

"Yeah, I think she was making a scene. Amy has a real sense of the dramatic." Dunbar took a bite, and his eyes indicated that his opinion of reduced-fat muffins was roughly the same as mine. "Calling me a murderer was sure dramatic."

"I don't know about the dramatic," I said. "I run a comedy theatre."

"I know. Vince was sorry he hadn't found your place sooner. You should do more advertising," Dunbar told me. He didn't mention where I'd get the money for that, and I didn't ask.

I had to be careful with the place I was about to go. "How about another woman? Someone in the theatre thought they saw Mr. Ansella with a blond woman. Any idea?"

Even if I hadn't been watching Dunbar closely—and I was—it would have been obvious that he was unnerved by the question. He coughed into his napkin and took a swig of coffee. "No idea. Vince never mentioned a blonde," he said. But my eyes were telling me another story: *he knew something*. Problem was, I had no idea how to call him on it in a constructive way. So I pressed on as if I believed him.

"Do you have any idea why someone would want to kill Mr. Ansella?"

I'm sure Dunbar wasn't *trying* to do an impression of someone who's guilty and trying to cover it up, but he looked away and coughed again to avoid answering. I just waited him out, and eventually, while turned away from the table, Dunbar exhaled and bit his lip.

"I can't think of one reason anybody would want to hurt that man," he said. "He was the sweetest human being I've ever known. Vince Ansella should never have died."

Maybe he wasn't badly hiding his guilt. Maybe he was badly hiding the fact that he was crying. Dunbar snorted, blew his nose into a Dunkin' Donuts napkin, and kept looking away.

"All he wanted was for everybody to be happy," he continued. "Who would want to hurt a man like that?"

I didn't know, so I didn't say anything.

"Did Vincent and Amy get along well? Was there trouble in their marriage?"

That seemed to focus Dunbar, and he pretended to have an eyelash in his eye and brush it away. He turned to me with red eyes. "The cops asked me about that," he said.

"I'll tell you what I told them. Vince and Amy weren't the love story of the century, but they got along fine, as far as I know. Vince would have told me if there were problems, at least, until the last few months."

"His behavior changed?" Marcy had told me the same thing.

Dunbar nodded. "He started, I don't know, closing up. He didn't invite me over to watch comedies. He didn't come out bowling, like we did once a month or so. He didn't seem to want to be alone with me, because . . ."

"Because?"

"It's stupid. I got the feeling he was afraid he'd tell me something he shouldn't. Isn't that dumb?"

"I don't think so. What do you suppose he didn't want you to know?"

Dunbar discarded half his muffin in a trash bin directly behind him. "These suck," he said. "Reduced-fat muffins. I should have gotten a double chocolate donut."

"What do you think—"

"I don't know, Mr. Freed, but there was something bothering the man. He was a completely changed person, and not for the better."

I took a shot. "Amy thinks he was having an affair."

"Amy should know better," Dunbar said.

"He was seen at the theatre with another woman," I offered. "Amy wasn't there, but someone else might have seen him and told her."

"What do you mean, Amy wasn't there?" Dunbar asked.

A large firecracker went off inside my head. "You mean Amy *was* there?" Then, I thought another moment. "Were *you* there?" I can't remember everyone in the theatre every night. I leave that to Leo.

"No," Dunbar said. "I wasn't there. Do you think I'd just leave my best friend dead in a movie seat?"

"What about Amy? Was she at the theatre that night?"

"I would have no way of knowing." But Dunbar's eyes were saying something other than what came out of his mouth.

21

○○○○○○○

FRIDAY
The Thin Man (1934)
and *Phat Ho* (today)

The theatre had been packed again Saturday night, and while every seat wasn't filled on Sunday, a good number of them were. I had made all the reel changes myself both nights, and there had been no further evidence that Anthony was anywhere near the place. I imagine Dutton and O'Donnell were both watching the theatre pretty closely, just in case.

The crowds were still larger than usual, but starting to diminish, and I knew that sooner rather than later, Comedy Tonight would be back to the depressing audience levels it averaged before becoming the Crime Scene du Jour.

Leslie had been on the night shift the whole week, so I didn't see her again until Friday. During the week, I'd invented a few more newspapers and talked to some of Ansella's coworkers. And that was where it had gotten a little weird: two of them confirmed that Vincent had been acting "angry" for about two weeks before he'd been killed. But they each contradicted Marcy's story that she and Vincent hadn't been close.

"They were the best of friends until right before he

died," one said. "Something happened—I don't know what—but after that, he was a different man." The woman went on to suggest, in terms that were not terribly subtle, that she knew *why* Vincent and Marcy had stopped getting along, but she was far too principled a person to say. I made a mental note not to tell her anything even slightly personal, and moved on.

I'd also spoken to two more of Anthony's professors, who hadn't heard from him and were waiting for term papers, and another of his roommates, a kid named Lyle who was so stoned he called me "dude" seventeen times during a six-minute conversation. Dolores wasn't home, he assured me, but they were "just friends," anyway. I got the feeling Dolores had a lot of friends. Amy Ansella's friends didn't have any news, either. But her neighbor, a Mrs. Nelson, confirmed that Amy and Vincent were shouting at each other the night he died. "It was mostly Amy," Mrs. Nelson said. "I'm not sure Vince could get a word in edgewise."

I didn't tell Leslie any of this when she showed up at the town house without warning just around noon on Friday, even though she knew I hadn't cleared enough money to buy furniture—at least, not yet. She appeared at the door, with her own bicycle strapped to the back of her car.

"Let's go for a ride along the canal," she said. I didn't bother to tell her that I consider a bicycle to be transportation, not recreation. *You wanted to know where this relationship (if that's the word for it) is going,* I told myself. *Here's your chance.*

The Delaware and Raritan Canal towpath is a bicycling route of about twenty-eight miles that runs from Frenchtown to Ewing, a ride of roughly two and a half tree-lined, scenic hours (thus trashing, one hopes, the vision most people have of New Jersey as a toxic waste dump run by the Mob). The problem is, you have to leave your car (assuming you have one) at one end, and ride back up the same path in the other direction, making it a ride of approximately fifty-six miles, which is more than I'm willing to do unless being chased by a very determined bear on roller skates.

We solved this problem by calling my dad, who agreed to meet us in Lambertville and drive us back to Leslie's car in Frenchtown. Luckily, he still had an old truck which could accommodate two bicycles and a pair of weary riders, one of whom he was no doubt anxious to meet. I'd get back to the theatre in time for the night's showing, tired but without the saddle sores those who don't ride regularly might have. Leslie might have a slightly more tender behind when we got back, but my philosophy was that this ride hadn't been *my* idea.

Leslie rode in front for a while, which allowed me the luxury of watching the aforementioned behind for an extended period. When the path widened after a while, I pulled out and rode next to her. It was a weekday, so there were few other riders, and not many pedestrians on the path.

But I was regretting the decision to get close enough that she could talk to me once I'd told Leslie about my conversations with Amy Ansella and Joe Dunbar. "You went to her *house*?" she pretty much screamed as we rode over a wooden bridge somewhere to the left of the Delaware River. "How could you do that? Why can't you just leave this to us?"

"Everybody's so bent out of shape about some copied DVDs that I don't see anything being done about the murder," I told her, a bit unfairly, since I had no idea what was being done about the murder. "Besides, with all the circumstantial evidence, Anthony's being hung out to dry, and I'm the only one who seems to care."

"I've heard this before," she said, pedaling harder and making me catch up.

"Well . . . his father came to see me, and he cried."

There was a small decline, and we coasted for a few welcome seconds. Leslie didn't speak for the moment; she felt the breeze in her face, then looked at me. She smiled.

"You're a real softy, you know that?"

"Not where it counts," I said.

She pretended to ignore that. "All right, what did they tell you?"

I recounted most of what I'd learned—which wasn't much—over lunch, which we had in a coffee shop in

Lambertville, a town so adorable you want to wrap it in a little pink blanket and feed it pastina. Alas, there was no outside seating, but we could look out the window at the fine day, and at our well-chained bicycles attached to the cast-iron fence of a church across from the restaurant. I had my front wheel with me in the coffee shop. Leslie, being a law enforcement official, chose to live on the edge, and just ran the chain through her front wheel spokes.

"So, do you believe Amy about the affair her husband was having with Marcy Resnick?" Leslie asked. She was eating a small salad and refused even to touch the croutons, which I thought was just a little showy. I had a steak sandwich because there was no way I was riding twenty-eight miles unless I got a reward for it. I even ordered french fries.

"I don't know," I answered. "Everybody seems to agree that Ansella was not himself for a few months before he died. You could attribute that to guilt, I suppose. Some people at their office clearly thought something was going on between Vincent and Marcy. Amy admits they fought before he left for the movies. I would suspect her, but it just doesn't add up."

"What doesn't add up?" She had put so little dressing on the salad, I was practically embarrassed to look at it.

"The murder couldn't have been that spontaneous. Someone had to know where Ansella was going that night, get hold of the medication, grind it up and put it in the vial in advance, get to the theatre and sit next to him, sprinkle it on his popcorn and leave undetected. That's not something that just happens; it's something that is planned and executed."

Leslie stopped spearing romaine to ask, "So? The crime was premeditated. No kidding. It's not an impulsive act. We knew that."

"So, it's not the act of someone who just found out her husband had been cheating on her. It's not an act that comes from a shock. It was something done after long, careful thought. And from the description Leo gave me, the woman sitting next to Ansella that night sure wasn't his wife."

"Marcy?"

I shook my head. "Not unless she put on a blond wig and about thirty pounds before she left the house, and hit herself in the face repeatedly with a bag of loose change. Leo said she was the ugliest woman he'd ever seen, and he was a good few rows behind them, in the dark."

"So how reliable is his description, then?"

"Leo's a nut, but he's a smart nut. If he says that's what she looked like, you can bank on it."

"Joe Dunbar's wife looks roughly like that." Leslie was all cop now. I don't know why, but I found it exciting.

"Yeah, but Leo said this woman was ugly. Christie Dunbar isn't ugly."

"Not everyone has the same standards of beauty that you do, Elliot," Leslie said.

I thought about what Dunbar had said. "But there might have been someone else there . . ."

Leslie looked up sharply. "Who?"

I didn't have time to answer because my father was walking toward us, but not even pretending to look at me. His gaze was fixed directly on Leslie, like many men's often were, but to his credit he was looking directly into her eyes. He's a class act, my father.

"So this is Leslie!" Classy, but not restrained. He took her hand between his own two, and held it. "It's so nice to meet you," he said.

"It's nice to meet *you*," she answered. "Come sit." There was no question which side of the booth Dad would choose; he sat next to Leslie, who had to scoot over. I could have warned her about his brimming affection for anyone whom his son deems worthy, but it's not the kind of thing you can adequately describe.

"So, Elliot says you're a cop," Dad began. Nice opening, Dad.

"A police officer, yes," she corrected gently.

"Sorry." He caught the distinction immediately.

"You know, I'm here, too, Dad," I interjected.

"You I've seen before," he noted without shifting his gaze. "So Leslie, why is a pretty girl like you out there carrying a gun?"

I love my father deeply, but the man can drive you nuts without half trying. "Dad," I started.

"It's all right," Leslie cut me off. "It's what I want to do, Arthur," she continued (he had instructed her to address him that way). "I've always wanted to be one of the good guys. Whether or not I'm pretty doesn't really enter into it."

Dad thought that over, and nodded. "Makes sense. So. Are you two done? I'm ready to drive."

"You just drove here from Manalapan, Dad. Don't you want something to eat?"

He made a face. "Your mother made me lunch before I left." My mother is a lovely woman, but family legend has it she learned to cook from the Marquis de Sade.

"You sure you don't want anything, then?"

He considered. "Maybe a little something."

We sat while he hunkered down with a brisket sandwich, cole slaw, and a side of creamed corn before ordering rice pudding for dessert. Maybe my mother couldn't cook, but she certainly understood cholesterol, and would never have allowed such a repast if she'd been present. Which is why I didn't say anything to Dad about it; I knew he didn't get to enjoy himself this way too often.

He insisted on paying for everyone's meal, over our protests, and then ushered us to his truck where we lifted the bikes into the bed, over *his* protests (he wanted to do the lifting) and got in to drive back to Frenchtown. Naturally, Leslie got the window seat, and I was stuck in the middle, feeling the drive shaft heat up beneath my . . . beneath me. Being one's son only goes so far in my family.

In between my father's fawning over Leslie and her enjoying it immensely, we discussed where Anthony might be. Dad was still convinced there "must be a girlfriend somewhere," despite his having met Anthony on a few previous occasions. Of course, he was convinced that I had been the most popular kid in my senior class in high school, and we were living under the same roof at the time. So his assessment of teenage males might be a tad suspect.

Leslie speculated that Anthony was "hiding out" with friends, and assumed, as the rest of the police did, that he had pirated the DVDs and might be somehow connected to Ansella's murder. I told her that didn't jibe with the pre-threaded reels at the theatre, and she pursed her lips and stopped talking for a while.

I wasn't prepared to agree with any of those assumptions, and I burrowed down deeper in my seat, trying to get into Anthony's head. If I were nineteen and people thought I'd committed a crime, where would I go?

He was only a year and a half out of high school, I thought. Anthony wasn't the type who would have made legions of friends in college, and probably not that many beforehand, either. If there were one old high school buddy he could trust . . . Where had Anthony gone to high school, again?

"You think he'd go back to his hometown?" Dad asked. There are times he can read my mind. Personally, it frightens me. "Wouldn't his parents see him around? Wouldn't he try to contact them somehow?"

"You're still operating on the assumption that he's guilty; that's where you're going wrong," I told him. "Anthony knows people suspect him, but he knows he didn't do it. He's enough of a movie maniac to think there's only one thing left for him to do."

"Oh, my god," Leslie said, "We'll never find him. He's pulling a Richard Kimble."

"What's a Richard Kimble?" Dad asked.

"It's from *The Fugitive*," she said. "He's searching for the real killer."

22

We stopped at Frenchtown to pick up Leslie's car, and parted ways with Dad, who expressed no regrets about having spent almost an entire day in the car without actually going anywhere. He twinkled at Leslie before leaving, and she kissed him on the cheek, which probably made his month.

She drove me back to the town house (I don't really think of it as "home" yet; I've only been there a year), where we liberated my bike from the contraption she had strapped to her car. We went inside for a quick soda and I took a shower (after she insisted we had to do so separately, the spoil sport). Leslie showered and got ready for her shift while I biked to the theatre, on the assumption that I hadn't spent enough time on a bicycle yet today.

The elves had threaded up the projector. I guessed the elves loved me again.

Since I wasn't busy rewinding and threading the film, I had time to think, and after I had finished checking the projection booth, I went down to the office, took out Anthony's employment application, and looked up his educational background.

He'd gone to Cranford High School. A place to start.

I read through the rest of the application, hoping some piece of information would jump out at me, but aside from his birth date (he was a Sagittarius), parents (two), grade point average (not bad), and reason he wanted to work at a crumbling movie theatre ("I love movies. I want to make movies. I have a script that I could shoot today if I had the money"), there was little to go on. In fact, nothing.

When Sophie arrived, I reminded her that in Anthony's absence, I'd be spending more time in the projection booth, and that she'd be in charge of most everything else. She seemed duly impressed, until I realized she still had the buds from her iPod in her ears, and was nodding along with the music, from Evanescence or some such band.

I motioned to her to take the buds out, and she sighed a little, but obliged. I repeated the instructions I'd just given her and Sophie looked more annoyed than she had before, if such a thing were possible.

"I *heard* you," she said. "I'm not deaf."

"It's hard to tell with those things in your ears. If I'm going to give you more responsibility, I have to know you're listening."

If Sophie hadn't already been doing her "cadaverous pale" thing, I'm sure the word "responsibility" would have made her look downright ashen. "Why would I want more responsibility?" she asked.

"So you can learn more about the movie business."

She half-closed her eyes and pulled in her lips. "Oh joy, my career can begin at last." Sophie put the buds back into her ears and began to undo the damage I'd done to "her" snack stand.

The house was still bigger than most nights, but clearly the novelty of going to the movies at the "death theatre" was beginning to wane. I'd have to either do better advertising or kill someone to keep the box office alive. It was a tough choice.

Our audience, I noticed, included a good number of teenagers (each of whom I'd personally asked for ID, as *Phat Ho* was rated R) dressed and made-up much like my lone remaining employee. When I could bear to pull myself away from William Powell and Myrna Loy (all right, so *The Thin Man* was a mystery; it was a *comic* mystery), I asked Sophie about the influx of Goth youth.

"They've come to experience the death," she said. I knew I shouldn't have asked.

I had just started the projectors on the second feature, a turgid sex comedy with remarkably little sex and even less comedy, when Sophie knocked on the projection booth door, and I came out.

"What are you doing here?" I asked her.

"Can fresh popcorn go bad?" she asked.

I could feel my eyebrows crowd together into one big eyebrow. "No," I said. "You just popped it, right? You did it yourself?"

"Yeah."

"Then, no. It can't go bad that fast."

She nodded, and headed back downstairs, but I stopped her at the top of the staircase. "Why?" I said.

"Why, what?"

"Why did you ask about the popcorn?"

"Oh, because it's all white and powdery." Sophie headed downstairs again, and I stood there for what I hope wasn't the fifteen minutes it felt like, then ran down the stairs to the snack bar.

Sophie was alone there, standing with the iPod buds back in her ears, bagging popcorn. Luckily, she didn't sample any as she bagged.

It *was* white and powdery. It looked like white cheddar corn. We didn't sell white cheddar corn.

I motioned for Sophie to take the buds out of her ears. "Did you sell any of this to anyone?" I asked.

"Popcorn?" She clearly figured I was a complete idiot, and I was starting to feel like one.

"*This* popcorn. The fresh batch. *The white and powdery stuff.*"

"Oh. No, I popped it just at the end of the intermission, but I still had some left from the last batch. Nobody's been out here since then." She picked a piece up, and was about to put it into her mouth.

I slapped at her hand and knocked the popcorn out. Before she could complain, I said, "Call Chief Dutton and tell him to come here *right now*. And don't, under any circumstances, let anyone eat this popcorn. Understand? Don't sell anybody any popcorn, and don't eat any yourself. And wash your hands."

Chastised, Sophie nodded, and reached for the wall phone behind the snack bar to call Dutton. Just before she dialed, however, she turned to me. "Elliot?"

I was heading to my office, but I turned back to face her. "What?"

"Are the Milk Duds okay?"

○ ○

Dutton showed up fifteen minutes later, with Sergeant O'Donnell and a Midland Heights cop who was not (to my dismay) Leslie Levant. O'Donnell, who by dint of his county affiliation appeared to be in charge, made sure the officer bagged some of the popcorn in plastic.

"Are you sure nobody ate this batch?" O'Donnell asked me.

"Sophie had just finished making it, then she had to walk away from the snack bar for a minute," I told him. "She says when she got back, the popcorn looked, and I'm quoting, 'white and powdery.' So she came upstairs and got me."

"Why'd she have to leave the snack bar?" O'Donnell said.

"We're down to a two-person staff these days," I emphasized for him. "After the intermission, sometimes one of the people needs to walk away for a minute. You know."

"I spoke with her," Dutton reported. "She didn't notice anybody near the snack bar before she left or when she got back."

"Could whoever put the stuff on the popcorn have given it to someone in the audience already?" O'Donnell asked, looking nervously at the auditorium doors.

"Then why put it on *all* the popcorn?" Dutton said. "They could just dose the box they wanted the victim to eat, like with Mr. Ansella."

"What do you think it means?" I asked. "Is someone trying to sabotage my business, and poor Mr. Ansella died randomly?"

"It's all about you, isn't it, Freed?" O'Donnell said.

"Well, somebody was trying to poison everybody in *my theatre*," I answered. "They can't be mad at the entire audience individually."

"We don't even know it's the same stuff on the popcorn," Dutton pointed out. "For all we know, it's flour. It could just be a prank, Elliot."

"A prank? One man is dead, we don't know how many others were just prevented by a matter of minutes, and you call that a *prank*?" My heart was pounding, my stomach was churning, and I'm sure I was in a sweat. It was a good thing I hadn't eaten any popcorn, or I'd be really concerned.

"Well, we can't take any chances," O'Donnell sighed. "We're going to have to close down the theatre again, Freed."

"Close down the theatre? When?"

"Now."

"It's the middle of a showing," I said. "People are going to want their money back."

Dutton grimaced. "For *Phat Ho*?"

I protested, but it was hard to argue with an attempt to spread low blood pressure throughout Central New Jersey; I lost. The uniformed cop went into the auditorium on Dutton's orders and, after I stopped the film and brought the house lights up, made an announcement asking everyone to leave the theatre, mentioning something vague about "police business." Then he went ahead and told them not to eat any more popcorn, and the murmur that started when the projector had stopped running turned into a dull roar. People started running for the exits, and by the time I got downstairs, Dutton was surrounded by patrons demanding to know if they needed to go to the emergency room to have their stomachs pumped.

"There's no reason to believe that there's anything wrong with *any* of the popcorn sold tonight," he said, accurately. "Don't worry."

"Don't worry!" exclaimed one woman, whom I recognized as a cashier at the local Shop Rite. "A man died here the other night, and now you say we could be poisoned, and you want me not to worry?"

So much for the idea that only the information released by law enforcement officials is known to the public. Apparently, everybody in town knew Ansella's death wasn't a heart attack.

"I'm going to say it again," Dutton replied, louder now, and the crowd quieted down. "There is *no* reason to think there's *anything* wrong with *any* of the popcorn sold tonight."

"Then why can't we eat the popcorn?" a guy in the crowd asked. He must have been *really* hungry.

"Listen!" I shouted, hoping desperately to make nice with the customers. "Anyone who brings a ticket stub from tonight" (we use different color tickets for each day of the week, so I could know) "will get in free on their next visit."

"Sure," said the cashier, "*if* I survive tonight's visit."

They started filing out, after Dutton reassured them three or four more times. Bobo Kaminsky passed by me at one point, actually winked, and said, "I can trust the popcorn, huh?" I gave him a snide look, and he left, chuckling.

Before I could blink, Bobo had been replaced by Professor Bender, who had emerged from the auditorium shaking his head. "A pity," he said as soon as he was within earshot. "Of course, *The Thin Man* isn't W.S. Van Dyke's best." Pompous ass. Then he added insult to insult by saying with a sly smile, "I was so enjoying the second feature as well." In a feat as heroic as any ever witnessed in Central New Jersey, I refrained from slugging him.

I confess I retreated to my office at that point, but frankly, nobody—besides Bender—seemed terribly upset at having missed *Phat Ho*. If Anthony had pirated this movie, the charge would probably be downgraded to a misdemeanor.

Sophie came into the office at one point. "My friends want some of the popcorn with the, you know, stuff on it, but the cops say they can't have it."

"Sophie, that stuff could be poison!" Although she seems bright, Sophie can sometimes act like the dimmest bulb in the package.

She gave me a pitying look. "That's why they want it." Of course. As usual, *I* was the winner of the dim-bulb derby.

"Well, they can't have any," I said. "We have to do what the police say."

"Yeah, and when you're in trouble, the helpful officer is your *best friend*." Sophie's voice dripped sarcasm.

With no idea how long we'd be closed *this* time, I told Sophie I'd call when she could come back to work, gave her a check for her wages up until that night, and shut the place down myself after a gaggle of O'Donnell's investigators once again searched the place from dome to cellar with no visible results. If this kept up, I'd be able to cancel the weekly cleaning service and just let the cops do the job.

I was getting tired of closing the theatre up on my own. Usually Anthony and/or Sophie would help get the place into some kind of shape, but with Anthony missing I didn't like the idea of keeping Sophie late, especially with someone trying to kill my patrons. I was getting tireder still of riding my bike back to the town house at absurd hours of the morning. Despite what everyone seemed to think, I realized that all this mayhem hadn't been directed at me personally, but I'd be damned if it didn't feel like I was bearing the brunt of the consequences. Well, after Vincent Ansella. And Anthony, wherever he was.

There's nothing like fatigue when it's combined with frustration: you're guaranteed to be up all night, desperate for a short nap to fuel your insomnia. I was looking forward to a long evening, and unfortunately, virtually nobody plays baseball at two in the morning. Luckily, there's the YES Network, which shows baseball games of no consequence at all times of the day and night, 365 days a year. Including Christmas.

I arrived at the town house and put the bicycle down in

the hallway, then locked my emphatically green door. If I was, indeed, going to be up all night, the least I could do for myself was cause a tremendous case of heartburn, so I decided to indulge in the one thing I was craving which was absolutely certain to keep me up until roughly sometime in February: a grilled cheese sandwich. I had bought cheese and bread the day before, in anticipation.

Once I got to the kitchen, though, I saw something sure to make me lose sleep for a period far longer than that.

Sitting on my kitchen counter was one of the popcorn boxes from the theatre, with the Comedy Tonight logo on the side. I knew I hadn't left it there, and I don't even eat popcorn, so that was strange enough.

But that wasn't the most disturbing part, by far: the popcorn in the box had a white, powdery substance on it, as did much of the counter. And the box was secured to the counter with one of my larger kitchen knives, which had been driven through the box and straight into the countertop by someone who was clearly very strong. Butter from the popcorn had leaked out through the hole in the bottom of the box, leaving the distinct impression that the popcorn had been bleeding.

This time, I was pretty sure it really was all about me.

23

✿✿✿✿✿✿

Nothing in man is more serious than his sense of humor;
it is the sign that he wants all the truth.
—Mark Van Doren, quoted in *The American Scholar,*
Summer, 1957

I don't mind dying;
I just don't want to be there when it happens.
—Woody Allen

Dutton showed up ten minutes after I called him, despite
the town house being outside his jurisdiction. He had made
sure to call the New Brunswick cops, and two of them, in
uniform, arrived only a few minutes after he did. For the
moment, it was a local police matter, so O'Donnell hadn't
been summoned.

I didn't call Leslie. Think about it: you've been out on
one dinner date and a bicycle ride with a guy, and he calls
you the very first time his home is vandalized by a maniac
with incredible strength and a sharp knife. Might put you
off the guy. Make you think he was somehow less than
macho.

Anyway, Dutton surveyed the situation, which consisted
of a box of popcorn with a knife through it, bleeding melted
butter onto a Formica countertop. "What happened?" he
asked.

"Well, I decided to unwind after a rough night, and invited Jason Voorhees over for some Jiffy Pop," I said. "What
do you think happened, Chief?"

"You found it like this?"

"Yeah. I cleaned up the theatre a little after you left, then rode back over here. When I got in, there it was."

"Did you touch it?" Dutton asked. The New Brunswick cops had put on gloves to examine the . . . object, and they actually took pictures of the popcorn box, and then bagged it along with the knife, which took some doing, as the thing didn't want to come out of the countertop.

I gave him a "what am I, stupid?" look. "What am I, stupid?" I asked.

He looked heavenward for a moment. "I withdraw the question," Dutton said.

"What do you think it means?" I asked him.

"Clearly, you think you know," he answered. Dutton was insightful, and/or I was transparent.

"I have a theory, but I can't prove it," I said.

"Let me hear it," Dutton said.

"I think someone doesn't want me asking questions about who killed Vincent Ansella."

"*Nobody* wants you asking questions about Vincent Ansella," Dutton said, grinning. "*I* don't want you asking questions about who killed Vincent Ansella, and strangely, it didn't occur to me to assault a box of popcorn in your kitchen."

"I'll admit, whoever it might be is taking things to extremes, but if you have another idea of what the message might be, I'd be happy to listen." Dutton stayed silent, which I took as a very small victory.

One of the uniforms came over to tap me on the forearm. "We can call the detectives if you want, but since there's been no violent crime committed here . . ." he said.

"Unless you count what's been done to my countertop," I said. He looked confused for a moment, so I said, "Forget it. I'm sure he used gloves. They're not going to find anything." The cop nodded, and walked back to his partner.

"You would have ended up with fingerprint dust all over your apartment, and they would have only found your prints, anyway," Dutton agreed.

I thought of Leslie, and hesitated. "Well . . ." But I didn't continue the thought. Dutton gave me an odd look, but let it go.

The cops indicated they were leaving, and I nodded to them. They carried the evidence bag with the knife and the popcorn box out to the car, and after a few minutes, the flashing red lights that were keeping my neighbors awake stopped bleeding through the front window shades. Dutton took another look at what I insisted on calling the "crime scene," and shook his head.

"You're going to have to get that countertop replaced, you know."

"Replaced? I can't just get it fixed?" Like an idiot, I walked over to look more closely at the gash that went all the way into the countertop, as if a closer angle would suggest a better alternative.

Dutton shook his head. "Nah. These things come in one piece. You're going to have to get a new one. You got homeowners?"

"I rent."

"Your landlord's problem, then, I guess," he said. Dutton zipped up his jacket and headed for the door. "I've seen all I can see of this 'message' of yours. Did it work?"

"Did what work?"

"The message. Did they convince you to leave Ansella's murder alone?"

"Hell no, it didn't work. Now they've just pissed me off."

Dutton sighed. "That's what I was afraid of," he said.

24

ᗡ◯ᗡ◯ᗡ◯ᗡ◯

Anthony Pagliarulo's high school yearbook, provided by his father, was a very useful tool. The great thing about a traditional (that is, paper and not CD-ROM) high school yearbook is that classmates sign them, quite often with elaborate messages, and you can tell (if you're willing to be a serious invader of privacy) who the one or two closest friends were.

In Anthony's case, it wasn't difficult to gain that information—only one classmate in ten had signed the book at all, and most of those (particularly from the more attractive girls) were terse "best wishes in college" messages.

Two classmates were more verbose: William "Tajo" Rosenblad took half a page to remind Anthony of their trips to New York City (which he referred to as native New Jerseyans north of Trenton do: "The City"; those south of Trenton are generally talking about Philadelphia) to see independent films and attend the Tribeca Film Festival ("remember when we saw DeNiro, like, across the street?"), and looked forward to seeing him "at Sundance in a couple of years." Clearly, he and Anthony were kindred spirits.

More interesting was the entry from Carla "No Nickname" Singelese, who not only seemed to have noticed that Anthony was alive, but took an entire page (with a jump to the inside back cover!) to reminisce. Carla wasn't gorgeous, but at least physically she exceeded what I would have thought would be Anthony's expectations. You had to wonder just how dense Anthony had been if Carla was not, in fact, his girlfriend. Still, a close reading of the message she wrote— and I'll always feel guilty about reading it—indicated that whatever feelings Carla had been badly hiding from Anthony had gone unnoticed ("I really, really love you—you're my best friend!"). I had to wonder what Anthony wrote in Carla's yearbook.

Mr. Pagliarulo told me that neither Tajo nor Carla had followed Anthony to Rutgers, but both were still in the state. Carla had moved on to Montclair State University in (duh!) Montclair, while Tajo was going to NYU, but still living at home with his parents in Cranford. So I started with Tajo, since it was a shorter bus ride.

It had been less than two years since he had graduated from Cranford High, but William "Tajo" Rosenblad no longer looked much like his graduation picture. He had grown a very unconvincing mustache, had cut his hair, and had gained that "freshman fifteen" pounds plus maybe a few more, but the gain was all muscle. Rosenblad had been working out, a lot, and his room was decorated with pictures of "serious" martial artists, all covered in something approximating sweat, various limbs extended to unbelievable proportions.

Insisting I call him Bill, and not Tajo, Rosenblad sat on his bed under the lone remaining movie poster—from *Seven Samurai*—and closed the door to his room, to better keep his mother from eavesdropping. She, eyeing me suspiciously, had allowed me into the house but didn't seem happy about it.

"The Tajo thing came from Tajomaru, the character played by Toshiro Mifune in *Rashomon*," he explained, as he and Anthony were "serious (Akira) Kurosawa fans." But he said I should call him Bill, since Tajo was "so high school."

"Have you and Anthony kept in touch?" I asked.

"Yeah, I hear from him every couple of weeks," Rosenblad said. "I've gone down there a few times and hung around for the weekend. Not as much this year as last year."

"Did he call you after what happened at the theatre last week?"

Rosenblad shook his head. "I haven't heard a word from him since before then. Only way I even knew about it was the story in the paper, and it took me a while to realize it was the same theatre where Anthony works. You own the place?"

I admitted that I did.

"Cool," he said, the first person (except Anthony) I've met who had that response. "So where's Anthony now?"

"Actually," I answered, "I came here hoping you would know."

Rosenblad made a face very much like a duck would make if he were asked the same question. He pursed his lips, then flattened them out, and his eyebrows seemed to be circling his forehead with intent to land there sometime soon. "Me?" he said. "How would I know?"

"Well, you're a good friend of his, aren't you?"

"In high school, I was," Rosenblad said. "Sure, and I see him once in a while, but it's not like we're best friends or anything now. I spend more time in the city now. I'm more into martial arts now than movies, and Anthony, well, Anthony's got his film."

"You mean *films*. Anthony loves a lot of films."

He shook his head. "No, I mean the movie he's making." He must have seen the baffled look on my face, because Rosenblad went on. "You know, that thing with all the shooting."

I regained the power of speech long enough to say, "Shooting?"

"Yeah, Anthony decided he was Quentin Tarantino, but without the skinny ties, so he wrote this script—what the hell was it called? Uh . . . *Killin' Time*; that was it. I guess he's shooting it now, because when I talked to him about a month ago, he said he thought the money was going to be in place soon. And that he never dreamed it would happen so fast."

I was afraid to ask the next question. "How much money was he expecting?"

"Ah, it's a low-budget thing, you know, unknown cast, except for Steve Buscemi, and he only has a small part. So the whole thing was only going to cost two hundred grand."

"Two hundred thousand dollars?"

"Yeah. It's practically nothing, in Hollywood terms. Anthony wants to show he can work on a budget."

"So the money was on its way?"

"Uh-huh. Anthony said a big deal was going through, and he'd have the money in a couple of weeks."

This wasn't good.

25

⬦⬦⬦⬦⬦

TUESDAY

"**Powdered** sugar," said Sergeant O'Donnell, once again mistaking my office for his own.

"Powdered sugar?" Perhaps this was some sort of new game they taught the county investigators, to get witnesses to open up. Next he would say, "vanilla extract," and it would be my responsibility to come up with another ingredient.

"That's what was on the popcorn," he explained. "Powdered sugar. No poison, no chemical substance of any kind. Somebody was trying to scare you."

"They did a very professional job," I told him.

"You can reopen tonight," O'Donnell said. I was starting to wonder if I really *wanted* to reopen the theatre anymore, but a man has to do *something* to occupy his time.

"Thanks."

I must have conveyed some of what I was thinking, because he said, "Try to contain your enthusiasm." I shook my head.

"Sorry. It's not you. It's me."

"Oh dear," O'Donnell said, standing. "Our first fight."

He left shortly after that, and I started to get the place ready for company. But my mind kept returning to Anthony, and what possible connection he could have had to Vincent Ansella's murder.

I'd spent a few days, since I had no theatre to run, trying to get Carla Singelese's phone number through a directory at Montclair State. That proved to be not so easy—colleges aren't nuts about giving out students' phone numbers—so I called Carla's mother and explained my predicament. She called Carla, who called me, and agreed to meet, but not right away, as she had exams.

The best thing, of course, would be to ask Anthony himself, but since Rosenblad had remembered Anthony saying that his movie would have to shoot "in Ukrainia, or someplace that sounded like that; I'm not too good at geography," locating him might be just a little difficult.

I'll admit, it didn't look good that Anthony had been expecting a very large infusion of cash at the exact moment a large shipment of pirated DVDs was found in the basement at Comedy Tonight. And it didn't look good that Anthony had the very substance that killed Ansella in his possession at the time he disappeared, which was almost immediately after the murder. And it *really* didn't look good that Anthony was almost certainly doing his best to avoid begin seen by anyone in Midland Heights soon after both Ansella's body and the illegal movies had been found.

It didn't make sense: there was no connection I could see between Vincent Ansella and the pirated DVDs, but there had to be. It was too big a coincidence that the discs were discovered the day after Ansella's death. Could Ansella have been financing the DVD operation? Was that where his huge collection came from? Did they have anything to do with his death?

Could Anthony have killed Vincent Ansella?

"You're thinking about Anthony," said Leslie. She stood, in full uniform, at the door to the office. I have no idea how long she'd been there, one hand on her hip (lucky hand), watching me.

"You're getting to be like my father," I told her. "Wait. I didn't mean that the way it came out. I mean, you seem to know what I'm thinking. He does that. Stop me before I speak again."

She stood up straight and walked into the office, leaving little room for, say, oxygen. I didn't mind. "It's not a really hard thing to figure that you're thinking about Anthony," she said. "You've been thinking about little else for a week now."

"Occasionally, I think about you," I said. It probably wasn't a wise thing to say, because Leslie's face tightened just a bit. She looked directly into my eyes to emphasize her point.

"Don't get attached, Elliot," she said. "It's much too soon."

"Absolutely," I agreed. "I'll be sure to think of you as nothing but a sexual object for the foreseeable future."

Leslie smiled a crooked smile that looked a little sad. "We've only been out a few times," she said.

"A guy can dream," I answered. "At other times, however, I'll think about Anthony." I told her what Rosenblad had told me. She listened very carefully, nodded at times, and her eyes widened at the part about the two hundred thousand dollars.

"You see, Elliot?" Officer Levant asked. "Anthony was more concerned about money than you thought he was, and he had a plan to get a large chunk of change all at once. Does this alter your thinking at all?"

"Of course not." I shook my head. "Anthony's a gullible kid, and anybody could take him for a ride if they wanted to. If he was at all connected to the piracy deal, he got involved through his own naïveté. I'd be willing to bet on it."

Leslie shook her head slightly and smiled. "You only see what you want to see, don't you?"

"It gets worse," came an all-too-familiar voice from the doorway. "He only hears what he wants to hear, too." Sharon, arms folded, stood in the office doorway, grinning a very irritating grin and talking to Leslie but looking at me.

I made the necessary (if awkward) introductions, noticing Sharon's gleeful expression contrasting with Leslie's
considerably warier one. "I was on my way home, and
wanted to drop off the alimony check." Sharon beamed,
offering it. I snatched it out of her hand. "I forgot to give it
to you earlier," she added, now watching Leslie for a reaction. She didn't get one, and was clearly disappointed.

"I've already explained our settlement to Officer Levant," I told my ex-wife.

Leslie had been leaning on the corner of the desk, but
now she stood. "I really need to be going," she said. "Nice
seeing you, Elliot. And nice to meet you, Doctor." She tried
to extract herself from the office, but Sharon was in the
doorway.

"I'm sorry," my ex-wife said, "I didn't mean to make you
uncomfortable. I'm really the one who should be leaving."

"I'm still on my shift," Leslie countered. "I can't stay."

"Now I feel bad," Sharon kept on.

"Do I get to choose?" I asked. "Because if you two are
going to fight over who gets to leave first, I'd love to state
my preference." I stared at Sharon, and not in a nice way.

"Sorry," Leslie said. "Have to go fight crime, you know."
She nodded at Sharon and walked out.

I gave Sharon my best jaundiced look, which probably
looked like I had a bad head cold. "We don't work and play
well with others," I finally said, my voice sounding like a
rusty bicycle gear (and believe me, I know what that sounds
like).

Sharon exhaled, and leaned on the side of the desk. "We
do fine with others; it's each other we can't seem to work
and play well with," she said. "I'm sorry. I'm actually happy
you're getting past, you know . . . me, and making forays."

"Is that what I'm making? Forays?" I looked around. "I
knew it wasn't money."

"Not to worry," said my ex. "I have that department
covered for you."

I scowled. If you've never scowled, trust me when I say
that you're not missing anything. "Thanks. I really needed

another reminder that you're footing a good number of the bills."

"Aw, Elliot, you know that's not what I meant." Sharon looked truly concerned that she'd hurt my feelings, and—*damn it!*—I started to remember why I'd fallen in love with her to begin with. "I don't mind it. I really don't. I just want to stop feeling like I ruined your life all by myself."

"Not *all* by yourself," I admitted. And I could see that she was starting to remember why she had fallen out of love with me.

"That's right," she said pointedly. "*You* were a big help." Sharon stood, with the clear intention of huffing out the door, but to do that she'd have to turn around first, and in this closet, that wouldn't be easy. I stood, since all that required was a little vertical space, and put my hands on her shoulders.

"I'm sorry."

Her eyes softened a little as she looked at me, since she could tell I meant it. "Honestly. That's not what I meant," I added. "Well, yes it is, but I was wrong."

"I know. We really have to stop bickering like we're still married." Sharon stared into my eyes, and I remembered other things about our relationship.

"Yeah," I said. "I'd rather remember how we used to make up." And on what can only be described as an impulse, I leaned over (although I didn't have to lean very far) and kissed her.

She didn't stop me, and I didn't go any farther than that, but we shared a puzzled look with each other when we were done. Sharon made some noise about having to get home and order dinner, and I mumbled something about cleaning up before the show, and she left without looking into my eyes again. I wasn't sure if I was disappointed or relieved.

The elves had once again spooled up the reel when I got to the projection booth, but this time, I didn't even bother looking for Anthony. For all I knew, my projectors were now being run by the benevolent ghosts of deceased projectionists. Like in *Topper*, only probably not as suave as Cary Grant, and definitely more technologically proficient.

What the hell. It was one less thing for me to do.

There was a decent crowd for a Tuesday night, less than half full, but not so few that I considered having "the Guy in the Third Row Buys Everyone Popcorn Night." I'd given that serious consideration a few times before (except that the only guy I could count on being there every night was Leo, and he never sits in the third row). The shows went without incident, although I almost mixed up reels accidentally and avoided by seconds a segue from Myrna Loy to Carmen Electra in the blink of an eye, a switch that might actually have caused some people in the audience motion sickness.

Things didn't get really freaky until I started riding home.

It had been raining, but now the air was just a little clammy; it was cool but not cold, and the streets were damp, not soggy. This time of night, there was almost no traffic, and it should have been a calm, mind-clearing ride home.

It wasn't.

I didn't notice the silver Lexus behind me until I was almost into Highland Park, heading for the Albany Street Bridge, where I would cross the Raritan River into New Brunswick. Maybe ten minutes to my extremely green door.

Tonight, at one in the morning, I wasn't being especially careful. While there is some traffic on Raritan Avenue at virtually any hour of the day, it's not exactly Forty-second Street and Broadway. If there were cars coming, I'd hear them well in advance.

I don't have a rearview mirror on the bike, although I've seen some that do. To me, that's just a little too carlike, and besides, I figure if I don't hear it coming, it's probably not there.

And I did hear the Lexus, which I noted with a quick look over my left shoulder. It was a generic luxury car, nothing special about it, and could have been a Hyundai or a Toyota for all its expense. Luxury car buyers get ripped off, in my opinion. If the car gets you where you're going, and brings you back, who really cares if the seats are leather and you can go from zero to sixty miles per hour in two fewer tenths of a second?

But I digress.

The car was driving behind me, but since it *was* a car, and I was self-propelled, I felt it wouldn't be behind me for long. For some reason, though, the driver, whose face I couldn't make out in my repeated backward glances, seemed to be in no hurry to pass me. In fact, he (and I was only guessing that it was a man) appeared to be determined to let a bicycle beat him to the bridge.

I waved him around me as we approached, trying to get him off my back, and the car seemed to respond, closing the distance between us and moving to my left. I kept pedaling, but when the car came even with me and we were shoulder to shoulder, the driver didn't accelerate, and the Lexus didn't pass me.

Instead, it veered to the right, and came very close to hitting me. I reacted quickly, pulling the handlebars hard to the right, and luckily there were no cars parked on that side of Raritan Avenue. Riding home at one in the morning has its advantages—fewer shoppers are parked on the road as you go.

I yelled, "Hey!" at the top of my lungs, and pedaled harder, the most useless thing I could do at the time. A man on a bike isn't going to outrun a luxury car (he won't outrun a 1939 Hudson, for that matter), but when the ol' adrenaline starts pumping, it's hard to keep a level head. The impulse is to get the hell out of there.

The car swerved in after me again, just as I was starting down the hill that leads to the Albany Street Bridge. Highland Park, as the name might indicate, is built on the high ground, and the slope at that section of road is pretty steep.

There was no sidewalk to protect me there, and no parking meters to hide behind (the only time in my life I've felt

bad about the absence of parking meters). I was exposed.
There was absolutely no one else on the road to offer help.

And the Lexus was bearing down on me.

Luckily, Middlesex County, in its enduring concern for
the safety of people on foot and in motor vehicles (but not
on bicycles), had provided shelter—and some pretty serious shelter, at that: there's a concrete barrier between the
roadbed for the bridge and the pedestrian crossing next to
it. All I had to do was thread the needle and maneuver the
bike into the cutout on the road that led to the walkway.
Once I was behind the concrete, nothing short of a bazooka
attack would be able to penetrate.

Right now, I was trying to determine how to make it up
onto the sidewalk at high speed while headed straight down
a steep hill. Braking would mean that the car could reach
me more easily, and anyway, braking too hard could throw
me over the handlebars and into the road, where I'd be a
goner for sure. Trying to sneak onto a curb that could just
as easily throw me off the bike seemed too large a risk to
take. If I could keep the bike going down, actually pick up
speed, and then get behind the barrier, I could at least take
a moment to evaluate my chances.

But I had to make it to the cutout first. The Lexus, and
whoever the psychopath was driving it, seemed intent on
beating me into a bloody pulp before I reached the safe
haven. The driver made his most severe swerve yet, a violent and unexpected turn that could have knocked me off
the bike and into the middle of the road, where he might
easily have run me over and created an "accident."

That is, he could have done so, if I hadn't been trying to
anticipate his movements. I knew he didn't want me getting to the bridge, so he'd want to make his move soon.
And at the first hint of a move in my direction, I hit the
brakes and moved to the right as far as I could. I knew I
couldn't stop, but I could throw off the driver's sense of my
speed, and that might be enough. I hoped.

As it turned out, it was *almost* enough. He wasn't able to
broadside me, but the back fender of the Lexus just nicked
my left ankle as I swerved right. The concrete barrier was

only about twenty feet away, so I ignored the pain and didn't look to see if there was blood. I kept moving to the right, as if I were planning to turn onto River Road and go toward Piscataway.

The Lexus, whose driver was apparently disappointed he hadn't succeeded in killing me, also veered to the right, braking just when I picked up my speed again. I was riding downhill and I shifted hard to keep pedaling and gathering speed. It was fortunate that I knew the road so well, having ridden it almost every night for the better part of a year.

I pulled up on the curb and made it behind the concrete barrier just as the Lexus lunged right, banging its passenger-side rear fender on the edge of the barrier and then, apparently rocked by the impact (and with a nice-sized dent in that fender), drove off.

I stopped and ducked behind the concrete, just in case the driver had a weapon he wanted to wield. Apparently he didn't, and after a few seconds, the Lexus was nowhere to be seen. I hadn't gotten a good look at its rear license plate, other than to see that it started with the letter L.

Now that I had the luxury of time, I noticed the pain in my left ankle. I looked down, and saw the scrape wasn't as bad as it could have been, but there was blood, and I might need a few stitches. But I'd go home and ice it first, because a) I didn't feel like riding the bike to Robert Wood Johnson University Hospital, and b) I had no idea what would happen to the bike if I rode to the emergency room. A cab might be the way to go, if I decided I needed the treatment.

I got back on the bike and rode slowly across the bridge and to my front door. Sitting on the steps in front of my house was Leslie Levant, in jeans and a T-shirt. She stood as I rode up, and didn't notice anything odd until I got off the bike and started to limp to the sidewalk.

"What happened to you?" she said, grabbing for my shoulder and taking the bike's handlebars from my hands.

"I don't suppose you'd believe I cut myself shaving," I said.

"That's where *I* would cut myself shaving," she said.

"Well, it's a long story," I told her, and let her help me up the stairs. I pulled out my keys and opened the so-green-you-wouldn't-believe-it door.

"I have all night," she said.

26

⚬𝒟⚬𝒟⚬𝒟⚬

"I was coming to apologize," Leslie said.

We were lounging in my living "area," having just returned from the scenic emergency room at Robert Wood Johnson University Hospital, where I'd received six stitches on my left ankle, a tetanus shot, an elaborate bandage I intended to replace with a large Band-Aid the next morning, and a prescription for antibiotics in case the Lexus' rear fender was carrying an infection. My ankle stung a little, but other than that, I was fine. Leslie had cleaned up the blood from the entrance hall floor (there wasn't much), but I'd have to clean the bike more thoroughly tomorrow. Or later that day, if you wanted to be technical about it.

"Apologize? For what?" I asked. I didn't remember her doing anything worth apologizing for, unless it was the look she gave me when she saw my expression at the mention of a tetanus shot. I don't like needles. So sue me.

"The way I acted when your ex-wife was at the theatre today," she said. Leslie was used to being up this late (or early: see previous mention of desire to be technical), as she'd been on the overnight shift for a while now. But even though I worked late most nights, I was starting to fade. A growing boy like me is generally in bed by one a.m., and it was currently closing in on four. "I turned tail and ran as soon as there was competition."

"Yeah, but it's such a nice tail," I said. She scowled, so I quickly added, "Besides, Sharon isn't competition. She's married to someone else. That's all over with now."

"Sure it is."

I gave her my best innocent expression. "What's that supposed to mean?"

"It means, I saw the way you look at her, and I don't think anything's over yet." Leslie lay back on the sofa, which for a less fit woman would have meant she could never get up again. I was sitting on a folding chair that belonged in a park, blocking someone's view of Fourth of July fireworks. "I think you have unresolved issues about her, and you need to get through them before you can move on."

This conversation was heading in a direction I hadn't seen coming when she offered to apologize, and I can't say I was crazy about it. "This is sounding very much like a kiss-off speech," I told her. "You could at least save that for a time when I'm not coming home from the hospital."

Leslie stood up, which I considered a superhuman effort all by itself. She started to pace, and didn't make eye contact. No, this wasn't going to be one of our more enjoyable encounters.

"I don't have a problem with the way things are now," she said, talking more to herself than to me, from the way her voice sounded. "But I think we need to slow it down a bit."

"Slow it down? We've gone out twice and kissed a couple of times in almost three weeks. How much slower can we go?"

"You're dangerous," Leslie said softly. "You're on the rebound and you want to re-create the life you had with your wife. I'm not your wife."

"At the moment, you're not even my friend," I said. "You're a woman I'm getting to know, and I think you're overreacting. I'm not proposing anytime soon. For one thing, it would kill my alimony."

She didn't laugh. She didn't react at all. She just shook her head, said, "I'm going home, Elliot. I don't think we should see each other for a while," and left.

All in all, this was not one of my better nights.

I slept until one in the afternoon, and in the shower, took stock of my life. There's little else to do in the shower, since I really don't like to sing without a band, and there's no room for a band in my bathroom. Not even a combo.

I was a divorced man in his late thirties, living alone in a rental I didn't really call home, operating a business that didn't have a chance to survive, pining after a woman who had chosen to leave me for a guy who spends most of his day with unconscious people, and brooding over another woman I'd met less than a month before, and who had just dumped me, before I even knew what I was being dumped from. I didn't own my own home, my own car, or a stick of grown-up furniture, and my closest confidant was my father. It was a good thing a band wouldn't fit in the room, because all I'd be able to play would be the blues. And that goes so badly with soap and water.

Clearly, the only thing left to do was investigate a murder.

27

٥◌◌◌◌◌◌

FRIDAY
Help! (1965)
and *Too Many Kids* (today)

It took me a few days of phone calling and cajoling to set up more interviews with everyone I wanted to question. The people I'd talked to before at least understood why I was calling, even if they weren't all that thrilled about seeing me again. Others, confronted with a call from the owner of the local comedy theatre, were somewhat confused by a request to discuss the death of Vincent Ansella, and since I couldn't explain it to myself any better than I could to them, sometimes persistence was more convincing than logic.

Joe Dunbar's wife Christie, for example, was reluctant to grant an interview. I first contacted her via e-mail through her small business website. She took a while to get back to me, and didn't want to meet when I suggested it. But when I laid it on pretty thick about how Vincent Ansella had spent his last few moments enjoying himself at my theatre (even if his choice of refreshment was unfortunate), she relented, but said she wasn't going to tell her husband about the interview, so I should meet her at her office.

This turned out to be in an industrial park in Iselin, and Moe wasn't happy about loaning me a 2003 VW Beetle (brakes) to get there, but there I was. It was the least-descript building I'd ever seen, and I was once a government employee for a couple of months. The sign on the office door read "MediTek."

In her normal (non-funereal) clothing, Christie was brassy indeed. Her curly blond hair, almost platinum, orbited her head without really seeming to touch it. Her makeup was more reminiscent of Emmett Kelly than Sophia Loren, and her laugh reminded me of the horn on a 1977 AMC Pacer. I liked her immediately.

"Why didn't you want Joe to know we were talking?" I asked her. "I've spoken with him already."

"Ahh," (this might be the place to mention that "ahh" preceded everything Christie said, and I will omit it from now on) "he's been so upset since Vince . . . ya know, that I didn't want to tell him. Why bring it up again?" She adjusted one of her many bracelets.

"Do you know of anyone who would want to hurt Mr. Ansella?" I asked. No use beating around the bush with Christie; she was a straight-ahead kind of girl.

"I can't think of a soul. Vince Ansella was the sweetest, funniest, most joyful man I've ever known. Who'd want to bump off a guy like that?" She started to play with a plaque on her desk that read "World's Best Boss."

Obviously, I didn't know who'd want to "bump off " Ansella, so I didn't offer an answer. Instead, I shifted gears. "How did you meet your husband?" I'd put in another call to Meg Vidal to get tips on questioning people, and she said I should get them to talk about themselves. After a ten-minute lecture on letting the police do their job.

"Would you believe it? Vince's sister Lisa set us up. I think she was worried Vince would never get married if he kept hanging around with Joe. Maybe she thought they were queer, you know?" She laughed, which sounded like *PAH!* "They weren't. I've known some queer guys, and they're the nicest people on the planet, but Vince and Joe? Straight as a couple of arrows, believe you me. Anyway, she knew I wasn't Vince's type, so she figured she'd see if Joe was game. And he was."

I figured we'd established a rapport, so I moved into waters I thought might be a little choppier. "How do you get along with Amy Ansella?" I asked.

Christie's mouth, in a perpetual smile, drooped a little, but she was trying not to be obvious. "We weren't best buddies, but we got along," she said.

"I don't think you did," I said quietly.

She grinned a little, wickedly. "You're a smart fella, Elliot. But Amy . . . well, Amy is all about Amy, isn't she? And when someone's like that, and she takes on a guy like Vince, who just wanted you to be happy, she finds herself the perfect husband. He'll do whatever you want him to do."

"And you didn't approve?"

Christie waved a hand. "What's to approve? I'm not his mother. But it did drive a little wedge between Joe and Vince, toward the end. I don't know why, but it did."

"Christie," I began, not knowing how to phrase it less obviously, "you didn't happen to go to the movie with Vince the night he . . . the night it happened, did you?"

She looked at me as if I'd suggested that she plant a few magic beans and go kill a giant. "Me? No! Why the hell would I go see a movie alone with Vince Ansella?"

"So where were you that night?"

It was the only time I saw her actively evading a question. "I was . . . out."

"Out? Just out?"

Christie tried to snarl, but it just came out as a different kind of grin. "Yeah. You never been out before, Elliot?" She couldn't sustain it, and the grin reverted to her usual one.

I had one last question. "Why do you think Amy called Joe a murderer at Vince's funeral?" I asked.

Christie didn't hesitate. "Because she couldn't accuse herself."

♻ ♻

I told Amy Ansella I wanted to come back because I was interested in buying part of her husband's comedy library, and to a certain extent, that was true. I certainly would have to take a few of the more rare items, like *Flickers*, off her hands, just to ensure that they didn't end up on eBay, being sold to people who thought they were buying pornography or art house cinema.

I rode the bike rather than take the bus; it wasn't too far, and that way, I could set my own schedule. I needed to be back at the theatre in time to set up for the Friday night "crowd," which tonight would probably consist mostly of parents and children, since a family comedy was the contemporary draw for the week. The tainted popcorn incident had not produced the boost in ticket sales that the murder did, but crowds were still a bit above average.

Amy was not dressed in black when I arrived this time. I don't want to give the impression that I generally lust after recent widows, or that I do an inordinate amount of lusting overall. But Amy was a remarkably attractive woman in an indefinable way: she didn't look like a Victoria's Secret model or the girl next door with a naughty side, but she commanded attention.

She ushered me into the living room, and I immediately noticed that a number of the video titles were missing from their shelves. I breathed a sigh of relief that my favorites were still there.

"I see I'm not the first to inquire," I said as I assessed the collection. It had been haphazardly picked apart, with one title from a series missing and others randomly replaced on racks. The sight of it probably would have driven Vincent Ansella crazy.

"I gave some of them away," Amy said in a small voice. "I gave my sister-in-law some for her kids, you know, *The Pink Panther* and stuff like that."

It was true: the titles that were missing, as far as I could tell, were movies that parents would feel comfortable showing their children. For example, the Laurel and Hardy section was missing only *March of the Wooden Soldiers*, and the animated section was practically gone, with only things like *Fritz the Cat* and *Cool World* remaining (Ansella really *was* a completist!).

"I'm sorry I can't make you an offer for the whole

collection," I said. "I'd love to keep them together, but the theatre isn't making me enough of an income for that."

"I'd be happy to get rid of them," Amy said, looking me straight in the eye. "I don't want the reminders, and Vincent's insurance left me with enough money so that I don't have to worry about the value. Make me an offer."

Stunned, I did. I was even more stunned when she accepted it.

"I didn't think you liked me all that well the last time we met, Amy," I said after I'd written her an amazingly small check.

"I liked you just fine," she said, giving me the same reassuring attention I'm sure she would any man. Amy Ansella knew how she looked, and knew the effect it would have on men. But it seemed to have become reflexive, to the point that sometimes, I wondered if she even knew she was doing it. "I wasn't crazy about some of the questions you were asking."

"Because I mentioned Marcy Resnick?" Meg had said to prod in the sensitive areas, too.

Amy's face wasn't as attractive when I said that. She again mentioned a word that rhymes with Ipswitch, and said, "Yes, because you mentioned *her*." Nothing more than that.

"But I'm okay now that it's all about the collection?" I asked. Well, getting on her bad side hadn't helped much.

"You're fine, Elliot," she said, again almost by rote. "When can you come to take them away?"

"How's Monday?" I asked. "Comedy Tonight will be open during the day all weekend, but on Monday I can borrow my father's truck." Saying it out loud made me realize just how much sentences like that will take you back to high school. Maybe not owning a motor vehicle was a problem, after all.

Amy agreed on Monday as the moving day for her husband's enormous video collection, and I thanked her and said good-bye. She walked out to see me off, and just as I was adjusting my helmet, I figured it was worth one last shot.

"Why didn't you tell the police you were at the theatre the night your husband died?" I asked.

"Oh, Elliot," Amy said, disappointed. "And you were being so nice." She turned and walked back into the house.

28

I hadn't intended to schedule a talk with Marcy Resnick so soon after seeing Amy, but it was the only way Marcy's schedule worked out. Naturally, I didn't tell her I'd just come from seeing Vincent Ansella's widow, and there was no reason to bring it up. Best I didn't mention that Amy had called her names.

Marcy came to Comedy Tonight from her office, since I had to set up for the evening's showing (I was getting used to Anthony not being there, although I checked every night to see if the gremlins had threaded up the projector—tonight they hadn't), so I treated her to the Elliot Freed version of dinner: a sandwich from Tastee Sub Shop of Edison and a soda from the theatre's fountain. Never let it be said that I'm a cheapskate. At least, never let it be said to my face.

There was hardly enough room for us to both sit in my office, so I pulled two chairs up to the table we have next to the snack bar for popcorn salt, napkins, and straws. What it lacked in elegance it made up for in dreariness.

Marcy looked around at the lobby and nodded her head. "I like it," she said. "It's not like a multiplex at the mall."

"No," I agreed. "It's more like Pompeii after the eruption."

She covered her mouth to laugh. "It has charm." So did John Wayne Gacy, I thought, but I let it go.

Marcy looked more closely at me. "You didn't invite me here to discuss the decor, did you?"

"No." I felt awkward, but even Fred Astaire would have felt awkward in this situation, white tie or no.

"You're still looking into the thing with Vince, aren't you?" Marcy's gaze was probing, but it didn't burn through me like it could have. She wasn't accusing me; she was just trying to get it clear in her own mind.

"It's stuck in my head," I said, possibly to myself. "I can't stop thinking about it. And I'm concerned that the police think my projectionist is involved, when that doesn't make any sense."

Marcy watched me for a while, thinking. Then she said, "How can I help?"

"You can forgive me if my questions aren't tactful."

Her face clouded over. I was going to ask about the rumors again, and she knew it. "I didn't have an affair with Vince Ansella, Elliot," Marcy said. "I already told you that."

"So why do people think you did?"

She stood up. A theatrical move, but I understood it; I'm better on my feet as well. "People think what they want to think," Marcy said. "I had lunch with the guy a few times, and they turned it into this hot romance. By the standards of the office gossips, you and I are having a wild affair right now. But so far, I've managed to fight the impulse to jump your bones."

It was just as well. Marcy was a very attractive woman, though in exactly the opposite way that Amy was: she could very well have been the girl next door, if the girl next door had grown up compact, slim, and down-to-earth. But at the moment, my life was overstocked with women, and I wasn't prepared to add another. Not that Marcy was exactly making an offer.

"I understand how rumors get started," I told her. "But Amy Ansella believes it's true, and she doesn't really have contact with the gossips at the office, does she?"

Marcy's mouth puckered a bit at the mention of Vincent Ansella's widow. "I don't know what her problem is," she said. "She knows I didn't have an affair with her husband, but she's resentful of me."

"If you only worked with Vincent, and had lunch with him on occasion, how would his wife even know enough about you to be resentful?"

She sat back down. "From . . . being around, you know. Office Christmas parties, Fourth of July picnics, that sort of thing. The company's really into pretending we're a big happy family."

Marcy didn't seem too keen on finishing her sub, and I thought it would be rude to scarf it up while she was sitting there, so I cleared the table and threw out the remains of our dinner. I gave her the tour of the theatre, showed her the projection booth and screened a three-minute trailer for *Help!*, the classic film of the evening, which she found, and I'm quoting now, "groovy."

"You're off by a few years," I told her. "Actually, it's 'fab.'"

"Gear."

I smiled and nodded, but I'd killed our chance at easy conversation by talking about her rumored liaison with Ansella. "I'm sorry if I've upset you," I told her as I walked her to the theatre entrance. "Are you sure you won't stay for the movie?"

"I'd like to, but I have to walk the dog," she said. "He's probably sitting home with his legs crossed as we speak."

"Another time, maybe."

"Yeah."

I unlocked the front door and reached over to open it for Marcy, then stopped. "Can I ask one last impertinent question?" I said.

She nodded, a little hesitantly.

"Why do you think Amy called Joe Dunbar a murderer at the funeral?"

"I really don't know."

"Speculate. I could use your perspective."

Marcy thought about that, searched my eyes, and nodded. "I don't think she loved Vincent as much as she should have, as much as he wanted her to," she said. "Once he was dead, I think she felt guilty, so she had to shift the blame to *somebody*."

"You think Amy killed her husband?"

Marcy shook her head. "No. I don't think she cared about him enough to kill him. You can chalk that up to the word of a suspected adulterer, but that's what I think."

"You're not a suspected adulterer," I told her.

"I'm not?"

"Of course not. You're a suspected *adulteress*." Marcy chuckled, but there wasn't much mirth in it. "I have one last uncomfortable question." She nodded, accepting. "Where were you the night Vincent died?"

"I had a date," she said. "The police asked me that, too."

"Have they confirmed it with the guy?" I asked.

"No."

My eyebrows dropped. "Why not?" I asked.

"I haven't told them who I was out with." She clearly wasn't going to tell me, either.

I repeated the offer to stay and watch the movie, but Marcy seemed to want out of Comedy Tonight as soon as possible, which made me feel bad. I unlocked the door for her, thought about what a nice person she seemed to be, and wondered why what she'd said had unsettled me so badly. And then I wondered if Sharon had ever loved me as much as I wanted her to. I wondered if anybody ever loves someone as much as that person would like.

And I was willing to bet Marcy didn't have a dog.

29

○○○○○○○

The showing that night went by uneventfully, which was a blessing, considering how hard my mind was racing. Having immersed myself in the investigation of Vincent Ansella's murder, I used my most trusted mental tool—obsession—to attack the problem, and so far, I was coming up empty.

Beyond a few gut feelings, a rumor or two, the observations of relatively unreliable observers, and a succession of women of varying degrees of attractiveness, I had pretty much nothing to go on. Ansella was just as dead as he'd been three weeks earlier, and there had been no arrests.

Meanwhile, back at the theatre, the projection booth was still unmanned, the basement had been cleared of its illegal booty weeks ago by a team of armed men and women from an agency of either the county, state, or federal government (I never could get a straight answer on that one), and worst of all, the novelty of seeing a film at the Scene of the Crime had worn off, so my crowds, as I was still euphemistically calling them, had dwindled to their pre-murder numbers. New furniture in the town house would have to wait.

None of that would have bothered me, but the more I thought about it, the more it seemed that whoever had killed Ansella seemed to have it in for me, too, these days. Besides the unsettling image of a bleeding popcorn box affixed to my countertop with a deadly weapon was the even more unsettling image of my left leg, now an adorable shade of purple under its bandage, and the equally upsetting thought of what would have been if my reflexes had been just a hair slower or the concrete divider just a little less strategically placed.

Not to mention, I wasn't having sex with anybody, and while I'd gotten used to that since the divorce (actually, a while before the divorce), my first chance since then was gone, and that was a real downer.

Other men have a best friend or a spouse off of whom they can bounce feelings and ideas like this, be told they're acting ridiculous, and get on with their lives. I, on the other hand, was vacuuming the lobby of an ancient movie theatre while a sixteen-year-old girl trying her best to look like Wednesday Addams listened to Alien Sex Fiend on her iPod and tried very, very hard to pretend I wasn't there.

I decided to reach out. "So Sophie," I said, immediately sounding ridiculous. "What's new?" It was a way to kill the time until we could both go home. And I assumed anything with the word "kill" in it would appeal to Sophie.

She stared, as I was surely speaking some obscure dialect known only to bush people in a single remote African village. "New?" Sophie asked. "What is this obsession with newness? Don't the ancients have anything to teach us? Have you ever read *The Tibetan Book of the Dead*?"

"Still don't want to tell me what you're hiding from your folks?" Stare. "You're not doing drugs, are you?" *Big* stare. I walked away.

It's a full life I lead.

Turning over in my mind all the information I had on Ansella's murder—and believe me, it didn't take long—I kept coming to one conclusion: the only person who had any reason to want Vincent Ansella dead was his wife. If he was indeed having an affair with Marcy Resnick, or anybody else, Amy Ansella could certainly have become enraged. It happens. It doesn't as a rule happen much to men who looked like Ansella, but love is a funny thing. I'm told. Even if Vincent *wasn't* having an affair, Amy certainly believed he was, and therefore the whole "enragement" scenario could still apply. Maybe the front she showed—that she barely cared about her husband—was just that: a front.

But if Amy *didn't* really believe Vince was prowling around outside the marriage bed, did she have a reason to want him dead? Considering that he'd worked for an insurance company for many years, his own policy was substantial, but hardly winning-lottery-ticket substantial. There were easier ways to end the marriage than by spicing Ansella's popcorn with blood pressure nukes.

Okay, I thought, putting away the vacuum and locking the storage closet, so riddle me this, Batman: if Amy Ansella didn't kill her husband, who else had any motivation to see him dead? As far as I could tell, the answer to that was: nobody.

So I settled on Amy Ansella as my chief suspect, lacking trifles like proof. But that still didn't answer a lot of questions. For example, who was the blond woman who gave Vincent a good-bye kiss in the middle of the movie? Christie Dunbar? She had only offered the lame "I was out" defense, which I believe was dismissed in the case of *I.M. Lying vs. O. Please*. Whomever the mysterious blonde was, did she give him the poison as a parting gift? Was there another person somewhere out there who hated Vincent Ansella enough to end his life? Not to mention, ruin his appreciation of a classic comedy?

Sophie nodded a couple of times in my direction, both an indication she was through for the night and an appreciation of the beat being drummed into her head. I walked her to the door, unlocked it, let her out, watched as she got into her father's car and drove away, then locked the door and went back to the lobby. It drove Sophie just a little crazy that her father had to pick her up after work, but in New Jersey, sixteen-year-olds can only have a limited learner's permit, and can't drive without a licensed driver in the car, and not at all after midnight. The look on her face was priceless. The look on her dad's face, one of absolute adoration for his baby girl, was heartbreaking. One finds entertainment in strange places.

Everything was just the way it had been before the doors had opened this evening. Mostly clean, mostly painted, mostly restored. I lived in a world that was defined by the word "mostly."

I was mostly over my marriage, mostly healthy (the only flaw being the stitches in my leg, which were beginning to itch), mostly independent, mostly doing what I wanted to do, and mostly content with my life. But I was finding that the gap between "mostly" and "sufficiently" was widening.

Was this it for the rest of my life? Pushing the rock that was Comedy Tonight uphill every evening just to see it roll back down every night? Reveling in my self-reliance, only to find that it meant I had nobody else I could rely upon? Banging my head against the wall trying to solve riddles no one had asked me to solve?

Okay, so that last one probably wasn't going to last the rest of my life. Not unless the driver of the Lexus was waiting for me on the way home again tonight. A thought I'd had every night since he tried to run me down.

I finished shutting the theatre down and walked outside, steering the bike without getting on. Suddenly, the prospect of my daily commute back to New Brunswick wasn't quite as pleasant a thought as it had been before.

As I walked down Edison Avenue, trying to convince myself to mount up and start pedaling, I noticed a car slowing in front of the theatre, and turned instinctively to ready myself. But this time the car was a Honda Accord, and behind the wheel was Chief Barry Dutton.

"You want a ride?" he asked. "I'm going your way." I nodded, thanked him, and took the bike's front wheel off so the rest would fit into the trunk.

"What are you doing driving into New Brunswick at this time of night?" I asked him when I got in. "Don't you live in Midland Heights?"

Dutton nodded. "Sure. We have a residency requirement."

"So what's this about?"

He hesitated. "Officer Levant told me about your . . . mishap the other night, and I want to see if that mysterious Lexus of yours is back again."

"You came out to give me a ride home? At midnight?"

"My wife's at a convention in San Diego," he said. "I didn't have anything to do."

We drove south into Highland Park, and Dutton pulled over just short of River Road, and turned off his headlights. It was warm enough to leave the windows open, so he did.

"I asked the Highland Park police chief to watch for a Lexus around this time each night since you reported the . . . attack," Dutton said. "They've pulled over two so far, but neither of them had an L on the license plate, and one of them was dark blue."

"So what are we doing here?"

"We're on a stakeout," the chief said. "I brought you a cup of decaf and a bagel." And sure enough, he produced both items from a Dunkin' Donuts bag he had on the floor behind him.

"A decaf?"

"I didn't want to keep you up all night."

"Very considerate," I said.

"To protect and to serve. Here." He handed me the bagel and put the coffee in a cup holder in the console.

We sat for a while as I ate the bagel and Dutton sipped on a coffee (he hadn't brought any food for himself). Finally, he turned to me. "Are you sleeping with Leslie Levant?" he asked.

I came very close to a coffee spit-take that Jerry Lewis would have envied. "Did you really just ask me that?" He nodded. I shook my head. "No," I answered honestly. And the odds were, I never would be. Thanks for reminding me, Chief.

"Good," Dutton nodded. "I don't think she's good for you right now."

"Since when are you Dr. Phil?" I asked.

"I'm just making conversation." He stopped doing that,

and we watched the road silently for a while longer. "You know, she can bench-press two hundred pounds," Dutton said out of the blue.

"That's great; I'll put it on the back of her bubblegum card. What are we talking about, Chief?"

"I'm just watching the street." And he stopped talking again.

The Lexus seemed determined not to show up tonight. "Where did you first notice the Lexus that night?" Dutton asked.

"In Edison, about a half mile up." I finished the decaf, which would have been fine without the sugar.

"So what are we doing here?"

I shrugged. "You're the cop."

Dutton started the car and said something quietly to himself. I didn't ask.

Silently he drove me the rest of the way to my front door, which hadn't gotten any less green since I saw it last. I got out and took my bike out of the trunk. Walking to the driver's side, I saw Dutton lower the window, and I stood by his door.

"Thanks for driving me. I was a little nervous about riding home tonight."

He nodded. "I was, too."

"Aw, Chief. You go on like that, and people will talk."

He gave me a patented look to indicate that he was a practicing heterosexual, and began to raise his window. I held up my hand. "One thing," I said.

"Yeah?"

"What was this all *really* about? Maybe you were concerned, but you're not going to come and drive me home every night. What am I missing?"

Dutton considered me for a long moment. "That's what I'd like to know," he said, raised his window, and drove away. He didn't even wave.

It had been a less than satisfactory evening. But on the plus side, nobody had made an attempt on my life, which made it an improvement over other nights I'd had recently. It wasn't much, but it was something. Sort of.

You should never assess an evening before you're asleep in bed, however. When I got inside, against all logic, the phone was ringing. And the caller ID indicated an out-of-area call with no number listed.

Usually, I let those calls go, assuming they're from people trying to sell me insurance or heavy breathers who can't read a phone book properly. But it was after midnight, and the insurance salesmen are mostly off work by then. If it was a heavy breather, I could have the satisfaction of telling the idiot I had his phone number and would be giving it to the proper authorities, even if it wasn't true. So I picked it up and said, "Yeah?"

"Mr. Freed?"

Anthony.

30

✿✿✿✿ ✿✿

My head was reeling, and it being the wee hours of the morning didn't help. I gripped the cordless phone so hard I truly expected to find finger indentations when I hung it back up later. I wondered if I could use *69 when I got off.

"Anthony!" I sounded just a little less frantic than Oliver Hardy when a piano was plummeting down 150 stairs directly at him. But perhaps this wasn't the moment for a classic comedy reference.

"Yeah, hi?" His voice betrayed a little confusion, like he was expecting someone other than me to pick up the phone. Someone who could speak rationally.

I tried very hard to control my tone. "Where . . . are you?" I asked.

"I'm on set," he said with great pride. "We're shooting the bakery scene, and I have to get off in a minute before the light shifts."

Okay, so he was shooting the bakery scene. Sure. The bakery scene. *What* bakery scene? The kid's on the lam from every law enforcement agency in the country and he's filming a cookie transaction?

"The bakery scene?"

"Yeah, and we have to clean up from the last take. There's fake blood all over the cheesecake."

"Anthony," I said, biting my lip so hard I had to wonder if they make Band-Aids for lips, "tell me where you are. Maybe I can help you."

"I don't see how," he said. "The script is locked. Believe me, it's not that I don't respect your opinion . . ."

One of us was insane, and I wasn't entirely convinced it wasn't me. "Listen to me carefully, Anthony. The police are after you. The FBI is after you. For all I know, the United Federation of Planets is after you. You have to tell me where you are, and let me help you get out of this mess."

There was a pause. Then I realized Anthony had put his hand over the mouthpiece of his cell phone. "Sorry about that," he said when he came back, "the DP was asking me about a gel on the key light. What were you saying?"

"I was saying that you are wanted by the police in connection with video piracy and possibly murder, and you have to tell me right now where you are so I can help you."

At least this time he'd been listening. "You're kidding. Why do they think I had anything to do with the DVDs? And who got murdered?"

If the kid was faking, he was doing a really mediocre job of it. His delivery was fine, but the lines were awfully scripted—you ask about the murder *first*. "So you admit you know about the movies."

"Sure. I agreed to store them in the basement of the theatre." No biggie. A federal crime. What's your question?

"Agreed with whom?" Even under duress, I was being grammatical. I want that noted when the truth is finally told.

"I'm . . . not supposed to say. They told me not to call, not to call my folks, either. You know, so nobody gets in trouble. But I didn't do anything. I just unlocked the door a couple of times." Anthony sounded concerned, much as he would be if someone had told him that he needed to get a haircut or had to write another paper to pass a class. Not like he could go to jail for the rest of his life.

"They also think you had something to do with Vincent Ansella's murder."

You could hear his eyebrows rise. "Who's Vincent Ansella?"

"The guy in row S, seat 18."

"They think I killed him? That's crazy! He had a heart attack." I was starting to believe him.

"Anthony, why were you calling?" I had paced around the kitchen to the spot where the countertop had a permanent wound in it. If someone knew I was talking to Anthony . . .

"I felt bad about missing work." Anthony wasn't pulling a Richard Kimble; he was pulling an Alicia Silverstone: he was *Clueless*.

"Anthony, tell me where you are."

The tumult around him seemed to increase in volume again. "I've got to go, Mr. Freed. We're losing our light. I'll call you again in a few days."

"Wait! Who did you open the door for? Who told you not to call your parents?"

He hung up.

31

о◌◌◌◌◌◌◌

Carla Singelese lived in Bohn Hall at Montclair State University, but even from her eighth-floor dorm room, you couldn't see the Yogi Berra Museum and Learning Center or the Abbott and Costello Center, so there was little point in looking out the window.

Neither of us was interested in the view, anyway. Carla, even with only one exam left in the semester, looked worried, sitting on her bed with a residence advisor (named Arnold) present, although Arnold seemed mostly interested in eyeing Carla when he wasn't perusing the copy of *Maxim* he'd brought with him. He was probably comparing Carla to Jessica Alba. Carla would come up wanting, but it wasn't really a fair comparison. She didn't have lighting, makeup, and a personal trainer.

Having seen her high school yearbook picture, I could say the ensuing two years had been good to Carla. She was what we would have called a "cute chick" back before "hot" became the only acceptable adjective to describe an attractive female. She was small and of average weight, neither overweight nor model-thin. She had large brown eyes, which were now widened at the news that Anthony Pagliarulo was found, having been lost.

"He called you last night?" she said. "How can he be missing if he called you?"

"He called me, but he didn't say where he was," I said. "Do you have any idea where Anthony might go?"

She made quite a show of thinking about it. Carla obviously wanted me to see how close she and Anthony were, how intimately she knew his thought process. "Probably, he'd go home to his folks," she said. "If he really thought he was in trouble, he'd go to his dad first. One time, he got in this fender bender, and even before he got out of the car, he was on the phone to his dad."

I rubbed my eyes, because I thought I'd already related the conversation with Anthony in excruciating detail. And since I had in fact called Michael Pagliarulo last night to tell him his son was safe, whereabouts unknown, I knew Anthony hadn't called his parents. "He didn't think he was in trouble." I tried not to sigh. "He said he was on set, shooting the bakery scene."

"The bakery scene." Carla chewed that over a couple of times. She ignored Arnold, who was taking turns staring at her T-shirt (which read "Stop Clubbing Seals") and the page of his magazine, where Ms. Alba was wearing a shirt on which it would have been impossible to fit that slogan, even in ten-point type. "I'm trying to remember what happens in the bakery scene."

"Anthony said there was blood," I attempted.

"There's blood in every scene." Carla dismissed me. "Somebody gets shot about once a page." She sat and put her fingers to her temples. "The bakery scene."

After I'd hung up the phone with Anthony, and determined that I couldn't trace the number from which he'd called (caller ID was blocked, so *69 didn't work), I had choices to make. I probably should have asked O'Donnell or Dutton to check into the phone records, but that would require that I actually tell one of them Anthony had called, which wasn't really my first choice. Or I could have ignored the call altogether, and concentrated strictly on

Ansella's murder, which was what I had been intending to do until the phone rang.

But as much as it irritated me that Ansella had died at Comedy Tonight, as much as I considered it a personal insult, the person I needed to help right now was Anthony. Even if he didn't really understand that he needed help. I knew it, and that was enough.

My mood hadn't been helped much by the fact that I'd needed a ride to Montclair (actually Little Falls, but why quibble?) to talk to Carla. I could have mooched a car from Moe, but for reasons even I didn't understand, I'd called Sharon.

We'd been unusually quiet for much of the ride, neither of us wanting to mention the kiss from the last time we'd seen each other. We spoke only about the directions I'd gotten from MapQuest and whether or not we wanted to eat after the interview. It was a warm May morning, but it had felt pretty chilly in Sharon's car.

"The bakery scene is where Antonio, the hero, confronts the baker, who is really a cruel monster who runs a whorehouse and gambling in the back room of the bakery," Carla said, eyes closed to better recall the details. "You think Antonio is going to get killed by the baker, but then he shoots the baker in the head six times."

I knew it wasn't going to get me closer to finding Anthony, but I couldn't help blurting out, *"Six times?"*

"Yeah. Anthony said it was accurate, because there would only be six bullets in a revolver from that period." Shooting a pastry chef six times in his head didn't seem to be a problem so long as the weaponry was accurately portrayed.

I decided to switch gears. "How close are you and Anthony?" I asked. It was a little direct, but I didn't really have the time to ease into the subject. Sharon was waiting in the car in the parking lot.

At the question, Arnold looked up, interested.

Carla didn't blush, but I could tell she wanted to. She closed her eyes halfway and made a sound that would have approached a giggle if she'd let it. "I don't know . . ." she said.

"Well, are you good friends? Are you dating?"

Arnold seemed to be assessing his chances with Jessica Alba, giving himself a reality check, and realizing that Carla was much closer to his level, although he probably overestimated his level and underestimated Carla's. She tilted her head back and forth for a moment, deciding.

"We're sort of . . . In high school, we had a thing for a while."

"You went out."

"More like we stayed in, if you want to know the truth." She turned to Arnold. "You don't have to be here, you know."

"Regulations," he said, clearly not wanting to miss this part of the story.

I considered the possibility that Arnold might drool his way through the rest of the conversation, and turned toward him. "It's okay if I'm her uncle, isn't it?"

"You said you were a newspaper reporter," Arnold said. I think this time, I was with the *Daily Tribune*.

"I am, but I'm also Carla's uncle," I told him. "Her dad wanted me to check on the security procedures here, and you have been an enormous help. I'll be happy to pass the word on to him that Carla is very safe here. Keep up the good work."

Arnold narrowed his eyes. "That true?" he asked Carla.

"Every word," she said.

Arnold curled a lip, deciding whether to protest, then sighed, got up, and took his magazine with him toward the door. "I've got an exam, anyway," he said, and left the room.

Once the door closed, Carla looked back at me. "If you're asking whether Anthony and I slept together . . ."

"I'm really not," I said. "I'm just trying to gauge how close you are now. Whether he'd confide in you, and whether you'd cover up for him. I want you to know that I'm on Anthony's side, I'm trying to help him, and I won't tell the police anything unless I think it will do him good."

"Well, I wanted to sleep with him," she said, seemingly having dozed through my speech, which is not unusual for me when I speak to women. "I love Anthony, and I think he loves me, but he was always obsessed with this *film* of his. His vision is so pure that he wouldn't give in to the temptations of the flesh." Great. I come for information, and I find myself in the middle of a book with a picture of Fabio on the cover.

"Carla, please listen."

"No, it's okay, really. I don't mind people knowing. Anthony broke it off with me a little after we started college."

Anthony broke it off with her? I would have been more surprised, but it sounded like there was nothing to break off.

"I understood. He needed to be thinking about his art. I love him enough to accept that," Carla continued.

Okay, that was the wedge. "Good. So help me help him. Tell me where he would be."

"He really didn't call his folks?" That seemed to amaze her. I shook my head. "And he's finally shooting his movie, huh? Well, I guess he's in Hollywood. I mean, that's where you shoot a movie, isn't it?"

"Not if you aren't employed by a studio," I told her. "Anthony got hold of some money . . . somehow . . . and he's using it to produce his movie independently. Now, where would he want to go if he was shooting on location? Where does the story take place?"

Carla raised her eyebrows. "In the Old West," she said. "In 1840. How do you think he went *there*?"

A good question. I got up to leave, and then had a sudden inspiration. "Do you have a copy of the script?" I asked her.

"Sure," Carla said, and climbed down to the floor to search under her bed. From my vantage point, it was hard to believe Anthony had *always* kept his mind on his film. Then I remembered: he was Anthony. I made a mental note to respect the fact that she was roughly half my age.

She found what she was looking for—a CD-ROM—and held it out. "You think this will help?" she asked.

"I don't know," I said. "But I do know Anthony is lucky to have such a good friend." I headed for the door.

Carla spoke very softly, and I could just barely hear her. "Lover," she said.

32

"I think this is the last ride I'm going to give you," Sharon said.

I almost spit out a mouthful of french fries, and that would have been an unpardonable faux pas in Sharon's car. It was a testament to the huge hurry she was in that she'd agreed to allow food in the car to begin with.

"What are you talking about?" I asked, as soon as I'd managed to swallow.

She went on as if I hadn't spoken. "And I think maybe we'd better stop having lunch together for a while, too."

"Jesus, Sharon, it was just one kiss. If you want, I'll pretend I didn't enjoy it, and we can go on like before."

She never took her eyes off the road, because she's Sharon, but I could tell this conversation was difficult for her. "It's not about . . . that," she said. "It's . . . I just don't think it's a good idea, that's all."

"You want to explain that?"

She wouldn't look at me, not even for a second, and I was beginning to think maybe it wasn't because the highway required every iota of her attention. In a wildly unconvincing voice, she said, "You know, you're not saving the environment by making people drive you all over or borrowing cars from Moe. It takes just as much gas for me to drive you as it would if you drove yourself. You're just saving yourself the responsibility and the car payment, and you're forcing us to spend time together."

"Yeah. That's why you don't want to see me anymore. It's an ecological issue."

"I'm just saying it's not healthy for the two of us to act like we're still a couple, Elliot. We're not. That part of our lives is over, and we both need to move ahead."

There's a face I make when something doesn't strike me as honest, which sort of looks like Jackie Gleason with a bad case of gas. I made it now, but Sharon was so intent on the road, it had no effect. "Okay, what's *really* going on?" I asked. "That didn't even sound like you talking."

She drew a deep breath, then let it out. Apparently, the act of respiration itself was supposed to be impressive. Finally, she spoke.

"Gregory thinks we spend too much time together for a divorced couple."

"Funny, I thought you and Gregory spent too much time together when we were a *married* couple, and that didn't seem to matter." Gregory? Now I had to worry about what *Gregory* thought?

"Don't be petty, Elliot."

There are certain things that push my buttons. Okay, there are a *lot* of things that push my buttons. But nearing the top of the list was someone I don't like telling me what I can and can't do. It's why I haven't voted in fifteen years.

"Petty! I love this. You and I try to have a civil divorce, unlike every other divorced couple in the country, and the guy who broke up our marriage to begin with decides we're being too *nice* to each other? What's he afraid of, that I'll steal my wife back from him?"

Sharon didn't talk for a while, and I stopped eating. I

confess, I even wiped a little of the grease off my fingers and onto her car seat. Okay, so maybe I am petty.

"It's just . . . you need to grow up, Elliot." Now, that *did* sound like her.

"I've never much seen the benefit to that, Shar."

She nodded. "But I'm not going to help you avoid it anymore."

"Fine. You want to let me off here, or can we make it all the way back home before we part ways and you can start living your life the way *Gregory* wants you to?"

Her mouth undulated a little as she tried hard not to frown disapprovingly, but it was a doomed effort. "It was going to happen sooner or later, wasn't it?"

"What?"

"That we'd start acting like all the other divorced couples."

This time, I was silent for a while. That one hurt. I looked out the window and tried to think of something else. The Garden State Parkway is a lot more attractive than the New Jersey Turnpike, and since they installed E-ZPass, it's not that much slower. If you have the choice, go with the Parkway. More trees.

"All right," I said after an appropriate pause. "You have to do what's right for your marriage." I didn't even mean anything by that.

Sharon put a finger to her left eye, but I couldn't tell if it was because it was tearing up, or because her mascara was clumping, which I understand from commercials can be a major hazard for women. "I'll call you when . . . things calm down a little, okay?" she said.

"You do what you have to do." Okay, that time I meant something by it. I never said I was the most magnanimous man on the planet. Or even the most magnanimous in the center lane of the Garden State Parkway. "Just step on it, will you? I have to get back so I can cheat a widow out of her inheritance."

Dad met me at the town house. Even though he's usually glad to see Sharon—he likes to think there's a chance we'll reconcile, despite her subsequent remarriage—this time he was a little more subdued, and as soon as she drove away and I hopped into the passenger seat in the truck, he gave me a look. He must have noticed the way Sharon and I were eyeing each other.

"What's going on with Leslie?" he asked.

"Can we talk about that later? I'm dealing with one disaster at a time right now." I'd left my bag of fast food, with french fries oozing oil, on the seat of Sharon's car. That would add at least a week to the time she'd refrain from calling, but I knew the rules. I couldn't call her until I heard from her. It was usually best to call her at the office or on the cell phone, anyway. When I called her at home, and a man—that is, Gregory—answered, I wouldn't hang up, but I'd generally wish I had.

"Disaster? What disaster?" Nobody can ignore a request to ignore something better than a Jewish parent. They can't help it; it's in the DNA. If I ever have kids, I'll be exactly the same way, and you can highlight those words right here and show them to me in twenty years if you like.

I gave Dad the rundown on my dealings with the women "in" my life. He listened, as he always does, with complete concentration. And when I was finished, he digested it all as he drove.

"This is what you're sending me home to tell your mother? I left the house this morning, and you had a new girlfriend she wanted to meet and an ex-wife she still loves. Now, I have to go tell her to expect you for dinner every Thursday night again."

"That's not going to happen."

"Sure it's not," he said.

"It can't. I have a theatre to run. Make it lunch."

We pulled up to Amy Ansella's Colonial and I helped Dad down from the driver's seat, which he resented. At the doorstep, he stood back, allowing me to ring the bell. After all, I was the one Amy had met before.

She was very charming with Dad, smiling her best flirtatious smile at him and calling him Arthur at his request. She had boxed up much of her late husband's DVD and VHS collection—at least twelve hundred titles, and that was a conservative estimate—but still had about fifty or so movies that she was loading into a carton from the shelves in her living room. Amy also handed me an inventory of everything I was buying, so that I could match it against the discs and tapes when I unpacked them, to make sure everything was there.

"Vincent kept the list," she said. "I just took the movies and put them into boxes. I didn't even look. But he was very careful about keeping the list up-to-date, so I'm sure it's still accurate. I crossed off the ones I gave his sister." I told her that at this price, the collection was beyond my expectations, and even a few inaccuracies on the list wouldn't have been a problem, but she assured me there were none. "Vincent kept it current until the day he died," Amy said.

I did my best to keep Dad from lifting heavy cartons (I had, in fact, tried to borrow the truck without him, but he'd seen through that), and was as successful with that as I had been generally for the past few weeks. When all was said and done, I believe I may have carried one more carton than he did out to the truck. I don't know about him, but I was exhausted.

Amy came out of the house with—I swear—a pitcher of lemonade, which she offered first to my father, who accepted gratefully, and then to me. I'm not a huge lemonade fan, but you have to be nice to a recent widow, so I drank four quick cups and waited for the cramp I knew would hit my midsection at any second.

"I still can't believe you're letting me have all this at such a low price," I told Amy. "Are you sure you want to do this?" Dad gave me a look that had its roots in the tradition of our people: *You're trying to pay more?*

"I'm sure," Amy said. "I told you, I just want them where I don't have to see them every day." Then she smiled naughtily and added, "Besides, you're a pretty nice guy when you're not asking me about my sex life."

The look Dad gave me then had no roots in the tradition of our people.

We sat on the bumper of Dad's truck while Amy refilled the plastic cups again. Cramp, be damned. "I didn't mean to ask you any impolite questions," I told her, although

I snuck a peek at my father to reassure him. "It's just that . . . what happened still gnaws at me. I'm just trying to make sense of it."

The pitcher was empty, and Amy sat on the grass, staring ahead with little affect in her tone or expression on her face. "There is no sense to it," she said. "I have to come to terms with that idea, that I'm never really going to understand it."

"I don't think you should do that," Dad told her. "If you give up, if you just tell yourself that it was 'one of those things,' you'll end up regretting it later. You're young now, and you don't really know about regrets. Trust me." I stared at him a moment. It was the least optimistic thing I'd ever heard my father say; usually he was so upbeat you'd swear he was Shirley Temple with a really bad sore throat.

"Dad," I said. He gave me a look that shut me up.

But Amy was giving him a sad smile. "You're probably right, Arthur," she said. "But I don't think I have the strength to do it. The police say . . ."

"The police are wrong," I told her. "Anthony didn't have anything to do with what happened to your husband."

"Then why did he run away?" My father. Helping.

"I won't know that until I get to talk to him again," I said.

Amy's body tensed, which wasn't entirely an unattractive thing. "Again? You've heard from him?" she asked.

Oops.

"No, not really," I said. "I heard a rumor that he was out of state, working on a project. But I have nothing to back that up. What I meant was, when I get to talk to him and ask him why he left, I'll know better."

Amy couldn't have been a terribly astute woman, because she leaned back and said, "Oh."

This wasn't getting me anywhere. "I can't stop asking questions, Amy. I don't want to embarrass you, but please tell me: where were you the night your husband died?"

"Here. At home. If you must know, Vincent stormed out. I thought he might go to your theatre; he'd been talking about *Young Frankenstein* being shown in the area. I didn't know where, and I didn't care; he'd made me watch it a thousand times."

"You really weren't at the theatre?" I asked.

Amy shook her head. "I prefer something a little more sophisticated. Like *Indiscreet*."

"So maybe you can tell me who I should be talking to," I tried. "Who would have a reason to want to hurt your husband?"

She thought about it. "I think it was his *pal*, Joe Dunbar, but nobody seems to agree with me."

"Dunbar had no motive," I said.

Amy looked sharply at me. "I don't know *why*. But I know men. And he's a man who could do something like that."

"Nobody saw him at the theatre. But . . ."

Amy saw it on my face; I'd said more than I had intended. "But what, Mr. Freed? You can't hurt me anymore; feel free to tell the truth."

"One witness saw your husband at the movies that night with a blond-haired woman. Not with Joe Dunbar."

"Have you seen Joe's wife?" she asked.

I didn't know how to react to that, so I said, "There was no one else? Nobody else who might have wanted to kill your husband?"

Amy laughed without humor, a hollow sound like a mallet hitting Curly in the head during a Three Stooges short. "He wasn't that memorable."

It slipped out: "So why did you marry him?"

Amy looked me straight in the eyes. "He made me laugh," she said.

33

It was getting late after Dad and I unpacked the boxes and carried them into the town house. He didn't say anything about the enormous gash in my countertop, although his eyes were filled with questions. My father is, if nothing else, a tactful man. I mumbled something about wanting to unpack (which I had no intention of doing now), and he said something about leaving my mother alone too long. Dad drove off, looking worried. Don't ever let them tell you Jewish guilt is the sole province of mothers.

I took a long look around the living room. There were at least twenty cartons of films in various formats, and the sad part was, they didn't clutter the room. Aside from the drooping futon-like sofa, there wasn't a stick of furniture to be seen other than a floor lamp that should have been banished two presidents ago. I would have to buy a decent home entertainment system to properly show the DVDs I'd just bought. And, since I was in a self-pitying sort of mood, I reminded myself that, in all likelihood, I'd be watching them alone.

With dark clouds gathering, this wasn't the best time to

be leaving for the theatre, but I had no choice—the doors had to open in an hour and a half. I got on the bike for the first time since the Lexus attack (I'd been taking cabs home and mooching rides around) and started toward Midland Heights.

Eight minutes into the ride, just when I was past the scene of the attack, it started to rain.

The fold-up poncho I keep in a pouch attached to the seat was all folded up (as advertised), but the rain wasn't hard, and going up the hill into Highland Park, I preferred not to destroy the momentum I'd developed. So I kept pedaling. And naturally, the sky opened up and buckets of rain began to fall. At least, they *felt* like buckets.

By the time I could have stopped the bike, gotten the poncho, and put it on, the whole exercise would have been pointless. It was beginning to feel like someone didn't *want* me to save the environment all by myself.

I arrived at Comedy Tonight wetter than if I'd just taken a shower, and considerably colder. Luckily, I keep some extra clothes in the office, so I went inside to change, and didn't bother to close the door, since I was the only person in the theatre.

At least, that's what I thought. I was lamenting my lack of foresight in not keeping dry towels in my desk when a sound came from the doorway. Leslie Levant was standing there, an amused expression on her face. Given the way my day was going, I assumed she'd come to tell me that not only did she never want to see me again, but also that she wanted to erase the memory of ever having seen me before.

"Have I come at a bad time?" she managed to say without guffawing.

I believe I said something on the order of "*argf*," and compounded my embarrassment by trying to cover myself with the sweatpants I'd picked up off the floor.

"Don't worry, Elliot," Leslie said. "I'm a professional."

"A professional voyeur?"

"Nonsense. You can't get paid for being a voyeur."

I pulled on the sweats and sat down, reaching for a

T-shirt from the bottom drawer of my desk. I never said Comedy Tonight was a classy operation. "Is there a reason you showed up, or do you want to arrest me for indecent exposure?"

"Depends on your definition of 'indecent.'"

I looked up. "Are we flirting again? Can you maybe carry a certain color handkerchief in your shirt pocket, so I'll know what our status is on any given day?"

Leslie leaned on the edge of the desk, a little too close for my comfort. I reached over to make sure my pants were properly zipped, then remembered I was in sweats. I left the hand there.

"I'm sorry about that," she told me. "I realize I was abrupt the other night, and I shouldn't have been. You scared me. I thought you were getting too involved too fast."

"I probably was. But you weren't getting involved at all, and I wanted to clarify the relationship," I said, sounding way too much like a TV psychologist for my own taste. "I wasn't interested in setting a wedding date; I just wanted to know where I stood, and you showed me."

She frowned. "I was abrupt."

"You could say that. At least you waited until I stopped bleeding from the leg to ambush me."

"You're not going to make this easy, are you?" Leslie couldn't seem to decide if she was irritated or hurt.

"I don't even know what 'this' is, so how could I make it easy?" I'd had a long day, and wasn't much in the mood to be charitable to a woman who'd put me in this state of mind to begin with.

"We've been going too fast," she said. "We met, we flirted, we dated, we kissed, and you were starting to look at me like I was your next Sharon. I was starting to look at you and Sharon and getting jealous. It was way too much, way too soon. I think we should start again, slowly." She stuck out her hand. "I'm Leslie Levant. Nice to meet you."

"*Man*, you blow hot and cold."

"I'm unpredictable," Leslie said.

"You're nuts, is what you are."

She withdrew her hand. "It's part of my charm." Leslie saw the look on my face, and stopped grinning. "Still. I think I've been unfair, and I want to try again. How about it?"

I closed my eyes and thought about that. "I don't know," I said.

That probably wasn't the response she was expecting, and I didn't blame her; it wouldn't have been the response *I'd* have expected if you'd asked me ten minutes earlier. "You don't know?" Leslie asked.

I opened my eyes again, and tried to look at her without anger, which I believe I managed. "I really don't," I answered. "If we can't define what we have, and what we hope to have, I don't know if I want to keep things the way they were. Not that it wasn't fine, but it's too iffy for me. I want to have something to do with your life, and for you to have something to do with mine. Or at least, I want to know that we're finding out whether that's possible. You seem to want something else, but I don't know what it is."

"I'm gun-shy, Elliot. I had a bad marriage, and I'm not in the least ready to even consider doing something like that again. I like you, but you're in a hurry. You want everything to happen in the next two weeks, and I can tell you now, that won't be the case with me." She stood up and made important eye contact. "I can't make any promises," Leslie said.

"Can you promise you'll at least think about it?"

"I don't know." Great. Now we *both* didn't know. This conversation was becoming more vague as it went along.

"Then I guess we need to keep our lives separate for a while," I said.

She looked at me for a very long time, and it seemed that Leslie was thinking of ways to counter my argument. "Do you really want to be alone tonight?" she asked.

"No, I don't. But I'm greedy, and I want more than just not being alone."

Leslie shook her head slowly and let out her breath. "You're not like other guys I meet, Elliot Freed," she said after a while.

"Maybe you should consider that."

"Maybe." She turned and walked through the door, then headed left, toward the lobby and the street. I got a good view of her on the way out, and I confess, it did shake my resolve. But I couldn't think of a way to call her back without sounding like an idiot.

Sophie would be showing up in fifteen minutes, and I had to get ready for her unspoken scorn. I still had to put on socks and shoes. There were things that needed doing. I hadn't threaded the projector or started the popcorn machine. Luckily, I had cleaned up pretty well the night before.

After all, a good thirty or forty people were coming. Everything had to be just right, didn't it?

I spent a few minutes setting up the popcorn and changed a couple of the two-sheets in the lobby to reflect the next week's movies, and then went and turned on the lights in the auditorium.

It really did reflect hours and hours of hard work, and I was proud of it. But it still wasn't within driving distance of the vision I had for the theatre, something that went back to my childhood and before that, when going to a movie was something more than watching a DVD on a really, really big screen.

In those days, there was a palpable excitement in seeing a film in a real movie palace, one of the over-the-top rococo structures that signaled a group experience. The idea was that it *should* be too much, it *should* be almost garish in its architectural excess. This was, in fact, the temple of moviegoing, and that made it a special experience, something that everyone could afford, but that gave us a glimpse of the better life.

At Comedy Tonight, it was more likely you'd get a glimpse of the better life as it was in 1948, but without cosmetic surgery. When you looked at Ginger Rogers, for example, in *Swing Time* (1936), it was hard to imagine a woman more beautiful. But in the last years of her life, while it was possible to understand that she had once been a great beauty, the present-day reality was only a reminder, and something of a tease. My theatre was like Ginger Rogers in 1995.

Luckily, the lights were never turned on high, so you couldn't see the cracks in the plaster and the missing pieces of the painting on the ceiling. (Michelangelo had nothing on the guy who climbed up into the cupola of Comedy Tonight.) The missing seats here and there didn't help, and the fact that not all the seats that *were* there actually matched wasn't a huge asset, either.

I stood another few seconds checking on the state of my *mostly* restored theatre and then remembered that I needed to take my huge asset upstairs to the projection booth.

Getting *Help!* to thread up had been a little tricky the night before—we don't always get what you'd call mint-condition prints, and this one's sprocket holes were a little cranky. I should have left myself extra time, and I hadn't expected to torpedo a budding relationship, so now I was in a hurry.

As it turned out, though, I needn't have rushed—the film was perfectly threaded and ready to go, and the projection booth was powered up and lit, as it always was whenever Anthony was in the theatre.

But this was different. I knew Anthony *couldn't* be in the theatre tonight.

Could he?

34

○○○○○○○

"**Don't** you see," I said to Chief Barry Dutton, who was sitting behind his desk the next day, looking like an African-American Transformer toy in "building" mode, "this means someone is trying to make it look like Anthony's here, when we know he's not."

"Let me see if I have this right," Dutton said, his voice rumbling somewhere beneath the tones of a lion who just came back to the den to find Uncle Scar hanging out with his lioness. "You received a phone call from a fugitive from justice, *didn't bother to let the authorities know about it*, and then when you think it might help that fugitive's case, you bring the information here to me. Is that about it?"

"No need to thank me. It's all part of the service."

"Mr. Freed, we don't know each other very well. But you can assume from this moment on that if I need to be irritated by a civilian who thinks he's witty, there are other places I can go." Dutton, I could see, could be very intimidating if he tried hard enough, and he was certainly giving it a shot. He didn't stand up, though, which might have helped. The man was roughly the size of Pike's Peak.

"I'm sorry, Chief. It's a reflex with me. From this point on, assume that you have successfully cowed me into submission."

He rumbled some more, which I took to be a sigh of resignation. "All right. So explain to me how the intruder or intruders who set up your projection booth for you provide any evidence whatsoever that your projectionist didn't have something to do with the pirated videos. And try to stick to something resembling facts, because theories that begin with 'you just don't know the kid like I do' really don't hold up all that well in court."

"It's simple," I said. I stood up, to pace around. It doesn't help, but it looks good. "The person—or people— trying to make it look like Anthony had a hand in the piracy and the murder don't know that I spoke to him. They don't know I'm aware he's away someplace shooting this movie of his. They think I'm still as much in the dark about his whereabouts as everyone else."

"Which you are." Dutton was listening closely, all cop now, his hands clasped in front of him, thinking.

"What do you mean?"

"I mean, all you got was a phone call that, for all you · know, came from across the street. Anthony could easily be here in town, operating out of someone's basement, or with some friends over on campus in New Brunswick. There's absolutely no reason to take him at his word."

"You don't know the kid like I do," I said with little enthusiasm.

"Uh-huh."

"He was shooting a movie. I heard the tumult and the crew behind him." It wasn't much, but it was something.

"You heard other people talking. It could have been a bowling alley or a Laundromat for all you know." Okay, maybe it wasn't something, after all.

"You could probably get my phone records and see where the call came from, couldn't you?"

Dutton was about to answer when the door opened, and a uniformed officer I hadn't seen before walked in and handed Dutton a sheet of paper.

"Yeah," Dutton said. He took the paper from the uniform, nodded, and watched the officer leave. I wondered why I was there for any of this.

Dutton spent a good deal of time scanning the paper.

"My phone records," I reminded him.

"Yeah, I'll have to get you to sign a waver for them before you leave," Dutton said. He scanned the papers. "They're not terribly interesting, really."

It took me a moment to realize what he was saying. "Those are my phone records?" I asked, pointing to the paper in his hand. Dutton nodded. "You just went ahead and got them without getting permission from me?"

Dutton looked at me over his half-glasses. "You obstructed an ongoing murder investigation for three full days after getting this phone call and you're going to lecture *me* on procedure?" he asked. Okay, so he had a point. I peered over his desk at the paper, and tried to make out the number highlighted on the sheet in front of him. I can read upside down, but not fluently.

"So, what do the phone calls show?" I asked. "If I'm not prying, what with it being my phone and all."

"Well, the call is here, Saturday morning right before one a.m.," he began. "But it doesn't really prove anything. It's from a cell phone registered in Los Angeles, but on the Verizon network. Call could have come from a lot of places."

"Is one of them across the street, or from someone's basement in New Brunswick?"

Dutton's eyes narrowed. "Let's assume for a moment that your projectionist isn't the one setting up the screenings at night. Who else could it be?"

"I haven't a clue," I told him honestly. "There aren't that many people who really understand the workings of that kind of machine."

"Okay." Dutton nodded in agreement. "Let's start with the basics. Access. Who could possibly have been in the projection booth on the nights when the Phantom Threader appeared?"

"The Phantom Threader?"

"What do you prefer? 'The Projectionist Who Wasn't There'?"

I tried to remember that I had to show some respect for the office, if not the man. It's like the president. "Don't go into film marketing as your second career, Chief," I said.

He ignored me almost as well as if Sharon had been giving him lessons. "How about the popcorn girl?"

"Sophie?" I laughed out loud. "Sophie doesn't even know how to work the popcorn machine. I have to set it up for her every night."

"She could be putting that on. Anthony could have showed her, since I'm assuming you haven't."

I shook my head. "You're giving her too much credit. Sophie can't even get Goth together on a convincing basis."

"Well, no one else is there every night except for . . . Who's that guy who's there every night? The one who told us about Ansella's supposed girlfriend?"

"Leo?" Dutton, who had been looking through his notes for the name, pointed at me: yes. I rewarded him with an expression of supreme skepticism. "Leo is a crusty little old guy who used to work in the merchant marine. He messed up his right hand with a fishhook, and doesn't really have the use of all his fingers. Believe me, you'd need all your fingers to work that monster in my booth."

Dutton pursed his lips, but nodded in agreement. "But it doesn't happen *every* night, does it?"

"No."

"So what can you remember about the nights when your gremlins were on the job? Was there anyone special who was there every time?"

I gave that some thought. And the more I thought about it, the more my stomach felt like I'd eaten a freezing plate of slush for breakfast. Nah; it *couldn't* have been. But Dutton saw it on my face.

"Who?"

I sat back down. "It can't be. No. Now that I think of it, it's somebody who wasn't even there one of the times . . . no."

His voice was considerably more basso this time, and his eyes darker. He drew the word out: *"Who?"*

"Leslie Levant."

And the scary part was, Dutton looked like that was the answer he'd expected.

35

○♡○♡♡○○

"It's not possible," I said. "Leslie wasn't there the night the powdered sugar was dumped on the popcorn. You can check your log books. She was on patrol that night. And the projector was threaded up when I got there."

Chief Dutton's house was a comfortable split-level on a quiet street in Midland Heights. He'd decided that our conversation was going to take a turn that might not be best expressed in police headquarters, no matter how closed his office door was. So we came back here, and were currently sitting in his eat-in kitchen. Dutton had taken out smoked turkey and rolls from his refrigerator, and was looking as domestic as he could, considering he resembled Gentle Ben more closely than Martha Stewart.

"She couldn't have been there ahead of you that day?" He spread mustard on one half of his roll and started assembling a sandwich. I rummaged through the refrigerator (with permission from the chief, of course) for low-fat mayonnaise, which is roughly the same as low-fat fat, an oxymoron.

"Nobody can be there ahead of me on any day," I

answered him. "I have the keys to the front door, and nobody else does."

"Not even Anthony? He let these piracy people in, didn't he? And would you get me a diet black cherry, while you're there?"

I got a can of soda as requested, which helped me find the mayo, since that was hiding in the far reaches of the second shelf behind the beverages. It was a very well-organized refrigerator. "No, not even Anthony has the front door key. He could get the keys to the basement, which he apparently used to let the pirates in, but not the front door. I have the only one. Nobody has the keys to Comedy Tonight except me. Nobody gets to the theatre ahead of me."

Dutton chuckled, Fred Flintstone in a mellow mood. "He let the pirates in. It sounds like Captain Jack Sparrow was running around in your theatre."

"Are you sure you're a cop? Is there a diploma or something I can see?"

He gave me a droll look, and said, "I'd be happy to give you a really good look at my gun, if you insist."

I ignored that, and narrowed my eyes. "You didn't look surprised when I mentioned Leslie's name," I said after a while. "You suspected her before I mentioned it, didn't you?"

Dutton's face betrayed him: he thought about denying it, then decided against it. He nodded. "I'm always concerned about things I can't explain, especially when they involve my officers," he began. "Officer Levant bought a new car recently. She moved into a new apartment, a larger one. Threw a party for her fellow officers when she moved in, and showed off the new furniture and appliances. Took a trip to Rome two months ago. That all costs money. Any one of them alone wouldn't be suspicious. All of them, in a relatively short period of time with no pay increase, makes you wonder."

I started filling a sandwich roll with sliced turkey. I looked across the table at him. Dutton never seemed to be seriously worried about anything—he maintained an aura of calm no matter what, and seemed to have a very strong inner barometer. He said what he had to say, but didn't tell you everything, ever.

"But there was no connection to this case specifically. Couldn't she have been taking kickbacks from businesses, protection, the usual graft?"

Dutton's eyes flashed anger. "Not in my town," he said. "That doesn't happen. In my department, there is no 'usual graft.' When I see someone spending more than they should, with no obvious increase in their income, I get suspicious immediately, and I act as soon as I can."

"Sorry," I said, and I meant it. "But couldn't the extra money be attributed to her divorce?"

"She's been divorced three years," Dutton said, and it occurred to me how little I knew about Leslie. "Where's the money been for three years?" I couldn't answer. "Besides," he seemed to think of something. "There was something else."

I waited. Dutton put his hands to his temples. "This can't go beyond this room, you understand?" he asked. I nodded my head. It seemed that speaking would be somehow inappropriate.

"Who found the pirated DVDs?" he asked me. "You were there."

"Officer Patel," I said.

Dutton shook his head. "No. Officer Levant led him down there. She discovered the cartons, and then sent him back up to tell O'Donnell."

That didn't seem so significant. "So?"

"Think about it," Dutton said. "An ambitious young officer makes a discovery like that, has a chance to impress her chief and the county prosecutor's investigator, and she goes out of her way to give another the glory? It doesn't make sense. Unless . . ."

"Unless she already knew the discs were there, and she wanted to distance herself from them," I said. "How did you know she found the discs? Patel told you?"

Dutton nodded. "He felt bad about taking the credit. But think: Officer Levant has been all over the murder case, but hasn't brought anything to the piracy case. And I had specif-ically assigned her to the piracy case to see what she'd bring in. Yet everything she's discovered herself has been about the murder: the bottle of clonidine and the idea that Ansella was at the theatre with his best friend's wife. The idea that Amy Ansella was at Comedy Tonight the night of the mur-der. Any idea where she might have gotten that one?" I re-mained silent. "That's what I thought."

I considered Dutton's argument. "No," I said. "I don't buy it. All that's circumstantial. And that still doesn't ad-dress the fact that Leslie wasn't there the night of the pow-dered sugar incident."

Dutton smiled. "Can't you stop saying things like 'pow-dered sugar incident'? It's hard to remain professional." He shook his head, seemingly to clear it. "If Officer Levant wasn't at the theatre that night, but she was all the other times the projector was readied ahead of time, what does that tell us?"

"That it wasn't her."

He shook his head, this time to say no. "It tells us it probably wasn't her *that night*," he said. "We have to as-sume there were others in on the piracy scheme. One per-son didn't do all of this."

"You thought Anthony did it all by himself."

Dutton looked amused. "Did I?"

"You did. And what makes you think Leslie even knows how to run the projector? I'm lucky *I* know how to do it. And I've gotta tell you, you and Leslie weren't having much luck changing reels the night I saw you in there." There! I hadn't thought of *that* before.

Dutton looked at his sandwich and frowned. "I should have gotten some ham," he said.

"Ha! I got you."

"You were the one who first brought up Officer Levant as a suspect, not me," he reminded me. Guilt isn't inflicted only by parents.

"I don't believe Leslie did it. I'm sorry I said anything." I put down my sandwich. It wasn't much of a gesture of anguish, but it was the best I could do in this setting. "There's no evidence, and here we are, convicting a lovely young woman of crimes we can't possibly know she committed."

"You *are* sleeping with her, aren't you?" Dutton pointed an accusing finger at me.

I looked away. "No," I said. "We're taking a break from each other . . ."

He looked heavenward, but didn't seem to get any divine inspiration for his effort. "Why can't you ever just tell me something the first time?" he scowled.

"Look, Chief," I said. "I've only known you a few weeks. I don't trust you, and you don't trust me. That's okay. But look at this from my point of view. My main concern here is Anthony. If I tell you something before I can consider it, and I don't know how you'll react, I could do him serious harm. And if there's someone I'm responsible for, and the question is whether to do them harm or not, I'm always going to come down on the side of not. That means being cautious with you."

"You're not Anthony Pagliarulo's father," Dutton said quietly.

"No, but his father asked me to find out what happened. His father thinks it's his fault because he asked Anthony to pick up a prescription."

Dutton washed down the remainder of his sandwich with black cherry diet soda, which is one step above drinking Drano, in my opinion. But to each his own. "It's not his father's fault. But the prescription presents more questions."

I sighed. "What *about* the prescription? What about Ansella's dying from poisoned popcorn? There's no evidence Ansella even knew about the pirated videos, let alone had anything to do with them. Even if Leslie did know how to thread the projector, a lot of this still isn't explained."

"That's the problem with this case. There's no evidence of *anything*." Dutton eyed the counter and, I thought, contemplated making another sandwich. He shook his head and started the cleanup.

I nodded. "Nothing adds up yet. But if Anthony calls again, I want to be able to tell him that he won't be arrested the minute he shows his face in Central New Jersey. Can I tell him that?"

"We're looking to question him, that's all," Dutton said. "There's no arrest warrant that I know about."

"How about O'Donnell?"

"If he obtained a warrant, I'd see a copy, and I haven't," Dutton answered. "Nobody's getting out the bright lights and the rubber hose just because your projectionist might want to surface one more time."

"That's good enough for now," I said. "What have you guys and the county been doing about Ansella?"

Dutton's face closed for business. "That's an ongoing investigation. I'm not telling you about that."

"Which leaves me to draw my own conclusions," I told him.

"Is that a threat? I don't like amateurs running around muddying the water in a murder investigation. I don't like it when they interview witnesses and visit the widow of the victim on three separate occasions." Dutton watched my face carefully as he said that.

"You knew about that?"

"You're not sleeping with her, too, are you?" He'd seen Amy Ansella and he'd seen me. It wasn't a serious question.

"I'm not sleeping with *anybody*. I'm sleeping with her late husband's video collection. It takes up most of my apartment."

"Let me know if any copies of pirated movies show up."

"Vincent had better taste than that. I haven't found a really bad comedy in the bunch."

Dutton stared at me a little more intensely, to make sure I wouldn't dodge his comment again. *"You let me know if any copies of pirated movies show up."*

"So I have to let you know everything I find out, and you won't tell me anything?" I dodged.

"I'm sorry, which one of us has the badge?"

I stood up, took my plate to the dishwasher, and put it inside. "The one who wants one," I said.

"Good. At least we have our roles straight."

"I'm going to keep asking people questions, Chief," I said as I walked to the front hall, where the front wheel of my bike was resting against a wall. "I don't want you to think I'm sneaking around behind your back." I picked up the wheel and walked toward the front door.

Dutton rumbled, but that might have just been the black cherry soda. "Just be a little bit quicker in reporting anything you might find out, okay, Elliot?"

I thought about that. "Okay," I said. "I don't think you're trying to screw anybody who's innocent. I'll let you know."

His face was solemn. "Thanks. The residents of Midland Heights will sleep more soundly tonight, knowing you're out there protecting them from evil."

"All in a day's work." I refrained from spitting (since there was no spittoon) or adjusting my ten-gallon hat (since I didn't have one of those, either) before I walked out.

But when I got outside and started walking toward my bike, which leaned against Dutton's garage door, I realized I had forgotten something very important. Not feeling completely comfortable with the situation, I went back and rang the doorbell. Dutton looked surprised when he opened the door and saw me there.

"Thanks for the sandwich," I said.

36

○◗○◗○◗○

I spent most of Tuesday mulling over what had happened, and it came to this: not much. I had theories, and some of the facts supported them, but others didn't. And I had the chief of the Midland Heights Police Department sort of on my side, but sort of not.

Not to mention, I hadn't heard from my ex-wife in a few days, and the woman I'd begun a relationship with had moved from police officer to suspect, and besides, wasn't talking to me. By my choice.

By Wednesday morning, having gotten through the slowest night of the week at the theatre, I was ready to push on. And Joe Dunbar, Vincent Ansella's closest friend, was taking the day off from work to attend to what he called "family business." He wasn't anxious to have me in his home, but he couldn't come up with a plausible excuse not to, so I rode the bike up to his neighborhood, which wasn't far from Amy's, on the other side of Piscataway.

"I'm actually cleaning up stuff for our yard sale on Saturday," he admitted when he let me in. "That's why the place looks like this."

"You must have a really understanding boss," I told him.

"I do," he said. "I work for my wife."

"Christie?"

"No," he said. "My *other* wife." Then Dunbar stopped. "You know Christie?"

I'd forgotten he didn't know I'd spoken to his wife. "Amy Ansella mentioned her."

Dunbar scowled. "I bet," he said.

I walked into the room, which was filled with cartons of vinyl LPs, VHS tapes, a couple of wigs, old clothing, and what my mother calls *tchotchkes*, knickknacks that serve little purpose beyond looking remarkably odd on people's shelves. There were New York Mets yearbooks, drinking mugs, and bobblehead dolls, as well as some exercise equipment (small free weights and the like) and cookbooks. And this was just in the living room.

"Why don't Amy and Christie get along?" I asked.

Dunbar didn't react outwardly; he just kept walking. "Their husbands were friends," he said. "Didn't mean they had to be."

"What exactly does your wife do?" I asked as we navigated through the room toward the kitchen. I already sort of knew from visiting her office, but I wasn't supposed to tell Dunbar I'd talked to Christie, so I was playing dumb.

"She runs a company that trains medical records personnel for hospitals, pharmaceutical companies, and support services," Dunbar said, clearly not for the first time in his life. "Christie provides the training, and then helps find jobs for these people. I mostly do the human resources work and run the office, and I handle all the interaction with employers that Christie doesn't do herself."

I'm embarrassed to say that the first thought that came to mind was: a guy whose wife deals with a lot of pharmaceutical companies might be able to get hold of some prescription medications.

Dunbar must have seen it on my face, because he said, "Don't even think it. Pharma companies are very closely regulated, and you can't just get a prescription for something because you want it."

"So Christie doesn't have high blood pressure?"

He moved some boxes out of the way as we walked from the kitchen to the "family room," where there were yet more cartons. Dunbar made room on two chairs for us to sit. "No, she doesn't," he said. "But before you ask, yes, I do. And no, my doctor took me off clonidine six months ago. I don't have any."

"I'm sorry, Joe. But you know there are still a lot of unanswered questions."

He waved a hand to brush away the insult. "I understand," Dunbar said. "You're a movie theatre owner. You have to ask tough questions." He smiled.

I was playing cop a little too hard, and I smiled back. "I know. It's silly. But I can't leave it alone. If Vincent had been killed at the Loews in New Brunswick, you wouldn't be seeing me now."

"The Loews wouldn't be showing *Young Frankenstein*, would it, now?"

Dunbar's cell phone, which he wore clipped to his belt, rang. It was a simple ring, which I appreciated. Dunbar apparently didn't feel the need to express his individuality through the way his cell phone interrupted the rest of his life, and I found that refreshing. His conversation, which was clearly about business (he kept using words like "invoice" and "sessions") lasted only a minute or so, and then he turned his attention back to me, apologizing.

"No problem," I said. "It's a hazard of modern life. So, is the business doing well?"

Dunbar nodded enthusiastically. "It's still new, you know. We've only been doing this about a year. Christie used to be a beautician, you know, but she . . ." He got a little teary. "Christie is a cancer survivor, and when she came out of the chemo and the radiation with a pretty clean bill of health—for now; you know, they're never sure until a few years have gone by—then she decided she wanted to help the industry. Help people get better, you know. She wasn't a doctor or a chemist or anything, so she figured she could get them the best help they could have. And she asked me to give up my job to help her."

"What were you doing before?"

"I was a sales rep for a replacement windows manufacturer until she got sick. My territory was the whole East Coast. I'd have to be away too much, and I couldn't do that when she was sick. So I quit."

I never know what to say when someone tells me a story like that. "Well, I'm glad she came through it all right," I told him.

Dunbar nodded, and looked at me a while, waiting for something. I was wondering what to say next. "I guess you're going to ask me again about Amy calling me 'murderer,'" he said.

That seemed like a good place to start, seeing as how he'd brought it up. "It was on my mind," I told him.

"I've been thinking about it a lot. I really don't understand what she was getting at. I think she was just so emotionally out there at the funeral, you know, she'd say or do anything. She was in shock." Dunbar leaned back on his cushioned seat and stared at the ceiling. "The poor kid. It came so out of the blue."

"Joe, I've got to ask: where were you the night Vincent died?"

The response didn't come too quickly, like he had rehearsed it, and it didn't come too slowly, like he had to make it up on the spot. "I went out to dinner with Christie," he said. "And before you ask—because the cops already have—no, I don't have a receipt from the restaurant. We went out for a pizza, and I paid cash."

Christie had said she was *out*, but she hadn't said where, and that seemed odd, with an answer as innocuous as this at her disposal. If it were true.

"Would the guy at the restaurant . . ."

"Remember me?" Dunbar asked. "No. Would the guy at your pizza place know you by name, Elliot?"

Actually, he probably would, but that was a sad comment on my life, not Dunbar's. So I changed topics.

"Amy told me she and Vincent had an argument the night he died. She said he admitted to her that he was having an affair, and they fought bitterly. But it didn't seem shocking to her; it was almost like she expected it."

"Did she say who he was having an affair with?" he asked.

"She said it was with Marcy Resnick," I told him.

"Who's Marcy Resnick?"

"A woman he worked with." Strange that Dunbar didn't know the name.

"Strange that I don't know the name," he said. See? "Vince and I saw each other at least once a week. Up until the last few months, he told me everything. You'd think he'd at least mention her, if it was someone . . ."

"Maybe that's why he was so secretive the past few months," I suggested.

Dunbar shook his head. "It doesn't figure. Vince just wasn't that kind of guy. Besides, he was married to Amy. You'd think that would be enough."

I looked at him. "Who knows what goes on in someone else's marriage," I said.

"Yeah."

I took a look around the room, and the rooms I could see from where I sat. "You sure you're not moving out?" I asked Dunbar. "What's going to be left after you sell all this stuff?"

He laughed. "I'll be happy if we sell a tenth of it, to tell you the truth," he said. "I just want to clear out some storage space."

I couldn't think of anything more to ask, other than "how come Amy called you a murderer" again, but that was getting old, so Dunbar walked me to the door. The living room, filled with the first-class castoffs, was hard to navigate, but I'm pretty nimble on my feet, so I managed to get out of the house without causing myself a life-threatening injury.

Before I walked to the car, I turned back to face Dunbar, who was watching me from the open doorway. "Do you think Amy said that to deflect suspicion from herself?" I asked. Okay, so Marcy and Christie had given me the idea. I wanted to see if Dunbar would parrot his wife's opinion.

Dunbar's eyes opened as wide as if he'd been hit in the solar plexus. It took him a long moment to recover, and he exhaled. "I've known Amy a long time, and I think she was just lashing out at anything and anybody. She always sort of resented the fact that Vince and I had known each other for so long, and she was . . . jealous of me in a weird way. She was just mad at Vincent, and she thought she could get to him through me."

"Except he's dead," I said quietly.

"Yeah," Dunbar said. "Except he's dead."

37

◌◖◗◌◖◗◌◖◗

It took me close to an hour to pedal home, but it wasn't a hard ride, and by the time I got out of the shower and dressed, my legs were back to normal.

Still, after an hour on the bike, sitting was a priority, especially on a nice soft cushion. Your butt gets conditioned to a bicycle seat, but never completely. I'll bet Lance Armstrong walks like Yosemite Sam.

I went into the living room to begin the mammoth task of uncrating and storing Vincent Ansella's gargantuan video collection. Trying to wrap my mind around the entire job would have given me a headache and led to a feeling of such intimidation that I'd never even begin, so I concentrated on the first box, which was what I'd decided to call the one closest to where I was sitting.

As I unpacked, I checked off each video from the list Amy had provided. Ansella had the most eclectic, yet comprehensive collection of classic comedy I'd ever seen, making my own—which numbered in the hundreds—seem puny and superficial, like someone who claims to be a major rock and roll fanatic because he has all of the original albums the Beatles released in America.

Nonetheless, it took me about a half hour to check out the first carton of videos, mostly because I was checking each disc and tape individually, and I'd get distracted by the special features list on a DVD or the cover copy on a VHS box, and forget that I had approximately nineteen million more of these things to go through. I also had to contend with the small but significant percentage of doubles, since unsurprisingly, Ansella and I had similar taste. At this rate, I'd be completely finished sometime during the Chelsea Clinton Administration.

One major problem was that I had no bookshelves. I mean, none. And I really needed something to hold all these videos—if the water heater in the town house decided to blow up tonight and the living room flooded, I'd suffer the greatest blow to comedy since a major television network green-lighted *Hello, Larry*. (Look it up.)

So the first step would be getting some shelves from someplace that would deliver, since I couldn't actually drive somewhere and pick up large pieces of furniture. I could ask Dad to borrow the truck again, but I did have to become an adult at some point, and besides, have I mentioned that there are these places that actually bring the stuff to your house?

I walked, gingerly, into the bedroom, where I have the computer set up on one such assemble-it-yourself desk in one corner. I powered up the Mac and checked my e-mail. Apparently some ex-girlfriends had been talking out of school, since the usual ads for various enhancements to my anatomy still comprised the bulk of my messages.

I deleted all of those, read one or two from actual humans I knew, particularly one from a fellow Marx *freres* fan in New Hope, Pennsylvania, and then turned my attention to the task of finding shelving that could accommodate well over one thousand movies in various formats.

But before I got to that, something caught my eye. And I could have kicked myself.

On the corner of my desk was Anthony Pagliarulo's

screenplay, *Killin' Time*, on the CD-ROM his "lover," Carla, had given me. I had placed it on my desk with every intention of reading it, but my attention had been distracted by, well, everything that had happened since that moment. I got the impression that if the disc could have grown arms, it would have been waving frantically at me, trying to remind me it was there.

I put it in the disc drive and waited for it to show up on the screen. I don't really know why, but I was sure that reading the script would give me a clue to Anthony's whereabouts. Understanding the kid the way I did, as a devoted and possibly fanatical film freak, I'd be able to get into his head and follow the train of thought toward whichever station Anthony might have bought a (one-way?) ticket to visit.

Killin' Time was, as anyone who'd ever met Anthony might expect, a very referential script, which included plenty of artsy camera angles; no character development of any kind, ever; a barely recognizable story; and dialogue that (remember, this takes place in the 1840s) featured lines like "the African-Americans in town ain't gonna like this."

As advertised, it also included depictions of gore so lovingly described it was like a new father pulling baby pictures out of his wallet: oh, look here, how he shows the eye-gouging from the *inside* of the skull, and here, look at this one, where the intestines are actually *visible* after the slashing. It would probably make untold millions at the box office and be lionized by critics everywhere.

I have to say, though, that it wasn't until the second time through the script that I began to realize what Anthony was getting at. Not with the violence, which was strictly there to show how many different ways he could depict violence. But there was something in the description of the surroundings that conjured up images in my mind so familiar as to be almost iconic. I could practically see the settings, because from his loving detail, Anthony had told me which movies he'd stolen them from.

The Searchers. Fort Apache. My Darling Clementine. Even, yes, parts of *Easy Rider.*

I could have smacked myself in the head for not figuring it out sooner. Any movie nut/film student shooting a Western, if he had any budget at all, wouldn't have been able to resist the allure, not to mention think he was the first to create an *homage*, just by using the location. A quick call to the Utah Film Commission confirmed that permits had been issued, and a film called *Killin' Time* was completing principal photography as we spoke.

Anthony was in Monument Valley, Utah.

38

Now, the question became what to do with my newfound information. Of course, I had promised to tell Chief Dutton whatever I had discovered, without hesitation, but the whole question of what *he'd* be required to do after that slowed me down. I hadn't had the need to test Dutton's word, yet, and I wasn't sure whether he'd agree to find out more, or simply have Anthony picked up by the Utah State Police.

To avoid deciding what to do about Dutton, I considered my other options, which were, in a word, limited. I could try calling the number Dutton had gotten for Anthony's cell phone, but I had tried to read it upside down from a distance of about seven feet two days ago. It wasn't the most reliable information I'd ever gathered.

I even toyed with the idea of flying to Utah—what the hell, I'd always wanted to see Monument Valley—but then thought of Sophie running the theatre all by herself, and immediately banished that thought. By the time I got back, she'd be showing *The Seventh Seal*, followed by *The*

Exorcist, as a tribute to the great comedian Max von Sydow. Even Leo wouldn't sit through *that* double feature.

I couldn't just close up, either. That's the problem with owning a movie theatre—there are no days off. We're open on Christmas, we're open on Thanksgiving, and we're open on Yom Kippur. We're open on my birthday, when I'm sick, and when a distant relative dies. If Mr. Ford had been running a movie theatre, he probably would have been showing a matinee the day after Lincoln was shot. Well, not if O'Donnell was running the investigation, but otherwise.

If I couldn't call Anthony and I couldn't go see him, I could try to get a message through to him via Carla or Tajo Rosenblad. But they had both seemed genuinely amazed at the idea that he was missing, and equally surprised he was not in touch with his folks. It was possible, though not likely, that he'd gotten in touch since then, but my urgency on the phone had probably spooked Anthony into going farther underground. Once again, my superior investigative technique had shown through. I had a real future in this pursuit.

Staring at the computer screen in frustration, it occurred to me that a film student let loose for the first time would know when he was in over his head—at some point he'd *have* to be in over his head—and he'd call the closest thing he had to a mentor for help.

I put in a call to Professor Bender at Rutgers, and he immediately asked me to come to his office, as "just the tone of your voice is causing me vociferous anxiety." You have to love college professors: they can't just say something creeps them out.

It wasn't a long ride to Bender's office, and I chained the bike outside this time, carrying only the front wheel with me up the stairs. Bender, ponytail all a-twitter, was sitting behind his desk, with a poster over his head for *Repulsion*, an early Roman Polanski thriller. You had to figure it wouldn't be a *Back to the Future* poster. Film professors.

"What news is there of Anthony?" he asked as soon as I sat down, and I was tempted to answer, "Belike, 'tis but a rumor," but I was way too common a man to make Shakespeare references before four in the afternoon.

"I think I might know where he is, but I wanted to see if you'd heard from him at all," I said. "I thought perhaps I could confirm it." I'm also usually way too common to say "perhaps," but some of the snootiness in that room was bound to rub off.

"Indeed." Bender stroked his beard as if it were a pet. "I'm sorry, but I haven't heard from Anthony at all, or I'd have called the police. But I'm intrigued, Mr. Freed." That made him look and sound even more like a Bond villain. "Where do you believe Anthony might be?"

I told him I'd spoken to two of Anthony's friends, and they had each confirmed he was trying to film a low-budget (by Hollywood standards) Western. I asked Bender if he'd read the script, and he said Anthony wouldn't let him see it before it was "perfect," so I gave him a brief summary of what Anthony might have un-ironically called "the plot." I included a few key sequences, and described the settings almost verbatim from Anthony's script.

"And this information leads you to believe . . . what?" he asked, still stroking. A white cat for his lap would have cemented the Ernst Stavro Blofeld image. And, of course, he would have to shave his head.

"Think about it, Professor. Anthony is a film . . . student." ("Geek" seemed a little harsh.) "He's very familiar with past films and the way they were shot. He knows a good deal of film history, as I'm sure you've taught him most of it yourself." (In reality, Bender had probably distracted Anthony with pretense and opinion masquerading as fact, but sometimes you have to blow a little smoke.)

Bender nodded. "Of course. We want our students to have a solid background in the classics. We have separate tracks of study in cinema history, cinema appreciation, cinema criticism . . ."

I interrupted the recruitment pitch. "So given all that, and given that Anthony is dedicated to the idea of cinema tradition" (now he had *me* saying "cinema"), "if he were to try to deconstruct the classic Western, where would you expect a film student to go?"

The light seemed to go on over his head. "Ah. Monument Valley. John Ford's idea of God's movie set."

"Exactly."

"Don't you think, though, that Ford overused the location? After a while, Monument Valley became something of a cliché. Why, even the Warner Brothers animation series with the Road Runner made fun of . . ."

"Professor."

He caught himself. "Of course. My apologies. We were talking about Anthony."

"Yes, we were." I stood up. The cramped office didn't offer much in the way of pacing room, but it did give you a lot to look at: movie scripts (with titles written in marker on the spines) ranging from *The Magnificent Ambersons* to *The Devil Toupee*, which I was hoping was some student's idea of a horror spoof; a dust-encrusted fake Oscar statuette with the words "Prof. Bender" inscribed on it; a 16-mm. projector, DVD recorder, and all-in-one TV/VCR/DVD combo; an autographed picture of Ingmar Bergman (the inscription was in Swedish); a stack of term papers to be graded. It looked like the archives of the Academy of Motion Picture Arts and Sciences had gotten hold of a piece of bad whitefish and thrown up all over this tiny room. "You're Anthony's faculty advisor."

"I am," he agreed. If he were any more solemn, he could have been presiding over a war crimes tribunal.

"In his absence, I could use some advice," I said. "Let's assess the situation: a student accused of a crime that could get him serious jail time, who could be a suspect in a murder, leaves the state before he can be questioned. He suddenly has a lot more money than anyone thought he did. His closest friends and relatives, even his parents, haven't heard from him. Then he calls me—of all people—out of the blue and it appears for all the world that he's making a low-budget Western in Utah. I feel some responsibility for the young man, since I'm his employer, and I've been asking around about his involvement. I promised the local law enforcement that I'd keep them informed on anything I found out, but I'm worried that they might not have Anthony's best interests in mind, and I'll just be handing him over for arrest and an appearance in kangaroo court. On the other hand, if I don't turn him in, I could be making things worse for him, and I'll certainly be making things worse for myself, possibly to the point of an obstruction of justice charge. So I'll leave it to you, Professor: what do you think I should do?"

Bender made quite a show of thinking it over, with his best Arlo-Guthrie-as-Sigmund-Freud manner. I began to worry that his beard might actually dissolve under his fingers.

"I don't think there's any question, Mr. Freed," he said after an eternity or two. "You must turn the boy in."

39

❀❀❀❀❀❀❀

Lisa Ansella Rabinowitz lived in Red Bank, New Jersey, a town that had become the sad-eyed puppy of the Jersey Shore. It was just so *cute.* In New Jersey, we don't go to the beach; we go Down the Shore. And until recently, Down the Shore has meant the kind of carnival ride saltwater taffy mixture of excitement and cheapness that a good coastline experience should be. But now, with real estate values skyrocketing, Down the Shore has become a more aggressively upscale experience, with muffin shops; liquor stores that specialize in fine wines, not cheap beer; and bistros where pizzerias used to be. In short, Down the Shore had gotten to be so enjoyable, it was no longer any fun.

Like in Red Bank.

It had taken me a bus ride to Woodbridge, a train from there, and a ten-minute walk from the train station to arrive at Lisa's door, so I wasn't taken in by all the cuteness. Having fewer friends to drive me places was becoming a serious drag on my scheduling. I could only prevail upon Moe in emergencies, and really long trips.

At the moment, though, Lisa was providing me with an iced coffee in a large glass, and her younger daughter Ashley (*Ashley Rabinowitz?*) was watching me with great curiosity, so it was hard to be too gruff. Not that I wasn't trying.

"When I married Mark, you know, being Jewish and everything, I thought my mother would disown me and kill my husband," Lisa said. "Mama's not at all religious, but I'm afraid she is a little anti-Semitic." Apparently, telling tales about her grandmother wasn't considered too upsetting for Ashley's four-year-old ears. When I was a kid, my mother would shoo me out of the room if there were so much as a slur on my grandmother's matzo ball recipe, so times have apparently changed in the child-rearing arena. "But Vince calmed her down," Lisa went on. "He was the glue that held the family together." She misted up a little, but bit her lip and managed not to sob.

We were sitting at the dining room table in Lisa's very nice, yet not intimidatingly neat home, where everything was freshly painted and toys were left all over the floor. It was an amiable contrast, and it worked. I asked Lisa if she knew of any trouble in Vincent and Amy's marriage, in language I thought was discreet. Ashley stared directly at me and completely ignored anything her mother did. Clearly, I was fascinating.

You may notice that I did not go directly to Sergeant O'Donnell or Chief Dutton to rat out Anthony. That is mostly because, in addition to my own problems with a vanishing backbone, I had decided that Bender was a pompous ass, and therefore I was under no obligation to heed his advice. He already had me using words like "heed." You can't trust a man like that.

"I did get the impression there was something going on in the marriage," Lisa said. "Well . . . hell, I *knew* something was going on. Especially the past few months. Vince just wasn't the same guy, and when I saw him with Amy, he was . . ."

"Angry?" I asked. Ashley's eyes widened and she swiveled to look at her mother. But Lisa smiled and shook her head, and Ashley's attention was immediately back on my face.

"Sad," Lisa said. "Other people probably would have said he was angry, but I knew him better. He was sad. And that was so not Vincent. My brother could be a lot of things, Mr. Freed, and not all of them were wonderful, but he wasn't ever sad, not until those last few months. It worried me to see that."

"Do you think . . ." I hesitated, and put a hand up to indicate confidentiality. Lisa leaned over to hear me as I whispered. "I'm sorry, Lisa, it's none of my business, but some of the questions I have to ask are a little . . . adult. Should we be talking that way in front of your daughter?"

Lisa's face took on a wise, resigned expression. "Ashley is hearing impaired, Mr. Freed," she said. "She can't hear a word we're saying. She can read lips a little, and she can sign, but at the speed we're talking, she's only picking up the tiniest bit of the conversation."

"I'm sorry," I said. "I didn't know."

Lisa shook her head. "No need to be sorry. I'm glad you couldn't tell, because it means her lip-reading is getting better. But if she had spoken when you came in, you would have been able to tell. Don't let it concern you. She's not really listening to you; she's just practicing."

It concerned me a little, but I decided Ashley's mother would know best. "Well, I was going to ask whether you think your brother was having an affair."

I thought Lisa would be shocked, but instead, I got explosive laughter. She made a sound like *HIE!* and rocked back and forth on her chair for a moment. Even Ashley turned abruptly to look at her mother.

"*Vincent?* An *affair?* You've got to be kidding me, Mr. Freed. Vincent absolutely worshipped his wife. He wouldn't even have *considered* something with another woman."

Egotistic idiot that I am, I decided to defend my position. "Well, Amy said the night Vincent . . . the night it happened, they had been fighting, and Vincent told her he was having an affair with a woman in his office."

"And you believed her." It wasn't an accusation; it was a statement of fact. Lisa expected that.

"I had no reason not to," I said. It wasn't much, but it was true.

"Oh, I don't blame you, Mr. Freed. Amy can make a man believe pretty much anything she wants him to. It's chemical, I think. She's the kind of girl who can play a man and make it look like there's no effort involved. Natural. I'll bet she gave you a gift or something, too, right? One of Vince's videos that you really wanted?"

I mumbled, "Yeah, or the whole collection," so softly and with such a lack of lip movement that Ashley put her hand under my chin, pulling up, to get a better view. Lisa asked what I had said, and I admitted to the sale of the collection. Her eyes didn't widen, but she also didn't blink for a good few seconds.

"Wow," she said finally. "She must have really wanted to convince you."

"Convince me of what?" I asked. "Why would she care what I thought?"

Lisa stood up and put her hands on Ashley's shoulders. She drew her daughter's attention, then signed something very quickly. Ashley signed back, but Lisa shook her head "no," and Ashley, with a quick look over her shoulder at me, slunk out of the room.

"I'm sorry," Lisa said, "but I didn't want to risk her understanding any of what we're going to say now. I'm not sure I'll be able to control my language."

I nodded. "I don't understand this. Why would Amy make up a story about Vincent?"

"My sister-in-law is the one who was being unfaithful," Lisa said plainly. "The bitch was having an affair."

"Amy was having an affair? Did Vincent know?"

"How do you think I found out? Vincent told me. She'd admitted it to him. It was driving him crazy."

"How long was it going on? When did your brother tell you this?"

Lisa sat back down. "Oh, man. When was it . . . six

months ago, eight maybe? I think it was last fall, early in the fall. I don't remember exactly."

"So he was walking around with this for eight months?"

"That's what made him sad, Mr. Freed. That's why he was having such a hard time with . . . you know, everything."

"Do you know who she was having the affair with?"

"I don't know. Vincent either didn't know, or he was so . . . embarrassed, he wouldn't tell me. Can you believe that? Embarrassed? Like it was his fault his wife was a lying bitch who could make a man do whatever she wanted. But she couldn't get him to do what she wanted. Not in the end, she couldn't."

"What do you mean?"

Lisa's face was cold, thinking about Amy. "She told him about the affair for a purpose, and it was just to hurt him. That coldhearted . . . well, you know . . . didn't just want to cheat on him—she wanted him to know he wasn't enough for her. But she never told him who she was seeing. And when she saw that he was going to pretend everything was all right and go on living his life, she saw she couldn't hurt him enough. So I think she killed him."

Something occurred to me. "Forgive me, Lisa, but the night Vincent died, he was seen at the movies with another woman. Are you *sure* he couldn't have been cheating on his wife?"

She put down her cup. "Mr. Freed, you never met Vince when he was alive. I'm here to tell you, he was the most devoted husband on this planet. I don't think he was capable of cheating on his wife, even if she deserved it. As long as he had the old comedy movies to hide away in, he'd sooner live a life in hell with her, knowing she was making a fool of him, than do something he considered wrong."

It was going to be a long train-and-bus ride back. But at least the scenery would be cute.

40

ｏＯＤＱＱＤＱｏ

The theatre was about a third full that night, which under the circumstances wasn't bad. It's hard to go wrong with family movies, since there are usually only one or two out at a time, and parents are hungry for something to take their kids to see. It made me wish I'd held the feature over another week, but it was too late for that now.

Maybe I hadn't been paying enough attention to my business lately.

It was Thursday night, and the last evening for these two films. I loved *Help!* almost as much as *A Hard Day's Night*, but six viewings in six days was getting to be enough, especially since *Rubber Soul* had better songs. And the family movie *Too Many Kids*, with its predictable waiting-for-the-bathroom jokes and budding teen romances, had worn out its welcome for me somewhere around the middle of the second screening. People were bringing their children, though, and we do appreciate that in the theatre business. Adults don't buy nearly as much Buncha Crunch.

I'd had to thread up the projector myself, leading me to

believe that I had in some way offended the Projector Elves.

Where I'd felt only a few days ago that I knew nothing about either the situation with the pirated DVDs or Ansella's murder, now it seemed like information was bombarding me from all sides, and none of it was adding up. I knew where Anthony was, but not what to do about it. I knew that someone had been trying to make it seem that Anthony was still nearby, but who, why, and how were all unanswered questions. I knew that one, if not both, of the Ansellas was believed to be having an affair. And I knew that Vincent Ansella had excellent taste in comedy videos, but was still, unfortunately, dead.

I also knew calling Dutton and telling him my suspicions about Anthony's location (I didn't trust O'Donnell enough to impart the information to him) was the right thing to do, but it didn't help much. After I got off the phone with the chief, I knew I wouldn't be able to look at myself in the mirror. Lucky for me, I'd already shaved today.

Finally, I knew I had a sinus headache that would kill a normal man, and there's never been a medication on this planet that reduces the pressure, no matter what the ads on TV say.

Leo was in his usual seat, near the center of the theatre, and would no doubt leave after *Help!*, a film he saw as only marginally a comedy. "Are you getting a *real* comedy for tomorrow?" he'd asked on his way in tonight.

"Yes, Leo, I promise," I'd told him. "No rock and roll at all."

"Better not be," he'd answered. "You don't want to drive away my business."

"Yeah. You could go to one of the *other* all-comedy theatres in this area." Leo had given me a look that indicated I might want to switch to decaf, and started to take his business inside the auditorium. I'd stopped him.

"I'm sorry, Leo," I'd told him. "It's been a rough few weeks."

"You don't know rough," he'd answered with great compassion. "This one time in Bulgaria, we almost had to throw our cargo overboard to right the boat. We were in a storm that had come out of nowhere . . ." I'd stopped paying attention, and had made a mental note never to apologize to Leo again.

Instead, I'd reached into my pocket and pulled out a photograph of Christie Dunbar that I'd printed out from her website. I passed it to Leo, who'd looked at it, then looked back at me.

"So?"

"*So*, is that the woman you saw with Vincent Ansella the night he died?"

Leo's eyes had practically crossed. "Are you kidding?" he'd asked. "I told you that was the ugliest woman I've ever seen. This one's a *babe!*" He wouldn't leave until I agreed to let him keep the picture. I don't like to think about what he wanted to do with it.

If the truth shall set you free, innuendos, assumptions, and apologies will give you a sinus headache.

The rest of the audience was comprised of parents and children. None of the glittering hoi polloi who had graced the old barn on the night of our "reopening" had become regular customers, and on a Thursday night, you were lucky to get drop-ins. The weekend is where you make your money.

I had just done a reel change and was walking downstairs to the lobby, replacing the velvet rope to indicate the balcony was closed. Sophie looked more bored than usual, since not much ticket or snack business was being done an hour and ten minutes into our first film. Maybe a straggler or two would come in just to see *Too Many Kids*, but it was a little early for them, anyway. The movie was advertised for almost an hour from now.

When I was foolish enough to enter her orbit, Sophie looked at me, cracked some gum in her mouth (I've talked to her about that), and said, "When are we going to get a *real* movie here?"

"These looked real enough when I threaded them up," I said.

"This is just Hollywood's attempt to keep us all quiet

and happy," she moaned. "It's not a depiction of the *real* human condition, like *Final Destination*."

"Cheer up, Sophie. I promise to get more death movies for you."

Her eyes widened. "Really?"

"Yeah. For Halloween, I'm getting *Abbott and Costello Meet Frankenstein*."

Sophie scowled at me and cracked her gum again. I walked away, making a mental note to book *Beetlejuice* just for her. I'm such a soft touch.

I'd have to decide, based on the weather and how tired I was, whether to change the marquee tonight or come in early tomorrow to do it. It's not hard work, but it takes time, and you have to stand on a ladder, which I prefer to avoid whenever possible. I'd probably end up leaving it until the sun was out.

Sergeant O'Donnell opened the front door and walked in, surveying the place as if it was his name on the deed. And tonight, for fifty dollars and a ride to the airport, I'd have been happy to turn it over to him. The fight was knocked out of me.

It was worse when I saw that he'd brought Leslie with him. We didn't look at each other as she followed him in.

He walked right past me and made a beeline for Sophie, who didn't seem to recognize him (she'd spent most of the night Ansella died and the following day staring at her shoes, possibly in the belief that they held the secret to the *real* human condition) and was reaching for the roll of tickets under the counter. O'Donnell waved his hand to get her to stop, and I moved toward Sophie. As her employer and a really nosy person, I felt I had every right to listen in on the conversation. Besides, it would get me to the other side of Leslie, where we wouldn't have to make eye contact. It's hard being a grown-up. Or so I'm told.

"Miss Beringer, I want to know what you know about Anthony Pagliarulo," O'Donnell was saying as I approached. Sophie looked up to meet his eyes, but hers were not comprehending.

"You don't want a ticket?" she asked.

"No, I don't want a ticket!"

I nudged my way into the conversation with my trade-mark grace and tact. "Back off, O'Donnell," I said. "She didn't recognize you, okay? And keep your voice down. I've got a full house in there." In my world, "full" was a relative term. I was showing off. I'm not sure for whom.

"She's not cooperating, and I'm tired of getting jerked around." O'Donnell seemed to be taking the argument to me now, and Sophie, staring as if it were happening on a television screen in front of her, seemed less interested than simply transfixed, watching something really awful, but being unable to change the channel.

Leslie started to say, "Why don't we take this out—" O'Donnell cut her off with a look that said "I'm in charge." She stopped talking, and the angry look I would have expected on her face never materialized. This was more one of resignation.

"What makes you think Sophie knows anything about Anthony?" I asked him. It seemed a little late in the game for him to be going all bad cop on us out of the blue.

"Her cell phone records," he said. "Miss Beringer here has been getting calls from Anthony Pagliarulo's apartment at least once a day since he supposedly disappeared."

Well, that didn't make a lick of sense. I knew Anthony was in Utah, but I couldn't tell O'Donnell that. If Dutton hadn't made the information available to the county, *I* certainly wasn't going to be the one to do it.

"Sophie?"

She looked up, startled, as if the TV had begun to address her directly. Sophie looked at me, but didn't say anything.

"Have you heard from Anthony?" I asked.

"You mean, like, today?" Wow. Those iPod ear things must really do something awful to a person's brain. I'm usually a big fan of Apple products, but there was definitely some erosion going on, and I rarely saw Sophie without those buds hanging out of her ears.

"No. I mean, like, since he left." Now she had me talking

like that. "Since we saw him sleeping in the theatre the day after Mr. Ansella died."

"Mr. who?" Maybe she was playing dumb. Yeah, that was it. And she was doing a really professional job.

"Mr. Ansella," O'Donnell seethed. "The guy who croaked in your theatre a few weeks ago."

"Oh. Yeah." Sophie took on a sad expression, thinking she was supposed to be sorry Ansella was dead. We all stood there, looking at each other. Finally, O'Donnell couldn't stand it anymore.

"So?"

"So, what?" Honestly, Lisa Kudrow at the top of her game couldn't play clueless this well.

"Sophie," I said in my best fatherly tone, *"Sergeant* O'Donnell here, the *county investigator*, says you've been getting phone calls on your cell from the phone in Anthony's apartment."

"Oh. Yeah." And what was your question?

"So, you have?"

"Uh-huh. I'm dating one of his roommates. But don't tell my folks, okay? They don't like me going out with college guys." So *that* was it! That was what she and Anthony had been discussing the night he vanished. Sophie looked from me to O'Donnell, worried only that her parents would be upset with her.

O'Donnell looked suspicious, and frankly, given Sophie's performance, I couldn't blame him. "You're dating one of Pagliarulo's roommates?" he reiterated.

"Yeah. This guy Danton? Although I'm not sure if that's his first name or his last. We never talked about it."

I turned toward O'Donnell. "He does have a roommate named Danton," I said. "I talked to him a couple of weeks ago. Nice enough kid."

"Yeah," Sophie said. "He has a Harley. Anthony made him come here to watch the movies a few times," she continued. "I gave him free popcorn, and he asked me out."

"I talked to Danton," Leslie said. "Didn't seem to know anything."

I gave Sophie a glare. "You gave him *free popcorn?*"

Sergeant O'Donnell's eyes might have been rotating in their sockets. "Miss Beringer," he said, "I think we're going to have to go somewhere where I can question you a little more privately."

"I don't think my folks would like that," she said.

"I can't say I'm crazy about it, either," I told O'Donnell honestly. "Plus, she's a minor, so you can't do a thing without her parents' consent, can you?"

"If you don't want an obstruction charge hanging over your head, Freed, you're going to stay out of the way. This is a criminal investigation, and I'm the investigator in charge. Don't worry, there will be a female officer present every step of the way."

Something clicked in my head. "Officer Levant?" I asked. Could *O'Donnell* be involved? Nah. That was too stupid.

Leslie, in fact, looked like she'd rather be anywhere than in a car with Sophie and O'Donnell discussing Anthony's whereabouts. She looked like she was trying to disappear, and doing a very bad job of it.

"I can't go," Sophie said. I think she was trying to fight off tears, as the reality of the situation was starting to set in. "Who'll sell the popcorn?" Well, reality means different things to different people.

O'Donnell responded by trying to take Sophie's arm, and she pulled away. "Don't worry about the popcorn, honey," he said. "Mr. Freed can handle it."

"Elliot . . ." she pleaded.

"O'Donnell, I'm not letting this girl out of my sight until you get in touch with her parents. Frankly, I think it's a little weird that you have to bring her in all of a sudden." I didn't really think O'Donnell was a child molester, but I needed something to stall with.

"What do you think, Freed? That I'm a danger to this girl?" He was genuinely offended.

"I'll be there the whole time, Elliot," Leslie said, but her voice betrayed her lack of enthusiasm. She coughed. "Mr. Freed."

"I don't know what to think," I told O'Donnell. "You

stomp in here in the middle of a showing, after weeks of investigation, and the only thing you can think to do is drag Sophie out of here? You're really grasping at straws, O'Donnell."

He looked like he was about to remind me of his rank, then settled for, "She's been getting calls from Pagliarulo's apartment."

"And she explained that. Go talk to Danton if you want to check the story out."

O'Donnell's face was red. "I don't need to justify my methods to you, Freed. This girl is a lead to Anthony Pagliarulo. The only way I'm walking out of here without her is if you produce Anthony Pagliarulo *right now*."

By the Ritz Brothers and all that is holy, I swear that is the exact moment the front door opened and Anthony walked in.

The four of us—O'Donnell, Leslie, Sophie, and me—stood there absolutely immobile, mouths open, staring straight ahead at him.

Anthony strode in with a sense of purpose I'd never seen in him before, and an expression on his face I honestly can't say I could remember seeing since I'd met him.

Anger.

"What did you do?" he shouted at me. "What did you *do*?"

I wasn't sure what I had done, so I didn't answer. Anthony walked straight past O'Donnell without giving him a glance, and got so close to me I could tell what he'd had for dinner. Airline food: could have been a corn muffin or chicken dinner; it all smells the same.

"What did you do?"

"Anthony," I croaked when speech became possible. "What are you doing here?"

"Mr. Freed! I talk to you for two minutes and my funding gets pulled! We had two more days left to shoot! Steve Buscemi's big scene was coming up! *What did you do?*"

"Anthony," I said as calmly as possible. "Do you see who's here?" I gestured with my eyes toward O'Donnell, but Anthony wasn't buying.

"Hello, Sophie," he said, icicles forming on his voice. "Now tell me, Mr. Freed. What . . ."

"Remain silent!" Leslie shouted suddenly, as if calling for one of the Miranda warning's greatest hits. I stared at her for a moment.

"Anthony Pagliarulo, you are wanted for questioning in association with violations of copyright laws," O'Donnell said. He produced handcuffs from somewhere under his coat, and grabbed Anthony's right wrist. It was only at that point that Anthony realized there was another person present in the lobby.

"Wait a minute!" I yelled at him. "Chief Dutton said he wouldn't be arrested!"

"Chief Dutton isn't in charge of this investigation," O'Donnell said, "and Mr. Pagliarulo is *not* being arrested. I'm taking him in for questioning."

"Then what are the bracelets for?" I asked, but O'Donnell ignored me and started to read Anthony his rights.

As Anthony was cuffed and Sophie began to cry, O'Donnell continued to recite the Miranda warnings to his prisoner, and eventually, to lead him out the front door. Leslie Levant followed placidly, looking like she was being taken to the principal's office. I saw a few people walk out of the auditorium, stop dead in their tracks, and stare as the young man was more or less dragged from the lobby. This would probably send tomorrow's box office skyrocketing. Two movies *and* live theatre!

And all the way out, Anthony's gaze never left my face. At least four other times as he was being moved out of the lobby, he said to me, with ever-increasing volume, *"What did you do?"* Finally, the front door closed, and all I could hear was Sophie sobbing.

It was a damned good question. What *did* I do?

41

◌♡◌♡◌♡◌

Tragedy is if I cut my finger.
Comedy is if you fall into an open sewer and die.
—Mel Brooks

Some Like It Hot (1959)
and What a Drag! (today)

I no longer lived in a world that made sense, and for a guy like me, that can be a problem. I tried to sort out everything that was going on, but it still ended up a jumble, and I continued to be powerless and frustrated. I hate that.

First, I had to call Michael Pagliarulo and give him the good news/bad news treatment: your son is home and safe but, oh yeah, did I mention he's under arrest? Just what every dad wants to hear. Would Anthony have thought to call? You only get one phone call—Anthony's would probably be to his film editor.

Then, I managed to get Sophie back into some semblance of usefulness (although the running black eye makeup made her look a little like a slim, timid Alice Cooper), and get through the final showing of *Too Many Kids*, which was a blessing in that it *was* the final showing of *Too Many Kids*.

I rode home that night. I know I did, because I woke up in my own bed in my town house the next day. I don't remember a thing about the ride, nor going to bed, nor anything else I did after leaving Comedy Tonight. It was a blur of confused thoughts. Confused thoughts are rarely clear and sharp, you know.

The next morning, I honestly couldn't think of anything to do. I tried to call Carla, because I knew she was worried, but her phone wasn't answered. She'd probably completed her exams and gone home.

I even tried calling Marcy Resnick, because I couldn't call Sharon and wouldn't call Leslie, but Marcy wasn't taking my phone calls these days, either. Some guys have a knack with women. Next time I meet one, I'll ask him for advice.

It occurred to me then that I didn't know if Anthony was still in custody, so I called Dutton in Midland Heights, but he was out of his office, so I left a voice mail. There was no point in calling O'Donnell. Even if he was in his office, he probably wouldn't have talked to me. I had been right—since she was only sixteen, O'Donnell couldn't question Sophie without her parents' consent. (He was probably just trying to scare her.) But Anthony, three years older, was an adult in the eyes of the law.

A really repetitive, thought-free task was just what I needed to clear my head. So I went into the living room and continued checking Vincent Ansella's vast comedy collection against the list Amy had given me. I spent three hours that way, and made some progress, but not a tremendous amount. Mostly, sitting on the floor, I succeeded in getting my legs to fall asleep. Ansella had been incredibly thorough, and had apparently spent all his retirement money on DVDs. Just as well.

Since I still had no shelves, but acres of floor space, I began organizing the discs in one area and the tapes in another. When I eventually got shelves, the two formats might not fit in the same space anyway, so it made sense to separate them now. Once I separated them, I could begin organizing by groups and classifications: all Bob Hopes in one section, all Red Skeltons in another, Cary Grants cross-referenced by Katharine Hepburn, who also had to be paired with Spencer Tracy. It became more elaborate as time went on, but it was a system that eventually would make sense to me, since I had invented it.

Each time I took a title out of the box, I crossed it off the list. And each time I started a classification by artist or series (the Pink Panthers were missing, but Blake Edwards was otherwise well represented, and I had *A Shot in the Dark* in my own collection, anyway), I would search for others that would be compatible, to complete the series and make sure all the titles were there. The Monty Pythons alone—both film and television work was represented—took the better part of an hour.

But all the while, I was concentrating on the murder and the film piracy. I couldn't let go of them, and I couldn't solve anything, either. Every answer led to another question, and each question simply turned in a circle and led to nothing.

"What did you do?"

Okay, let's start with that. What did Anthony mean by that question? Clearly, he thought that something I'd done had led to his source of funding being cut off, shutting down production of his dream project. Why would he think it was my fault? Because it had happened soon after he made his one mistake: reaching out to me on the phone.

So. Did that make sense? Could my talking to him have led to the end of his film? I couldn't know why his funding was cut off unless I knew the source of the money. Where had Anthony gotten two hundred thousand dollars to make *Killin' Time*?

Maybe I was approaching this from the wrong end. If contact with me *did* cause the money to dry up, what did that tell me about the source of the funding? Did it tell me *anything*? How could the people (or person) with the money know Anthony had spoken to me? Was my phone tapped?

His Girl Friday (1940) DVD, Cary Grant, Rosalind Russell, Dir: Howard Hawks, Scr: Charles Lederer.

I filed the disc away (cross-referenced with *The Front Page* (1931 and 1974), but not with its latest incarnation, *Switching Channels* (1988)—aside from a dozen or so exceptions, Ansella had not been a huge collector of post-1985 comedy—and considered. Maybe my suspicion of Leslie Levant was unwarranted, and I was a bad person. If I was to assume that the rescinding of Anthony's funding was a result of his phone call to me, and that the person/people responsible for his money were behind the pirated DVDs— which seemed logical, as that amount of money could have easily been generated through the stash I'd seen in the basement of Comedy Tonight—then did the mysterious threading of the projector have anything to do with the pirated movies?

It was, as Zero Mostel had often noted, a problem that "would cross a rabbi's eyes." And then he would chant some strange syllables that were meant to indicate he was an observant Jew. But what did Zero Mostel have to do with the popcorn box recently impaled on my kitchen counter, you might ask?

Good question.

The Frisco Kid (1979), DVD, Gene Wilder, Harrison Ford, Dir: Robert Aldrich, Scr: Michael Elias, Frank Shaw.

Now, here was a dilemma. Where do you put a movie about a Polish rabbi in 1850 going cross-country to get to San Francisco in the company of a bank robber? It's Gene Wilder, so it might go with *The World's Greatest Lover* and *The Adventure of Sherlock Holmes' Smarter Brother*, but some Gene Wilder is cross-referenced with Mel Brooks, as in *The Producers*, *Blazing Saddles*, and . . .

And . . .

I checked the box, and, incredulous, referenced the list Amy Ansella had handed me. Vincent had categorized the films much in the same way I was doing (which was eerie in itself), but his list seemed to be incomplete. Because he'd shelved the videos in the categories he'd listed, and Amy had simply taken them off the shelves and put them in boxes, the cartons I was unpacking generally had a theme to them; some link between the films that made it logical to display them together. It was still necessary, though, to check each title off the list and look for doubles, and, in some cases, Vincent's filing system and mine didn't mesh.

That was true of this box. In it were Gene Wilder films, from *Willy Wonka & the Chocolate Factory* to *Haunted Honeymoon* (and even some appearances on *Will & Grace*) coupled (inevitably) with Mel Brooks movies. Once again, Vincent was the ultimate completist: he had everything in Mel's canon, from appearances on *The Muppet Show* to *The Critic*, an animated short film that won Brooks his first Academy Award. There were the classics, and the duds, both *Life Stinks* and *The Twelve Chairs*. There was the remake of *To Be or Not to Be*, which probably drove Ansella insane when he tried to cross-reference Mel Brooks with Jack Benny *and* Ernst Lubitsch.

But that wasn't what bothered me. Ansella *should* have all those titles. It was the sort of thing that had made me salivate over the collection to begin with. But the weird part was that the collection *wasn't* complete, and it wasn't complete because it omitted a film that even the most casual fan would have.

Vincent Ansella's comedy collection didn't include *Young Frankenstein*. His favorite movie.

And suddenly, everything made sense.

But, of course, that's when the phone rang. I stood slowly, having been on my haunches for a while, and still stunned by what I'd discovered. So the phone rang a number of times (I turn off the machine when I'm home) before I answered.

"Were you in another area code?" Chief Barry Dutton asked.

"Sorry. I was . . . something odd . . ."

"You've been something odd since I met you," he said, but then his voice became more serious. "I just wanted you to know, Elliot, that something's happened."

I shook myself awake. "Something with Anthony? Chief, is he okay?"

"It's not something with Anthony," Dutton said. "He was sent home last night. O'Donnell hasn't charged him yet. But that could change. It's something else."

I waited. "What?"

"Amy Ansella just shot Joe Dunbar in his garage."

I was so stunned, I didn't ask what part of the body a 'garage' was. I hesitated. "Is he . . ."

"No," Dutton answered before I could finish the question. "He's alive. His wife hit Amy over the head with a vase just as she fired. It grazed Dunbar in the neck, but he'll be okay."

"Which hospital?"

"I don't think I want to tell you."

"Chief, if he can talk, or even communicate, he can confirm a lot of stuff."

"Yes. To *us*. You are not a law enforcement officer. Stay home. I'll call you from the hospital." Dutton had called me, hadn't he? Wasn't that like asking me to show up?

"I need to see him, Chief."

"Not yet." Dutton sounded stern. "The man's been through enough for one day, Elliot. Let him recuperate."

"You don't understand, Chief. I think I've got this thing figured out."

"How's that?" He sounded amazed. I inspire that kind of confidence.

"I promise I'll tell you when I see you. *Now* can I come to the hospital?"

42

I still couldn't call Sharon for a ride, although that routine was starting to get old, and while it was possible to ride the bike to John F. Kennedy Hospital in Edison, it would take time. I didn't want to use up a lot of time.

Moe, however, was not as forthcoming as usual. "I just don't have a loaner for you today, Elliot," he told me before I could even get the question out of my mouth. "Nothing I've got in the shop runs, and the body work isn't done yet, so I can't give you those to test-drive. Take a bus."

"I don't have time for a bus, Moe. Come on, there's got to be something."

"There isn't. Maybe this is a lesson for you." If Moe was the type to chew on unlit cigars, the picture would have been perfect, but in fact, he's a germophobe and a recovering nicotine addict. You can't always figure people. "If you had your own car, you wouldn't run into this kind of problem."

"Impersonating my ex-wife won't do it for you, Moe. Frankly, you don't have the legs for it." I looked around the lot, hoping there was a vehicle of some sort that I could talk him into loaning me. "How about the Nissan?" I pointed.

Moe shook his head. "Transmission."

"So it slips a little."

"It doesn't have one."

"Oh."

I couldn't see the entire lot from where we were standing, so I moved out into the center of the lot, and Moe followed reluctantly. I watched his eyes carefully. Sooner or later, he would slip. There was something he didn't want me to notice, and if I waited long enough, he would sneak a guilty glance in its direction.

Aha!

It was a silver Lexus with an obvious dent in its passenger side rear fender. A long scrape that looked like it had come in contact with a road divider, or . . .

Hey, wait a minute!

"Moe," I said, trying to control my breathing. "When did that Lexus with the dent come in?"

"Oh no, Elliot, forget it. You're not getting the Lexus."

I spoke slowly. "Answer the question. When was it brought in?"

He thought. "Yesterday, I think. The owner actually wanted me to give him a loaner, can you imagine? What am I, a Lexus dealer?"

"Yeah, imagine. You wouldn't happen to have the owner's name, would you?"

I think the look in my eye might have spooked Moe a little. "Not to give to you, Elliot. No chance."

"It's important, Moe." I'd have shown him the stitches in my leg, but only as a last resort. Even *I* didn't want to look at them.

It took another ten minutes of convincing, and I did actually pull up my pants leg to show the scar to Moe, which is what put him over the top. Moe would do anything to avoid having to look at my leg.

"Let's check the work order," he said, and we walked to the office. Moe checked the order number against the number on the key hanging on a hook over his desk, and pulled out the paperwork on the Lexus. He handed me the work order, which had the owner's name and address printed very neatly on top, in Moe's own hand.

"Can I use your phone?" I asked him.

"You don't have a cell phone, either?" Moe rolled his eyes to the ceiling.

"Do you know what those things do to your brain?"

"*Man*, you're cheap." He pointed to the phone. "Out of the area, you call collect."

"Oh, and under the circumstances, I think the owner of the Lexus owes me a ride, don't you?" He grumbled, but threw me the key.

"Gas it up," he said, and walked out.

I picked up the phone and called Sharon.

43

٥Ô٥Ô₿٥Ô

By the time I drove the Lexus up to JFK, O'Donnell and
Dutton were already in Joe Dunbar's hospital room. On my
way into the room, I saw Christie Dunbar in the hallway,
sitting between two uniformed officers on orange plastic
molded chairs. She looked up at me, gestured vaguely with
her hands, opened her mouth, and didn't say anything. I
took her hand for a moment, closed my eyes, and then let it
go. I couldn't say anything, either.

Dunbar, with an IV in his left hand, didn't look all that
bad for a guy in the hospital. The left side of his neck was
bandaged, and there was a bandage on the right side of
his head, where he must have hit the concrete garage floor.
His eyes were a little unfocused, but he was awake, and holding a little whiteboard and a marker in his hands. I assumed
that meant he was having trouble speaking.

The cops looked up when I came in.

"Mr. Dunbar has been telling us quite a story, as well as
he can," Dutton said. "But I forgot: you have it all figured
out, don't you?"

"I think I do," I said. "Can I test my theory against what Joe told you?"

I looked at Dunbar, whose eyes were at half-staff. He nodded, sort of.

"We're not here to play games," O'Donnell said.

"No, but I'll bet Dunbar can't talk all that well, and doing too much writing is going to tire him. He can nod to confirm what I say if I'm right."

"Go ahead," O'Donnell grumped. "Let's see how smart you are."

I walked to Dunbar's bedside and made eye contact. He perked up a little, at least opening his eyes all the way.

"You understand what we're doing, Joe?" I asked. Dunbar nodded. "You call me off if I'm wrong." Another nod.

I looked over at Dutton and tried not to smirk. "Amy Ansella was having an affair, wasn't she, Joe?" Dunbar nodded. "With you, wasn't it?"

Dunbar shook his head, no.

I stopped myself before asking, "Are you sure?" I could be relatively certain Dunbar knew whether he was sleeping with Amy Ansella. I tried not to look directly at O'Donnell and Dutton. "Then, who?"

Dunbar's mouth tightened, and for a moment, I thought he was going to cry. He looked at the whiteboard in his hand, but then gestured me over and whispered, "Marcy."

"*Marcy Resnick?* Amy was having an affair with the woman from her husband's office?"

Dunbar nodded.

I was reeling. "But you said you didn't know Marcy," I told him. *See? You're wrong!* Dunbar made a face that said, *I was* lying, *genius.* Then he went back to looking sad.

"Maybe you don't know the whole story, do you, Freed?" O'Donnell said.

I regained my composure. I had to prove myself, and I *did* know what I knew. I was pretty sure my theory would still hold up. I began again, more slowly, piecing in this new information as I went along.

"All right. Amy and Marcy met through company functions—or maybe after Marcy and Vincent became friends at work—and at some point, they began an affair. Amy and Marcy were together at Comedy Tonight the night Vincent was killed. Right, Joe?"

Dunbar nodded. He seemed a little more awake now.

"Vincent had known about the affair for months, or at least, he'd known his wife was cheating on him. His sister says he told her, and the change in his mood would be explained that way," I continued.

I looked at Dunbar. A tear was forming in his right eye.

"The thought of it was dragging him down. He confided in you. He would do that. You had to carry this around for a while, didn't you?" Again, a nod from Joe Dunbar. "And right after your wife had gone through a bout with cancer. It must have been awful. Seeing your best friend destroyed by something like that. He'd loved Amy so much. And you couldn't do anything. You felt bad that you couldn't help."

Dunbar hung his head. I was on the money so far. "And then something happened that you're blaming yourself for, but it's not your fault, Joe."

He looked up, wondering if I knew what had actually happened.

"You told him who Amy was cheating on him with, right?"

Dunbar nodded.

"How did you know?" I asked him, genuinely curious.

Dunbar took a moment and scrawled on the board, "Saw them together."

"So, you didn't know they were lovers; you just mentioned to Ansella that you'd seen his wife with his friend from work," Dutton said, piecing the puzzle together, filling in holes I hadn't. Dunbar nodded again and bit his upper lip.

It took him a long time to write on his whiteboard: "Vince mentioned to Amy in passing that I'd seen her and Marcy together. She went off, confessed everything. Like she'd been waiting to tell him." Dunbar showed us the board, then put his head down. It shook a bit.

"That set off the chain of events," I told Dutton and O'Donnell. "With the knowledge that his wife was having an affair with Marcy Resnick, Vincent confronted Amy, and they had the argument the neighbors heard the night he died."

Dunbar started scribbling again, and held up the board. "More," he had written.

This time, I nodded. "You guys already had a plan for Vince to get even with Amy, didn't you? You were going to make sure Amy saw Vincent cheating on her, too."

Dunbar wrote, "Before we knew it was Marcy."

"The timing was just a coincidence?" I asked, and Dunbar nodded. "So Amy was supposed to come to Comedy Tonight with Vincent that night?" But Dunbar shook his head, no.

He wrote, "In the car."

I got it, then. "Amy saw him getting picked up for the movies, and she saw who was picking him up, right, Joe?"

Dunbar nodded, and a tear crested over his cheek.

"So?" O'Donnell asked. "Who was it? Who was Ansella's mistress?"

Dunbar smiled a little and pointed to himself.

"In drag. The ugliest woman Leo had ever seen," I reminded Dutton. "And Leo is a veteran of the merchant marine."

"It was you?" Dutton said to Joe, who nodded agreement. "Why?"

"Vincent wouldn't ever cheat on his wife, no matter what," I answered. "But he wanted Amy to *think* he could, so he and Joe cooked up what was, for them, a logical scheme. Joe's wife, Christie, who used to be a beautician before her cancer, probably helped. She made Joe up as a woman, gave him one of her chemotherapy wigs, and probably had a good laugh when he went out the door."

Dunbar nodded and dropped his head again. He blamed himself.

"Do you know if that's when Vincent stole your last bottle of clonidine?" I asked Dunbar.

His eyes widened, and now he bit both lips. He shrugged; he didn't know.

"But you did discover it missing later?" I asked.

Dunbar nodded. He wrote: "My fault."

I shook my head. "No," I said. "Amy called you 'murderer,' but you aren't really a murderer, Joe."

Dunbar's eyes began to tear, and he nodded his head: *Yes, I am.*

"No, you're not. You inadvertently provided the means, but Vincent Ansella killed himself."

Dutton's head turned sharply, and he watched Dunbar for a reaction. Dunbar's eyes were still tearing, but they widened a bit. And he shook his head up and down, *yes.*

"Wait a second. Ansella poisoned his *own* popcorn?" O'Donnell said. "Why in god's name would he do that?"

"Because the world wasn't funny for him anymore," I said. "It was that important to him."

Dunbar's jaw dropped open. I was right.

"Vincent found out Amy was being unfaithful to him, even before he knew with whom." I turned to Dunbar. "He loved Amy, and tried to ignore it, but it went on for months, and it wore him down. But the real blow was when the movies, the classic comedies, the thing that always provided relief for him no matter what his problems were, stopped helping."

"What were you, his psychiatrist?" O'Donnell wanted to know. "How do you know what he was thinking?"

"Because I have his video collection, and I understand the way his mind worked," I answered. "He and I had similar tastes, and we catalogued the same way."

"Catalogued?" Dutton asked. "You're basing this on how Ansella listed his videos?"

"No, not exactly. But he had the most complete, comprehensive classic comedy collection I've ever seen."

"Nice alliteration," Dutton said.

"Thanks. I was working on that the whole way here. Anyway, Ansella had more comedy videos than anyone I've ever known, or known about. And I have some connections in the area, remember."

"So what's that got to do with suicide?" asked O'Donnell.

"I've been organizing the collection since Amy sold it to me," I explained. "And it's magnificent. But there's no copy of *Young Frankenstein.*"

They waited. For quite a long moment.

"That's *it*?" They both seemed to ask at once.

"That's enough," I said. "See, *Young Frankenstein* was Vincent Ansella's favorite movie. It was the one thing that was always guaranteed to pull him out of the doldrums, and there is no way—*no way*—that he'd ever consent to live without owning it. Unless he didn't think it was funny anymore. Unless he knew he wasn't going to be living much longer."

I looked at Dunbar. He scribbled on the whiteboard, and held it out for me to see: "That's why you're theater." I overlooked his spelling and handed him back the board. He wiped it off with a paper towel.

"Yes, I understand now," I told him. "See, Amy's affair was draining Vincent of his humor. People who worked with him, even his own sister, said that during the last months of his life, he wasn't the same man. He was humorless, he no longer found anything funny, and he seemed not to care about anything."

There wasn't a sound in the room now, as they were all paying attention to what I said. "When he didn't have comedy to lean on anymore, Vincent didn't have any internal support system left. He had you, and his sister, but I'm sorry, Joe. He needed something else." Dunbar was crying openly now.

"He started selling off his video collection, just a little bit. Especially the titles that had once meant the most to him. I checked. It was like they caused him the most pain now. As it stands, his collection has no *A Night at the Opera*, no *Sleeper*, no *Hail the Conquering Hero*. Some of the Laurel and Hardy shorts are gone. There's no Lucille Ball."

"Oh, come on," said O'Donnell. "You're going to base a suicide on holes in the guy's video collection? Suppose he never owned those movies. Suppose he just didn't like them."

"There were spaces for them on his inventory list, which he kept dutifully literally until the day he died. And he'd deleted them. You can see it; he listed them alphabetically and by year of release," I told him. Then I looked at Dunbar. "Did he own them, Joe?" Dunbar nodded. "Did he sell them off, at the end?" Yes, again. "I checked on eBay, and there are still a few items listed under the name VincAns. Things that didn't sell in time, I guess."

"I hate to say it, but you might be right," O'Donnell said. "He had one outlet, and that didn't work for him. He had access to the pills, and the fact is, Vincent Ansella was the only one who had a reason to want Vincent Ansella dead. Makes sense, Freed."

"Please, no autographs," I said.

Dunbar closed his eyes and lay back on his pillows, and we left the room quietly.

Chief Dutton approached the cop guarding the door. He tilted his head toward the room and said, "He's on suicide watch. Get in there and make sure nothing happens." The cop was inside before Dutton's voice stopped echoing, and he hadn't been speaking very loudly. O'Donnell and Dutton moved to a corner to confer.

I walked over to Christie Dunbar. "I'm sorry," I told her quietly. "You told me you were out the night Vincent died, and I thought you were covering for yourself. You were covering for Joe."

She nodded. "But I didn't know it would come to this."

"You were very brave," I told her. "Saving your husband's life when Amy tried to shoot him."

Christie curled her lip. "Brave?" she said. "I've wanted to hit her for years, and then I pick up a vase from that stupid yard sale and clock her with it. After all this time, I'm sorry."

"Sorry you hit Amy?" I asked.

"Sorry I didn't hit her with Joe's bowling ball, instead," Christie answered.

I nodded, took her hand, and let it go. Dutton, O'Donnell, and I headed out of the hospital. None of us said a word until we hit the parking lot. And it was O'Donnell who finally broke the silence.

"I can't believe you got all this from a few movies missing from the guy's collection," O'Donnell said.

.

"Well, I saw the wig at Dunbar's house, and he'd said that he was on clonidine six months ago. I just didn't put it all together until then. It really didn't matter who Amy was sleeping with; it just drove Vincent crazy he wasn't enough for her."

We stood there for a few minutes. I don't think any of us knew what to do next, and we talked about politics and sports (because we were men, and that's what men do) for fifteen minutes, before I said I had to get back to the theatre. I didn't really, but it sounded like a decent excuse.

"I forgot to tell you about the interview with your projectionist last night," O'Donnell said. "He admits to being an accessory to the piracy thing, but the kid is so oblivious, I don't think he even understood how serious it was."

"You plan on charging him?" Dutton asked.

O'Donnell shook his head. "His dad got him a lawyer, and the lawyer got him a deal. Immunity for his testimony. He did stuff wrong, but he's no criminal. He's just a young bozo."

"He's a young filmmaker," I corrected him. "They have tunnel vision; they don't see anything but the prize, and the prize is a finished movie."

"Yeah," O'Donnell said. "For a stake in his epic tale of adventure, this movie he thinks he's making, he let them use your theatre for a storage space. But it got screwed up when Vincent Ansella decided to sprinkle a little something extra on his popcorn, and all of a sudden there were cops everywhere and no time to get rid of all the discs without anybody seeing. As soon as the chief here got the autopsy report that night, he had cops watching your theatre, Freed. The video pirates couldn't get in to get their stock, and they were worried the projectionist would talk. So all of a sudden, the money got a lot better."

"Because now it was hush money. Do you think Anthony understood that?" I asked.

O'Donnell shook his head in wonder. "The kid fell asleep in the theatre, woke up when we were in the basement, didn't know where we were, assumed we were gone, and left through one of the fire doors. It wasn't until later, when he got a call from the real pirate, that he left town, and that was just because he was told that he had his money, and he had to start assembling a crew and shooting *now*. But it was contingent on his not telling *anybody*, not even his folks. He had to disappear for the duration. They just wanted him out of the way so he couldn't tell what he knew."

"Who? Who wanted him out of the way? Was it . . . ?"

Barry Dutton shook his head; no, it wasn't Leslie Levant after all.

"You won't believe it," he said. "But I guarantee you're going to like it."

"Wait, I'll bet I know," I said.

O'Donnell rolled his eyes. "Here we go again."

44

✿✿✿✿✿✿✿

Professor Aloysius "Ted" Bender did not look especially good in handcuffs. If the truth be told, he summoned up an image of someone else entirely. Bender would have disputed it, but the posture, with his hands behind him, slightly hunched over, and walking forward, was unmistakable. So was the widow's peak.

If it hadn't been for the gray ponytail, I decided, he'd be the spitting image of Richard Nixon, an analogy I'm sure Bender would find appalling. I'm not sure how Nixon would have felt about it, either.

As he was led out of Murray Hall, Bender couldn't stop talking, but he really wasn't saying much. Which wasn't unusual.

Mind you, I had not been invited to watch the arrest. In fact, Dutton and O'Donnell had been very clear about my staying away. But since I had correctly guessed the video pirate's identity, I figured there was no reason to miss this. They had decided against telling me his name, but the evidence was clear.

Cause and effect: Anthony called me and gave me information about what he was doing and where he was. I went to Bender, on the hunch that he might know more about Anthony's situation than he was letting on. Bender was, after all, pretty much Anthony's mentor, his source of all information about "cinema," and therefore, the person Anthony would have consulted on his film. I'm sure *Killin' Time* was a project in class, and that Bender knew the script intimately.

I gave Bender enough information to get him concerned. Anthony might talk if I found him on location. And almost immediately, the plug was pulled on Anthony's film. A stupid move, because that resulted in Anthony's coming back to New Jersey, demanding to know what I had done to sabotage him. It had taken me a while to realize the only connection could be Bender.

College professors do all right at Rutgers, but they're hardly making a fortune. Bender had all the duplication equipment he needed, and a student with access to a movie theatre, a small one where one employee would be trusted with the keys to the projection booth and the basement. Bender could get in, "borrow" the film overnight, duplicate it to his heart's content, and have it back the next day. Eventually, he'd had a copy of the projection booth key made. And Anthony let him store the boxes in the basement, possibly without even knowing what they contained. I wouldn't be surprised if Bender had told Anthony he just wanted to screen *Count Bubba, Down-Home Vampire* for his own amusement, or for a class on film comedy. Anthony was so focused on his own goals that he didn't really bother to notice anything that went on around him.

With a few selected nights of borrowed film, Bender had made enough (even bad movies are sellable at the right price, especially when they're still being shown in theatres) that he could afford to pay for Anthony's low-budget production and keep him safely out of the way. While I was in Bender's office, moronically spilling the beans that I'd deduced where Anthony had gone, and what he was doing, Bender was mentally cutting Anthony loose; assuming Anthony would never betray him, Bender advised me to turn

Anthony in, which was remarkably stupid and egotistical on Bender's part. But he'd cut off Anthony's flow of cash, and for that, the kid would probably never forgive me.

Of course, Anthony didn't realize that he'd been Bender's patsy, that Bender had placed the duplication equipment at Anthony's apartment in order to deflect suspicion from himself, and that he'd probably told the cops Anthony had been "acting strange and secretive lately."

I watched as two uniformed officers from the New Brunswick Police Department led Bender out of the building, and toward the street, where their patrol car was waiting. O'Donnell stood off to one side, but Dutton wasn't there. This was no longer a Midland Heights matter. I'm sure a few of the guys standing around campus in "inconspicuous" black suits were Feds of one kind or another. They must have found evidence that at least some of Bender's pirated videos had been sold out of state. Oops.

I moved up toward O'Donnell while they were marching Bender out. "You should get his class rosters," I said by way of a greeting. "You might find accomplices."

"Gee, thanks," O'Donnell answered. "We never would have thought of that. By the way, you should carry Raisinettes in your snack bar."

"We do."

Bender, still talking a mile a minute, made his guest appearance then, and I caught a quick snatch of what he was saying. The guy wasn't even waiting until he got to the station to spill his guts.

"It was me, all me, all me," he recited, almost like a mantra. "I did it for the money. Me. Education gets no funding in this country. I had to do it. It was me. I swear."

The thing was, nobody was asking him whether he'd done it.

"Methinks he doth protest too much," I said to O'Donnell.

"You'll get nowhere quoting the Bible to me," he said. "I'm an atheist."

"You don't look it," I told him.

45

"**I'm** surprised you asked to see me," I told Amy Ansella.

Amy didn't appear to have suffered any ill effects of her close encounter with Christie Dunbar's vase, but I couldn't see the back of her head, where the impact must have taken place. She looked at me through the bulletproof glass and spoke into the telephone. "I don't have anything to hide," she said. *Not anymore,* I thought, but I didn't say it.

Amy, from her cell in county lockup, had gotten a request through to O'Donnell: she wanted to talk to me. He hadn't been crazy about the idea, but granted the request.

"Why am I here?" I asked her.

Amy seemed surprised. "To set the record straight," she said. "They think this was all my fault, and they won't listen to me. But you seem to have their ear. You can tell them."

I had no idea who "they" were, but I did have this nagging curiosity, so I plunged in. "Why did you shoot Joe Dunbar?" I asked her. "You were in the clear; you hadn't committed any crime. Why screw it up by committing attempted murder?"

"It was self-defense," Amy asserted.

*Self-defense? To pick up a pistol and go after an un-
armed man in his own garage?*

"Self-defense," I repeated, by reflex.

Amy nodded vigorously. "He had destroyed my life,"
she said. "He told Vincent about my . . . arrangement
with"—and she hesitated—"that *whore*, and ruined everything. I had it all set up perfectly: my husband provided for
me, gave me a home and all the things I needed, and I
had . . . *her* . . . for the rest. But Joe Dunbar decides to be
the morality police and tell Vincent what was going on."

I curled a lip. It didn't hurt. "Vincent knew for months
before Joe told him," I said. "The only thing Joe told him
was that he'd seen you with Marcy." (*I* didn't mind saying
her name.) "Joe didn't even understand the significance of
it. You overreacted."

Amy all but launched herself at the glass. *"I did not!"*
she screamed into the phone, prompting a look from the
guard behind her. Amy composed herself and swallowed.
"It was a perfectly legitimate response. Dunbar threatened
my lifestyle, so he had to be removed. Any court in the
country will see it my way."

I wouldn't bet on it, I thought, *but we'll find out soon
enough.*

"I'm just curious," I told her. "If the relationship with
Marcy was so important to you, why did you two stop seeing each other after your husband died? You hadn't killed
him. Why not just continue the affair in the open, now?"

"I didn't know Vincent had committed suicide," Amy
said. "It wasn't until Dunbar approached me at the funeral,
and told me Vincent had taken the medication *from him*,
that I realized. And yet, here I am behind bars, and he
walks free. How does that make sense?

It occurred to me that Dunbar was in a hospital room
with a concussion and a bullet wound that had avoided
killing him by maybe an inch, but I kept that to myself, too.
I was a model of restraint today.

"You haven't answered my question," I reminded Amy.
"Why did you and Marcy break up?"

"Would you believe it?" she said. "She actually thought

I'd killed my husband. For *her*! So I told her never to contact me again. That woman seduced me, then accused me of murder. This is all her fault."

"Make up your mind," I told her. Someone else would have to model restraint for the rest of the day.

○ ○

Outside the Middlesex County Courthouse in New Brunswick, next to the facility where Amy was being held pending her arraignment, I spotted Marcy Resnick on a bench.

"I'm sorry," I told her. "They only allow one visit a day. I didn't know you were here."

Marcy didn't look me in the eye. "It doesn't matter," she said. "She won't agree to see me, anyway. I've asked."

"Someday, you'll have to explain to me what you see in her."

This time, Marcy did look at me. "Just what you saw when you first met her. She told me how you looked at her, and I could see it at the funeral."

I tilted my head. "She's very beautiful," I said, "but only on the outside."

"You don't know her the way I know her," Marcy said.

"Were you at the theatre the night Vincent died?" I asked her.

Marcy nodded. "After he told her he knew about us, she got mad, and they had this fight. Amy called me after Vincent left, apparently with some woman behind the wheel of the car. I don't believe Vince was cheating on her, but Amy insisted she'd seen this woman."

I didn't see any reason to tell her who the "woman" had been.

"I tried to talk her into coming over, see if I could calm her down," Marcy continued, unprompted. "But she was *mad* at him, can you imagine? She thought Vincent was having an affair, and she saw no irony in her rage at him for that. She insisted we go to the theatre where he was headed, just to rub it in for him."

"Did she confront him there?"

Marcy shook her head. "She never got close. We sat in the back row. I don't even think Vincent knew we were there. And he *was* with some woman, but I think they were just friends, from the way they were acting. They didn't touch, and she left before the end of the movie. Now that I think of it, she did give him a peck on the cheek then, but that didn't really count. I'd kiss Vince on the cheek when I saw him, too."

"And you two certainly weren't having an affair," I said.

"Of course not," she said. "I've never tried to hide who I am. I just don't broadcast my orientation. With Amy, I think she was always in denial. She knew, but she wouldn't admit it, and she married Vincent because he loved her and he made her laugh. She didn't love him; she didn't *want* him, but she could spend her life with him. Then I came along, recognized something in her that she didn't acknowledge, and one afternoon a little less than a year ago, I made a tiny gesture, and Amy was, I don't know, *released*. She couldn't get enough. And I thought she loved me. She didn't."

"I'm sorry for you," I told her.

"I'll be all right." Marcy tried to smile bravely, and did a semi-convincing job. "So tell me: how does she look?" She wiped away a tear and sniffed.

"Orange isn't her color," I said.

46

○○○○○○○

Suddenly, I had no one left to interview. I had nothing left to investigate.

I was just a comedy theatre owner again.

This would take some getting used to. For the past few weeks, Comedy Tonight had been something of an after-thought, running more or less on its own, and I hadn't thought a lot about doing the next level of renovation, or promoting to a wider geographical area in an attempt to draw an audience from a broader base. It was back to that, and I couldn't decide if I was glad or not.

I deposited the Lexus back at Moe's, with less than a quarter tank of gas in it, but no additional dents. It had taken effort, but I managed not to drive the stupid thing into a telephone pole on purpose.

Afterward, I walked back to the theatre. It was still there. Strangely, nobody had painted the walls or repaired the marquee in my absence, nor given a moment's thought to how a single-screen theatre that insisted on showing one old movie a week could possibly survive in the current marketplace. Funny how that never happens when I'm not around.

There wasn't much to do to set up, and I had three hours before the doors opened. For the first time in weeks, I didn't have very much to do. I could go home and sift through Vincent Ansella's collection some more, but at the moment, that didn't seem like a joyous thing to do.

Suppose, someday, for whatever reason, I stopped laughing. Suppose the jokes were just a part of a ritual for me, that I didn't appreciate the comic timing of Buster Keaton or the sublime facial expressions of Harpo Marx. What if, as I got older and spent more time alone, I no longer found solace in Bugs Bunny, or companionship from the Monty Python boys? Would I end up, like Ansella, wondering what my life had been about, and desiring only to end it before the pain became unbearable?

I had opened this theatre to show other people what I thought comedy was about, and instead it was teaching me what frustration and loneliness could be if you gave them half a chance. Who was I kidding? People didn't want to see black-and-white comedies made decades before they were born. No one under the age of forty (besides me) even knew half the names of these artists. Walk up to the average New Jerseyan and say "Ernst Lubitsch," and he'll probably call a cop and report you as a neo-Nazi.

Inside my office, where the smell of ammonia never really dissipated, I wondered if I'd made a huge mistake by sinking all my newfound wealth into this great big white elephant of a movie house. Here I was, in a room the size of a broom closet (let's be clear—it *was* a broom closet), without a wife, without children, without friends, trying to convince the world that I was right and it was wrong. Was this any way for a grown man to be spending his life? Maybe Sharon was right—I hadn't ever become an adult, and now, no matter how attractive the idea was, I had no idea how one went about doing so.

I walked out to the snack bar to see if we were selling Prozac there. I settled for a box of Milk Duds, and went back to the office.

Even if my professional "life" were going well, I had to admit that I'd loused up the personal side pretty well. I'd driven my wife into the arms of a chemical hypnotist with my aimlessness and contrary attitude. When I was ready to start seeing other women, I drove away the only one who showed any interest because she didn't want to commit to a lifetime with me after three weeks of dating, more or less. What was it about me that attracted really wonderful women just to see how quickly I could repel them?

I'd now solved the two problems I'd been wrestling with for close to a month now, and their resolution seemed to leave a void in my life—or to illuminate for me the one that was already there.

This trip down Melancholy Lane threatened to go on indefinitely until I saw a shadow growing in the lobby outside my office. I'd left the front door unlocked again, probably in the desperate hope that someone, *anyone*, would be interested in coming in to pass the time of day.

I'd done better than just anyone, though. When I looked up, Leslie Levant was standing in the doorway, and all of a sudden, things didn't seem all that bad. Maybe this was a new chance, maybe I could lighten up and just enjoy the moment with her. I'd tell her that I'd been thinking about what she'd said, and that she was right. Women love being told they're right. Especially if it means a man was wrong. That's their favorite. So that's what I'd do.

There were only two problems: I wasn't sure that Leslie was here to discuss our relationship, such as it was. I'd pretty much slammed the door on her the other day, and made it sound pretty final. I can be awfully pigheaded when I put my mind to it.

The other problem was the gun in her hand. Pointed at me.

I looked up at her. "Was it something I said?" I asked.

47

❁❁❁❁❁❁❁

Leslie's face was not the same face I'd seen at the microbrewery or on the bike trip down the canal. It was not communicative or evocative. There didn't seem to be any human emotion coming from it. She could have run for governor of California and swept the election, if she'd had an Austrian accent.

"You wouldn't stop," she said. "No matter how many ways I tried to warn you off, you wouldn't stop."

"I should have realized it was you," I told her. "I almost did, but Bender got arrested, and he didn't give you up."

She smiled the coldest smile I'd seen outside a Vincent Price movie. "He thinks he loves me," she said. "I don't know why; I never so much as kissed him. But he thinks so. He'll never give me up."

Leslie didn't move, but her presence in the doorway was imposing. This was a small room, and there was no back door. I had to keep her talking.

"I knew Bender couldn't drive a knife through my countertop," I said. "*You* can bench-press two hundred pounds.

And you were in the town house after I left that day. You said you were going to take a shower."

"I did take a shower. *Then* I drove a knife through your countertop. It was supposed to spook you."

"It worked."

She shook her head. "No, it didn't. Every time I did something to scare you, you pressed harder. You started asking more questions. You pushed and you bothered. Why couldn't you just leave it alone?"

"Because Vincent Ansella died in my theatre," I answered.

Leslie was so mad she almost stamped her foot. "This had nothing to *do* with Vincent Ansella!"

"I didn't know that."

"You know it now," she said.

"That's not very reassuring just at the moment. But you weren't here the night the powdered sugar was sprinkled on the popcorn. The projector was threaded that night, and then the thing with the popcorn. You were on patrol that night."

"That was Bender. He knows how to thread a projector; he taught me. When I wasn't there, he could do it. He came to the movie that night."

"He knows how to duplicate movies, too. He even has the equipment. You were in on the plot to frame Anthony, weren't you? You were the one who 'found' that prescription bottle. I bet you'd palmed it long before you showed it to me and Dutton."

Leslie nodded. "I'd had it a couple of days by then. It was in the projection booth, and when I threaded the projector, it couldn't have been more prominent."

"And you set up that situation in the projection booth to make it look like you didn't know how to operate the machine." The longer she talked, the longer I didn't get shot. It seemed worthwhile.

"It had to look like Anthony was still here. If he was found, we'd be discovered." She was giving a police report; just the facts, Sir, and that was it.

"So it was all a lie. Even when we were . . ." I needed to keep her talking until I could figure out a way out of this room.

"No. I really liked you, Elliot. I still do. It makes me that much sadder that I have to kill you." Well, *that* didn't sound promising.

"There's no need to lie now," I said, trying to distract her from that last thought. "You never had any feelings for me; you were just trying to find out what I knew. Then the night I assume you were coming to seal the deal and take me to bed, I showed up bleeding from the leg, and you got antsy. You thought Bender had gone off-message and tried to kill me, and you needed to get out of there fast. So you 'broke up with me' and went to check with Bender."

"You're not that far off," she said. "But that doesn't . . ."

"Don't interrupt." I was on a Sam Spade roll, and I was going to make it last. "When you found out it wasn't Bender behind the wheel, you had to repair our tortured 'relationship,' because it looked like I might be closing in on him, and you wanted to see what I knew about you. So you showed up here, flirting again. That's why you've been doing the relationship Hokey Pokey. So don't tell me you *really cared*. If you *really cared*, you'd put down that gun."

Women don't like you to tell them they're being emotionally dishonest; they think that is the exclusive province of men. I was counting on Leslie's wanting to prove she really had feelings for me, that she wasn't being as calculating as I'd said.

She smiled warmly. "You're right, Elliot," Leslie said. "If I really cared, I would." And she pointed the gun right between my eyes.

The phone rang.

"Don't answer it," Leslie said. She pulled the hammer back on the pistol she was holding, which I noted was not a standard-issue police weapon. I couldn't see from this far away, but it appeared to be something larger.

I looked at the caller ID on the phone. "It's Chief Dutton," I said to her. "He knows I'm here. If I don't pick up, he'll be suspicious."

"Let the machine answer it."

"I always turn the machine off when I'm here."

She thought it over. "Okay, pick it up, but put it on speaker phone. Make up an excuse."

I nodded, and hit the speaker button. "Comedy Tonight," I intoned.

"Elliot, it's Chief Dutton."

"Hi, Chief. You don't mind if we're on speaker, do you? I'm eating, and I don't want to get marinara sauce all over the phone."

I reached for the box of Milk Duds and started chewing on one to make what I hoped were extremely unrealistic eating noises. Leslie watched, still holding the gun on me. I figured it would start feeling heavy in her hand soon.

"No problem, Elliot," Dutton said. His voice would have echoed around the room, but there wasn't any air in here. Just papers, file cabinets, a couple of electric fans, and catalogues from film distributors. The place absorbs sound. It was a wonder I could hear myself talk. "I just wanted you to know, O'Donnell confirmed your suspicions about Bender's class rosters."

Uh-oh. Leslie's eyes narrowed.

"That's great, Chief. Thanks for letting me know." Maybe I could cut him off before he said anything that would get me even more shot.

"You were right. Leslie Levant was taking courses in the Cinema Arts Department at Rutgers, and she was in two of Bender's classes, Cinema Techniques and Cinema History. She was in Cinema History with Anthony Pagliarulo. The other class is probably where she got her experience working with projection equipment. Anthony says he never saw her in the theatre with Bender, so I guess she wasn't there for the actual duplication. She was usually assigned to patrol on the overnight shift then, anyway, and probably too smart to be on the scene while the crime was being committed." Leslie's eyebrows dropped and her mouth moved into a perfectly straight horizontal line. I'd seen her when she was simulating warm and loving, and this wasn't what it looked like.

"Yeah, thanks a lot, Chief. It really wasn't necessary for you to tell me. Really."

Dutton started to chuckle. "I love how they call it 'cinema,' like it's not just movies," he said. "Bunch of pretentious horses' asses, if you ask me."

"Yeah, ha-ha," I went along, sounding very much like a man whose life was being threatened. "What a bunch of nuts. Well, got to move along, Chief. Thanks for calling."

His voice deepened, if such a thing was possible. Dutton wanted me to know he was being serious now. "Don't take it lightly, Elliot," he said. "That could very well mean that Officer Levant was indeed in on Bender's pirating operation, and if that's true, she's probably heard about his arrest. She might be trying to cover her tracks, and you could be in some danger."

Leslie's hand never so much as quivered. A gun like that has to weigh, what, about twenty-four ounces, without any bullets in the magazine? That's like holding the weight of six baseballs in one hand, and it had been a good few minutes she'd been holding it steady. It was heavier than that now, I could be sure, and yet, she never moved it from hand to hand or showed signs of fatigue. Even under these circumstances, you had to marvel at the woman's control. I wasn't happy about it, but I marveled.

"Oh, I'm sure I'm fine, Chief," I said, trying to sound artificial. Dutton didn't know me well, but I was hoping he'd pick up something in my voice.

"You probably are, but you can't be too careful. Lock the door until it's time to open the theatre, okay?"

"Good safety tip, Chief. I'll try to remember it in the future, thanks." I chewed a bit more on another Milk Dud for continuity. The ultimate comfort food, Milk Duds. It wasn't working.

"All right. Bye-bye, then." What police chief says "bye-bye"? I pushed the button to cut the connection, and looked at Leslie.

"You were trying much too hard, Elliot," she said. "But it didn't work. The chief didn't hear anything in your voice."

"You can't blame a guy for trying."

"Sure I can."

I popped another Milk Dud into my mouth. Hell, if I was going to get shot, I didn't have to worry about empty calories anymore, did I?

I'd say she leveled the gun at me, but it had never been anything but level. "I'm sorry, Elliot," she said.

"How are you going to explain it?" I asked. It's harder to shoot someone when you're having a normal-sounding conversation. If the person begs and pleads for his life, I imagine it's easier, since you have in your hand the means to shut up this annoying pain in the butt, but to leave a question unanswered, well, it just doesn't seem polite. At least, that's what I was hoping.

It worked, for the time being. "Explain what?" Leslie asked.

"Explain me. Bender's being questioned by the cops, and Dutton knows you're involved somehow. If you shoot me, you're just making yourself the prime suspect. They'll find you."

"I wasn't planning on shooting you." Well, that was a relief. "I thought you'd have an accident, maybe fall off a ladder and hit your head on something hard, like the arm of a steel seat, or impale yourself on something sharp, if there's anything like that in the auditorium." That wasn't such a relief. "Now, get up."

I thought that one over. "No," I said.

"I'm sorry?" Leslie said. She finally moved the gun, but just to aim at my head, rather than my chest. There might have been a bit of a quiver in the hand, though.

"I said, no. I'm not getting up. You just blew it." I popped another Milk Dud. "You told me you don't want to shoot me."

Leslie sighed, a mother having to explain who was in charge, *again* to her ADD-rattled nine-year-old. "But I will if I have to," she said. "I'll shoot you, and then I'll burn this place down."

"You know they can always detect arson," I said. "And they'll find the bullet hole in my body." Somehow, it had seemed a better idea before I heard the sentence out loud.

"You're stalling, Elliot. Get up, or I'll shoot you in one of your favorite spots."

"That's cold."

She was having none of it. "Get up. Now."

So I stood up. We were eye to eye, but a few feet apart. You can't really throw something at a person holding a gun on you; that's just in the movies. If you do it, they're more than likely to shoot you just because they're startled. And it gives them something to aim at that is coming directly from your midsection. So you really can't throw something at a person holding a gun on you.

But, I discovered, you can *spit* something at them.

The three Milk Duds I had in my mouth made a lovely projectile, and we were just close enough that they appeared to be headed directly for Leslie's eyes. As soon as I shot them out, I ducked, and dove for her midsection, on the side away from the gun. Again, I got lucky. Her hand *was* tired, and drooped just a little as I hit her in the left side and went through the office door. The gun went off, over my shoulder. I didn't stop to see what it hit. My projectile, however, clearly *had* hit its target: there was a chocolate smear in the middle of Leslie's forehead.

Leslie didn't fall, but she stumbled out of the way enough for me to get by. She was blocking my path to the front door, so I turned right and headed for the lobby before she could regain her balance and fire.

Since Leslie was trained as a cop, in excellent shape, and younger than me, she recovered quickly, and charged after me into the lobby. I dove behind the candy counter and lay on the ground, trying very hard not to breathe audibly after the run from the office. I made a mental note to eat fat-free muffins more often and have a salad for lunch at least twice a week.

Suddenly, the world exploded. Leslie had fired a round into the glass candy case, destroying it and showering shattered glass over the lower half of my body. I shielded my eyes.

She was advancing. I picked up two Kit Kat bars—the

big ones—and positioned myself, still low to the floor, behind the popcorn stand.

Boom! Popcorn flew everywhere as I estimated insurance deductibles. I yelled out, "Do you have any idea what these things *cost*?" I was rewarded with another shot, a little nearer to my head than I would have preferred, which shattered the mirror behind the snack bar.

I dove out of the way, thankful that I didn't feel any glass in my shoes. That took me closer to the auditorium entrance. Inside, there would be more places to conceal myself. So I took my chances and ran for the doors.

I heard the shot fired, and felt something very hot crease my right calf. It seemed a silly time to worry about such things, so I just kept running. But it was obvious I wasn't going to make it to the auditorium before Leslie could fire again, so I changed my angle and headed for the stairs. If I could make it to the projection booth, I could lock the door from the inside and use the phone in there to call Dutton. I ducked under the velvet rope and started up the stairs. The "Balcony Closed" sign caught on my heel for a moment, but I shook it loose.

Leslie had to run toward the stairs to see me, and by the time she got to the landing at the bottom, I was halfway up the flight. She took aim, but didn't fire, as I ducked to the side away from her, where I'd be harder to hit. She'd have to shoot around the banister, and it was big.

So she started up the stairs. I couldn't stand straight up or my head would be in her line of fire, so I kept down and continued climbing, more slowly than before out of necessity.

In other words, Leslie was gaining on me by the time I reached the top of the stairs. I bolted for the booth door before she could aim. And I reached it just in time.

But the door was locked.

In the time it would have taken me to get the keys out of my pocket, isolate the one for the booth, and open the door, I'd have been dead four times over. The booth was no longer an option.

I cut left and flattened myself against the floor behind the last row of seats in the balcony. Leslie reached the landing just as I lay down. I hadn't turned the lights on in the auditorium, and I knew she couldn't tell where I was.

I certainly wasn't going to tell her.

"There's blood on the carpet, Elliot," she called. "I know I shot you."

Nice opening, Leslie. That's certainly the way to get me to stand up and let you shoot me again.

"Come on. You know you can't get out. It's not that large a balcony. I'm going to find you."

Yeah. And if you think I'm going to make your job easier, Sweetheart, you have been drinking from the extra-large size of the Crazy Cup.

I could see her feet coming up the aisle, slowly. At each row, they would swivel suddenly, one way, then the other. She was aiming the gun like a cop with a hostile in the room. She wasn't going to be caught napping.

"Maybe we can work this out. I don't have to kill you. We can share the money from the DVDs. Bender will be in jail; you can have his share. You keep quiet, and I can give you enough to really fix up this place the way you want it."

Did someone stick a sign on the back of my shirt that reads "World's Biggest Sucker"? Because that's the only way you might think this ploy could work.

She was only five rows away. And she knew she hadn't seen me yet. That meant I was in a very contained space, and Leslie was more confident. She stopped walking up the stairs.

She'd seen me. Or thought she had. It was still very dark up there.

"Stand up, Elliot. I know where you are now."

Yeah, let me give you a better target.

"We're done, Elliot. You can't get away. Just stand up."

I couldn't figure out a way to crawl silently, or I would have tried for the opposite aisle. And the pain in my leg was starting to become noticeable. I sure as hell wasn't going to get up and let her blast away, but my alternatives were narrowing rather noticeably.

Leslie realized then that with the dim lights that are always on in the auditorium (except when the place is shut down), and a little altitude, she would be able to see where I was. So she walked to the middle of the row, maybe ten feet from where I lay, and stood up on the arms of a seat in the center. She balanced herself, and looked around.

But before she could adjust her eyes to the light, I heard exactly what I had hoped not to hear. From beneath us, either in the lobby or the auditorium—it was hard to tell—came Sophie's voice. "Elliot?" she called. "Are you here?"

I couldn't see Leslie, but I could hear her triumphant smile in her voice. "Trentino! That's game!" she said, a line from *Duck Soup*. "Do you want to stand up, or shall I go and take a hostage?"

Shit. I couldn't let Sophie become a casualty of my meddling with things that weren't my business. For one thing, her parents would never forgive me. And I'd never forgive myself.

I stood up, painfully on the right leg. The wound wasn't bad, but it was enough to notice. The problem was, I knew it was nothing in comparison to what I was about to feel, and after that, I'd feel nothing.

I'd been right about the frosty smile on Leslie's face. It was exactly as I'd pictured it, but in this light, and with her towering over me like that, it was even more frightening. She kept the gun leveled at my head, and hopped down off the arms of the seat onto the floor of the balcony.

And then she just kept going.

The floor gave way under her, reminding me why I didn't allow customers into the balcony to begin with. She plummeted, gun and all, through the hole her impact had created, and disappeared from view entirely.

I hustled down the steps as best as I could (walking especially gingerly now, as I didn't want to join her, and after all had been shot in the leg) to the spot where Leslie had vanished. A sizable hole had opened up in the floor of the balcony just in front of row GG, seat 17, and when I looked down through it, I could see Leslie, on her back amid a pile of plaster, rotted wood, carpet, and candy wrappers from

1962, the gun knocked out of her hand. I was pretty sure she was breathing, but she was bleeding from a number of body parts, including her head, and her eyes were open, staring, and not seeing a whole heck of a lot.

"Now, *that's* comedy," I said.

48

ᗯᗪᗩᗯᗪᗩᗯᗩ

"She'll be well enough to stand trial," Chief Barry Dutton said. "Former Officer Levant suffered a severe concussion, a broken leg, a few cracked ribs, and cuts and bruises. She was lucky."

"She was lucky?" I asked. "*I* was lucky. Two more seconds, and she would have shot me. Again."

My right leg now had eight stitches in it, just to prove it could take more than my left (they're so competitive). The burning sensation was more of an annoyance, but the pain had subsided entirely. I could have lived without getting shot, but if this was the extent of the damage, I'd certainly tolerate it and consider myself fortunate.

"I had Officer Patel on his way," Dutton said, a little defensively. "He would have gotten there in another minute or two. I knew something was wrong by the way you spoke to me on the phone."

"You mean putting you on speaker phone?"

"No, I mean you were being polite."

I asked about Joe Dunbar, and Dutton said he was recovering nicely and would be out of the hospital in another

day or so. Christie hadn't left his side, and gave every
stranger who passed the hospital room door "the evil eye."
She was a mother lion and Dunbar was, apparently, her cub.

Amy Ansella was being charged with attempted murder
and a few lesser charges, though she still complained that
none of it was her fault, and had snagged some local reporter into covering "her side" of the story. The poor guy
probably thought he had a chance with Amy once she got
out of jail. In all likelihood, he wouldn't be disappointed
for quite some time.

There would, naturally, be no charges filed against
Marcy Resnick, since having a minority sexual orientation
was not illegal in New Jersey. As long as you call it a "civil
union."

Patel knocked on Dutton's door, then entered when the
chief waved him in. "Report from Sergeant O'Donnell,
Chief," he said, and placed the sheaf of papers on Dutton's
desk. Patel got a nod from Dutton, and left.

"Does that have anything about Anthony in it?" I asked.

Dutton scanned the top sheet of the papers over his
reading glasses, and nodded. "The Feds gave him immunity for his testimony," he said. "I doubt they'll be able to
use much of what the kid says, though. He lives in another
star system."

"It's Planet Film, Chief," I told him. "Many are called,
few are chosen."

I stood up to leave, and caught something out of the
corner of my eye. It stopped me dead in my tracks.

"Chief," I said, "do you ride a bicycle?"

Dutton, still reading the report, looked up at me over
the half-glasses. "No."

He seemed a little disconcerted when I walked around
his desk and reached behind a file cabinet to pull out the
object I'd spied there: the front wheel of a bicycle. "You
know, this looks strangely like one of mine that was stolen
from right in front of this building," I said.

"How can you tell? Does it have special markings on it,
or something?" Dutton said, but there was a hint of a grin
trying to peek out of his face.

I sat back down, stunned. "It was you," I said. "You took the wheel off my bicycle that day. Why would you do that?"

Dutton frowned. "You have no proof that I . . ."

"You *wanted* me to go home with Leslie Levant," I said. "You were behind that whole thing. That whole speech about how 'officers are freer to talk.' You were setting us up. Why?"

"Close the door," Dutton said, and I did.

Dutton pointed a finger and said, "If one word—*one word*—of what is said in this room is ever repeated to me by *anyone*, I'll deny it. Then, I'll have you arrested. For something. Whatever the worst crime on my desk is that day. Are we clear?"

Appropriately impressed, I nodded.

"You're right. I wanted you to get to know Officer Levant better," Dutton told me. "I didn't expect you to get to know her *that* well, but I wanted to be able to have a little different view of her than you get by being her boss."

"I didn't get to know her as well as you seem to think, Chief, but I don't understand why you wanted *me*, of all people, to provide that look."

"Because I suspected something was up with her. Like I told you, her spending was far exceeding her income, and I knew her income. Then this piracy thing shows up and she's the one who's finding all the information, and giving others the credit. It all seems to point at a kid who didn't even have a record of jaywalking. It didn't add up."

"You couldn't find out what you needed to know on your own, so you recruited a civilian?" I wasn't sure whether to be insulted or flattered.

"You were one of the first people we investigated," Dutton said. "I knew your background."

"What background? I don't have a background."

"I read your book," Dutton said. "You've spent some time around cops. And a friend of mine said you could handle it."

"You have friends?" I had no idea what he was talking about.

"The first day we met, I took a look at your book," Dutton told me. "I noticed a name in your acknowledgments, thanking a certain cop for being especially helpful in the research."

Oh, sure. "Meg Vidal."

Dutton nodded. "Meg and I have known each other for a long time," he said. "I called her up and asked her about you.

"Meg said you were very good; you had instincts. She said while you were doing your ride-alongs to research your book, she almost suggested you take the entrance exam to the police academy. Then she decided you were too impulsive, and you take everything too personally, so you wouldn't have made a good cop."

"She was right. After seeing what she dealt with on one case, I never wanted to go back again." I couldn't believe Meg had told Dutton all this; they must have been very close, because Meg doesn't open up to just anybody.

"She also said you thought I was a good cop, but an administrator who might not know how to work a case anymore."

My face must have been glowing red, because Dutton was grinning his best Yaphet Kotto grin. "I didn't say that last part," I told him.

"I asked her if she thought I could rely on you a little bit, and she said yes."

"Is that standard procedure around here? Dupe the civilian?"

Dutton frowned. "You'll recall, this is a small department, and I don't have many detectives. And all I expected was that you might be able to tell me, much later on, a few things about Officer Levant's lifestyle, not about a crime. I never anticipated there being any danger to you, or I wouldn't have asked."

"You figured I could find out, even without knowing that I was trying to, whether Leslie's upscale purchases were due to her terrific savings plan or something else," I said, thinking out loud. "You figured someone who knew about the movie business might notice things that would tie her to video piracy, and so you stole my bicycle wheel."

"I just wanted her to drive you home that night, that's all."

"Well," I said, standing up, "she did."

"I'm sorry," Dutton told me, and I think he meant it.

"So am I," I said.

49

"He saw us kiss," Sharon said.

It was a lovely warm day in late May, and we were sitting at an outdoor table at C'est Moi!, having a bleu cheese burger and fries (Sharon) and a Caesar salad with low-fat dressing (not Sharon). My fork stopped halfway to my mouth, and I looked at her, my eyes sending question marks out at regular intervals.

"Gregory. He came to the theatre that day because he saw my car outside on his way home, and he walked in just when we . . . kissed that time. That's what made him so crazy."

"I think what made him crazy was spending all that time inhaling gases meant to knock people out," I said. "After a while, it has to do *something* to your brain."

"Don't be mean."

I flashed a look at her. "Don't expect me to be diplomatic about Gregory," I said.

"I don't." She took a sip of iced tea, and then a deep breath. "We're separating."

This time my fork actually hit the salad bowl and stayed there. "You and Gregory?"

Sharon nodded. "Yes. He's moved out of the house."

Wow. After fantasizing about such a thing out of sheer spite for all this time, it was weird to have it really happen. I sat quiet for a long moment. "Because of me?" I asked her.

"Elliot, he tried to kill you with his car. I can't live with a man who would do a thing like that. To *anybody*."

"Still . . ."

"It's not about *you*; everything isn't about *you*, Elliot. It's about the fact that Gregory was upset with me, and didn't talk to me about it. Instead, he tried to run you down with his car and then told me he'd scraped it against a concrete barrier."

"Well, that last part was true," I said. "After he scraped it against me, he hit the barrier."

"You're missing the point, and you're missing it on purpose."

"Either way," I told her. "When our marriage broke up, I tried to blame it on Gregory. I thought that without him, we would have stayed together. Now I know that's not true, that if you had been happy with me, Gregory wouldn't have happened. I don't want your separation to happen because Gregory was jealous of me. Because maybe your marriage has problems that would have been there if neither of those things had happened. If it's about me, you should stay together."

Sharon pushed her plate away with half a burger and a healthy number of fries on it, which I believed meant that the food automatically became community property. But I didn't reach for her plate.

"That's very mature of you, Elliot. And it's true, Gregory and I have problems that would be there whether all this had happened, or not. We're going to go to a couples therapist and try to work them out."

"What does this separation mean for us?" I asked.

"I'm still married," she said, and I exhibited even more maturity in not remarking that she and I were still married when the Gregory thing began. I was just oozing maturity today. "You and I can go back to seeing each other for lunch when we want. It was stupid of me to stop being friends with you because Gregory didn't like it."

"And beyond that? Beyond being friends?"

"You said it yourself, Elliot. We had problems before Gregory. We'd have the same problems if we got together again. Right now, I'm committed to trying to make my current marriage work. Until that's resolved one way or the other, you and I are going to be friends, and that's all. I hope that's enough for you."

"It's not enough, but I can certainly live with it," I said.

She closed her eyes for a moment, and smiled sadly, something I've never seen anyone else do successfully. "You're really growing up, aren't you," Sharon said.

"Yes," I answered. "Someday, I might be a real live boy."

50

○🍪○🍪○🍪○

"This is going to take more than Spackle," Dad said.

We were eating lunch in the auditorium at Comedy Tonight, sitting beneath the hole in the balcony, which gave
one the uncanny feeling that he should see stars if he
looked up long enough. Most of the debris had been
cleared away, some of it bagged by the dogged Officer
Patel himself, and the rest was just a dustpan—okay, a
Dumpster—away from being forever out of my life.

Obviously, the theatre was not going to be open for
business tonight, or the next night, or in all probability for
ten or fifteen nights to come. I'd personally called Leo and
told him not to show up until further notice. The lobby was
a mess of what had once been our snack bar, although the
glass had also been removed. There were bullet holes in
various walls, some of which I'd already plastered once.
There was blood on areas of carpet.

In short, this was not something that your average
cleaning lady could handle in an afternoon.

"What do you think we need to do?" I asked my father.

He stood up and looked at the hole from another angle.

"That balcony wasn't much to begin with. If you were going to do it *right*, you'd probably need to remove the whole thing and replace it, but that could take months."

"And cost a year's receipts," I added.

"Yeah. So let's examine our alternatives. You can just fix the hole, keep the balcony closed for the time being, and concentrate on the snack bar. You can fix the snack bar *and* the balcony to the point that you'd be able to send people up there on nights when it's crowded . . ."

"Which would be twice since I opened the place, both times after a crime was committed on the premises . . ."

"Any way you look at it," Dad said, "this is more than we can do ourselves. You're going to have to call in carpenters, and maybe get a structural analysis of the balcony done to see if it can be saved."

"*If?* I've been climbing up those steps every night to get to the projection booth. What do you mean, *if?*"

"I mean, you've been really lucky."

"If this is what lucky feels like, I don't want to buck the odds. Call some of your contractor friends."

Dad nodded. I checked my watch, and walked out of the auditorium and into my office. I had to field some phone calls responding to my ad for more theatre help, which seemed a little . . . superfluous, considering that the only help the theatre needed at the moment was in not falling down.

Even when it hadn't been clear if I'd ever see Anthony again, I hadn't advertised for a replacement—maybe I was being sentimental. Maybe I was being cheap. Maybe I just thought that after it was all said and done, Anthony would be back trying to thread up films that probably hadn't been unspooled in twenty years.

But after a woman with a gun had fallen through the ceiling practically on their daughter's head, Sophie's parents had refused to allow her back into Comedy Tonight. So I placed an ad in the *Press-Tribune* for a replacement, despite the fact that the theatre would be closed until the repairs could be made. After all, I'd already paid for ads in the *Press-Tribune* for a week, and I couldn't advertise a movie. Might as well put the money to use.

Anthony had agreed to come back when we reopened, which was a huge relief, since only he and I (and Bender and Leslie, but they would be tied up for a while) knew how to keep the projector from blowing up on any given evening, and I wasn't that sure about myself. I promised him that if he could get a rough cut together, the first film on our return would be a one-night-only showing of *Killin' Time*. It wasn't a comedy, but there was no guarantee an invited audience would be able to tell that, and it was only one night. Anthony was editing fiercely, trying to make a deadline that I couldn't set yet. But I made him promise he'd bring Carla to the premiere. The kid shouldn't give up on something good, even if he doesn't see it himself.

Things changed a few days later, when Sophie showed up at the theatre to collect her last paycheck, and her parents were with her.

"I hope you know what you put her through," Ilsa Beringer told me. "The poor girl is traumatized."

"I am not," Sophie mumbled.

"Don't be brave, honey," her father said. His jaw was so tight you couldn't pry it open with a crowbar. "You don't have to impress us. We already love you."

Ilsa went on as if Ron hadn't spoken. "You create an environment where all *sorts* of things happen, and you don't think for a moment about what an impact that will have on an impressionable little girl, do you, Mr. Freed?"

The four of us jammed into my office, where I'd been trying to write Sophie a check for $262.47, was uncomfortable enough, but being blamed for not taking Sophie into account when someone was trying to shoot me—especially since I *had* taken Sophie into account, and that's why I almost got killed—was making things just a hair less enjoyable. But I didn't want to get Sophie in more trouble by defending myself. If that's what they wanted to believe . . .

"I'm not a little girl, *mother*," Sophie said, slightly more audibly than before.

Ilsa, having built up a head of steam, kept rolling. "We're considering legal action against you, for the pain and suffering you've caused our poor little . . ."

My mouth dropped open, but I never got the chance to say a word. "You're doing no such thing!" Sophie scolded, her eyes wide open and something approaching color actually showing in her cheeks. "It's not Elliot's fault that all this stuff happened, and I'm not even a *little* traumatized."

"You don't know what you're saying," Ron attempted, his voice sounding suspiciously like air being let out of a balloon. "Now Sophie, you know Mom is just trying to . . ."

"She's trying to control everything, like she always does," his daughter answered. "She's trying to make this all about what a good mother she is, but I'm telling you no. I'm *not* quitting my job and I'm *not* traumatized. I'm *not* changing the way I dress," (this was definitely aimed directly between Ilsa's eyes) "and I'm *not* going to private school next year."

Ilsa, of course, looked away from her daughter, and her face took on a very Margaret Hamilton–in-full-makeup hue when she said, "What have you done to her?"

It took me a moment to realize she meant me. "What have I . . . ?"

"He treated me like a *person*," Sophie answered on my behalf, which was fortunate, since I had no idea what to say after "What have I . . . ?" She went on: "He lets me call him Elliot, not Mr. Freed, and he asks me to do stuff that's important, and he trusts me to do it right. He doesn't stand over my shoulder and point out every little mistake I make before I have a chance to see it myself. And he doesn't call me a silly little girl. I'm his employee, and he treats me like that. I wouldn't give up this job for *anything*."

There was a silence that might have lasted ten seconds, or an hour and a half; I'm not sure. But while Ilsa's mouth opened and closed without any sound coming out, I kept my hand on the checkbook, where Sophie's paycheck was ripped halfway out. I couldn't seem to summon enough muscle power to finish the motion. And Ron

Beringer simply disappeared. I think he might have dissolved into a powder that I'd have to vacuum off the rug later.

"Go wait for me outside," Sophie said to her mother and the powder. They left wordlessly, with looks on both faces I'm sure neither had seen before. I woke myself up and pulled on the check, which tore in two.

"Another one," I said. Suddenly, I was capable of English only at the Tonto level.

"You can give it to me when the theatre reopens," she said. "Do you need me during the renovations?"

I shook my head. "Nothing to do," I said, slowly regaining the power of speech.

"Okay. You'll call me?"

I nodded, and Sophie turned to leave. I called to her before she made it out the door. "Sophie. Thank you."

She rolled her eyes. "Oh, let's not get all *dramatic*, okay?" she said.

After they left, I walked back into the auditorium. The workmen were just beginning on the balcony, and that meant they were tearing most of it down right now. (I had prevailed—mainly by pleading and begging—in getting them to retain the existing projection booth, thus saving me and my insurance company a small fortune.) There was a lot of nothing where something once had been.

On the other hand, I thought, this was also a place where something would once again *be*. I tried to picture Comedy Tonight the way it would look when all the work was done in a few weeks (hopefully): a new, sturdy balcony, new seats in much of the rear of the theatre, new snack bar, new carpet in many places.

Still not perfect, but closer to perfect than it had been before. In fact, right now, it looked worse than when I'd first bought the place. But, eventually, when I could get the business running the way I had always dreamed, it would be perfect, I was sure.

Like Ginger Rogers. In *Swing Time*.

FURTHER FUNNY FILM FACTS
FOR FANATICS

Young Frankenstein (1974)

Directed by Mel Brooks, screen story and screenplay by Gene Wilder and Mel Brooks. Starring Gene Wilder, Peter Boyle, Marty Feldman, Teri Garr, Kenneth Mars, Cloris Leachman, and Madeline Kahn.

The sound of the cat hit by a dart, the howl of the were-wolf, and the voice of Victor Frankenstein (in the quick sonic flashback) are provided by Mel Brooks. There were also scenes in which the voice of Beaufort von Frankenstein, Freddie's grandfather, was provided by John Carradine, but sadly, they were cut.

Gene Wilder and Mel Brooks were nominated for an Academy Award for the screenplay for *Young Franken-stein*. Instead, the Academy gave the award to Francis Ford Coppola and Mario Puzo for *The Godfather, Part II*. Not nearly as funny.

Horse Feathers (1932)

Directed by Norman Z. McLeod, screenplay by Bert Kalmar and Harry Ruby, S.J. Perelman, and Will B. Johnstone. Starring the Marx Brothers (Groucho, Chico, Harpo, *and* Zeppo), Thelma Todd, and David Landau.

When *Horse Feathers* was released, the Marx Brothers appeared on the cover of *Time* magazine for the only time, standing in a garbage can. The following year, when they made *Duck Soup*, considered by Marx purists to be their best movie, it was roundly panned. Go figure.

The first American artist to tour the Soviet Union after the United States recognized the country in 1933 was Harpo Marx. He scored a resounding success, although he claimed not to understand anything about the production in which he appeared. Harpo also claimed to have smuggled secret papers out of the country in his socks. This is unconfirmed to date.

The Thin Man (1934)

Directed by W.S. Van Dyke, screenplay by Albert Hackett and Frances Goodrich, from the novel by Dashiell Hammett. Starring William Powell, Myrna Loy, Maureen O'Sullivan, Nat Pendleton, and, of all people, Cesar Romero (playing a character named Chris Jorgenson).

Actually, *The Thin Man* of the title refers to the victim, not Nick Charles. But Powell and Loy went on to star in five more *Thin Man* films, despite the victim never showing up again. It didn't seem to bother anybody.

The role of Asta, the wire-haired terrier (in the novel, a schnauzer), was apparently played by the same dog in all six *Thin Man* films (but not on the radio or television series of the same name). While the dog was credited as "Skippy" when he appeared in *Topper Takes a Trip*, his name was changed to "Asta" when he started appearing in the *Thin Man* movies. Source: www.iloveasta.com (no, I'm not kidding).

Help! (1965)

Directed by Richard Lester, screenplay by Charles Wood, story by Marc Behm. Starring the Beatles (John Lennon, Paul McCartney, George Harrison, Ringo Starr), Leo McKern (later to play Rumpole of the Bailey), Eleanor Bron, Victor Spinetti, and Roy Kinnear.

It was on the set of *Help!* that George Harrison first encountered Indian musicians playing sitars. Thus was the history of popular music created.

Some Like It Hot (1959)
Directed by Billy Wilder, screenplay by Billy Wilder and I.A.L. Diamond, story by Robert Thoeren and Michael Logan. Starring Tony Curtis, Jack Lemmon, Marilyn Monroe, Joe E. Brown, and George Raft.

In 2000, the American Film Institute voted *Some Like It Hot* the funniest American film ever made. Among the other ninty-nine films in its top one hundred comedies: *Young Frankenstein*, *Horse Feathers*, and *The Thin Man. Help!* did not make the list. It is not an American film. In case you're wondering, number one hundred is *Good Morning, Vietnam*.

Penguin Group (USA) Online

What will you be reading tomorrow?

Tom Clancy, Patricia Cornwell, W.E.B. Griffin,
Nora Roberts, William Gibson, Robin Cook,
Brian Jacques, Catherine Coulter, Stephen King,
Dean Koontz, Ken Follett, Clive Cussler,
Eric Jerome Dickey, John Sandford,
Terry McMillan, Sue Monk Kidd, Amy Tan,
John Berendt…

You'll find them all at
penguin.com

Read excerpts and newsletters,
find tour schedules and reading group guides,
and enter contests.

Subscribe to Penguin Group (USA) newsletters
and get an exclusive inside look
at exciting new titles and the authors you love
long before everyone else does.

PENGUIN GROUP (USA)
us.penguingroup.com